THE RINGS OF VENUS

THE COMPANY'S MAN

DAVID PARKER-ROSS

The Rings of Venus

By David Parker-Ross

Edited by Tegan Bourke

Audiobook Performed by Aaron Smith

With Special Appearance by Tegan Bourke as Hannah Grant

eBook 978-1-959138-27-3

Hardback 978-1-959138-28-0

Paperback 978-1-959138-29-7

AUTHOR'S NOTE

Perceptions is a series that tells tales from different characters' perspectives. Each has their own ideas, their own values, their own beliefs, and their own memories.

The characters, including the narrator, have their own perception of the events that took place at the time of the stories. They may very well have political, religious, and social opinions. Those opinions do not necessarily reflect this author, or anyone involved with the creation of this work. Indeed, I have very much tried to keep my personal opinions out of the stories.

The whole idea is to leave it to you, the reader, to make up your mind on the rights and wrongs of the characters within the tales.

Memory is a fickle beast; not everyone will remember events similarly. One should not assume that a narrator is either accurate or, for that matter, even truthful.

Perceptions... It's all about who you believe.

Clear Skies to You,

David Parker-Ross

A Brief History of Grant Industries

By Hannah Grant

G rant Industries started its life around a hundred and fifty years ago in Adelaide, Australia. At the time, it was simply known as Henry Grant Tools. My great-great-times-whatever grandfather started out selling hardware online at knockdown prices, competing with a company known as Amazon. Although that company has long been forgotten, it once dominated the global retail market. However, Henry Grant was no fool, and he rapidly expanded into other areas.

The company began to grow, and while he sold some shares to private investors, he refrained from floating the company on the stock market, keeping the controlling interest in the family. In another canny move, he started investing in his competitor's companies. Frequent mergers happened worldwide, and the company was renamed Grant Industries. This had a knock-on effect for Australia. With income now pouring into the country from his various foreign investments, Grant Industries ultimately became the largest commercial employer in the country. He also maintained most of the manufacturing within its borders.

Henry Grant's takeover of Amazon is a matter of history, and I won't go into it here, other than to say that with that purchase, he became unstoppable. He was a powerhouse and carried political influence around the world. Not only did he have most of the major retailers under the company umbrella, but he also started gaining international contracts with governments for everything, from providing uniforms for janitors to military contracts, developing everything from firearms to the early starships that took humanity out into the solar system.

However, while Grant Industries maintained dominance of trade and industry for the next hundred and fifty years or so, that all ended with the Great War. Australia was classified as an economic superpower by this time, having overtaken the United States. And that in itself, gave us a seat at the head of world government.

As to who started the war is neither here nor there. Personally, I don't care, and nor should you. However, in a defensive measure against aggression from the European Union, Australia led the way in forming the Pacific Alliance since most of the countries within the organization bordered the Pacific. Not everyone, just the majority.

Grant Industries continued trading in the European Union and the Pacific Alliance, until the European Union gave an ultimatum. It turned out that they didn't like us selling weapons and military equipment to both sides. With much consternation, my mother, Marcia Grant, who was head of the company, didn't exactly pull out of the European Union, but she divided the company into two parts. Industries Européennes and Grant Industries.

She retained a controlling share in both companies, with the intent to reunite them after the war. However, twenty years later, the war continued. She'd pretty much lost control of the European wing of the company.

I know no other way to put it, but when the invasion of Australia happened, everything went to shit. While many executives escaped the destruction, my mother wasn't one of them. My sister, Annabelle, was next in line to take over the company, but she, too, perished in the destruction of Melbourne. I, however, managed to escape. My mother had apparently prepared for this, and Grant Industries Security Services managed to get me off the planet. En route to Mars, a ship failure left me stranded inside a M.E.T. system. I was considered dead for two years. When I returned, the company was in the control of Mr Tanner, my mother's former number-one associate, and he was rather reluctant to see my return.

To avoid facing a long, drawn-out legal battle in the American courts where the company was now officially registered, we agreed that I take a percentage of the company and control of my own division.

I was temporarily satisfied with this and used my resources to aid the Australian resistance back home. However, the time came when I decided the company needed restructuring with myself in charge of everything.

Drake wasn't going to just give up his seat as the head of the most influential organization in the solar system. But as part of our deal, we struck a very unusual settlement. Being genetically modified, I would neither age nor die, so

I made a practical argument that, in the event of his death, I would inherit his share of the company.

It would be the last mistake he ever made. This is where my dear Liam comes into the story, but I'll let him tell you all about that.

Hannah Grant
Joint Chairperson
HanWyn Corporation

CHAPTER ONE

THE GIRL

Two years before Last Day

The day was hot, and the beach was busy. I could've lived in Australia for the rest of my life, but I would never get accustomed to the extreme heat of summer in January. I had hoped to sit on the roadside in my air-conditioned vehicle and watch her, but I'm sure she deliberately moved further down the beach to where I couldn't see her. So, I found myself standing on the pavement, watching her and her friends set up their towels and umbrellas on the sand of St. Kilda Beach.

I wasn't expecting her to come here and, so wasn't exactly addressed for the occasion. I stood out like a sore thumb in my black trousers, white shirt, and matching black tie. It was still early morning, yet I could already feel the sweat on my back begin to stick to my shirt. Even the hottest day of the year back in London was no match for January in Melbourne.

I recognised one of the girls with her, but the other was unknown to me. I slipped my Grant Optical 5000 glasses out of my shirt pocket and put them on. There wasn't anything wrong with my vision, but these were connected to my phone, which was obviously connected to the Internet. I kept staring at the stranger whose back was to me, waiting for an opportunity to catch sight of her face. Only then did I notice that I wasn't the only one watching them. A group of young boys had caught sight of them and were clearly checking them out, dressed in their skimpy bikinis. My mark was always the centre of attention, for, despite the denials of her mother, she was clearly genetically modified. Whilst perfection regarding someone's appearance was subjective, there was no arguing that even at sixteen, she rivalled the top tier of models.

The girl turned round, and I could see her face. "Emily, zoom in." The glasses immediately enlarged the face of the young woman. "Emily, take a picture and identify."

"Subject: Sarah Monroe-Jenson. Student at Melbourne Grammar School," Emily replied in her soft, seductive tones. "Criminal record: Four speeding violations. Parents: Wade Jenson, C.E.O. of Jenson Ent..."

"That's enough, Emily," I muttered.

Emily was a GrantTech Companion Series Twelve computer program. My glasses were designed primarily as a personal organizer and day-to-day vocal interface. However, Grant Industries had provided me with an upgraded version that had access to what areas of the Internet the general public couldn't usually obtain. She'd proved an invaluable tool over the years.

It wasn't like I suspected this stranger to be some sort of threat. It was just an automatic routine to identify anyone around my mark. I turned my attention to the two boys approaching the girls. I quickly got Emily to do an I.D. on both, and they were all clean.

When the two boys came down the way, I weighed them up carefully. They sat down with the girls, and that wasn't a real issue. I could clearly see the girls were flirting with one of them, and he was reciprocating.

Not a problem.

Not yet.

Then they tried their move, and I fell for it.

The boy got up and walked away, but then one of the girls got up and started approaching me. I knew her quite well, for she was often at the family's Melbourne house.

"Hey, Mr Marshall, how are you doing?" she smiled at me, her eyes sparkling with mischief. She was dressed in nothing but a bikini and a very flirty attitude, which made me feel really uncomfortable. After all, she was only sixteen years old and could prove very problematic for me.

"Good morning, Miss Donovan. I'm doing very well. What can I do for you?"

"Oh, nothing. I just saw you here alone and thought you would like some company for a bit." She stood in the sand, directly between me and the group she had come from.

"Oh, I can assure you I'm perfectly fine, Miss Donovan. You should just go ahead and hang out with your friends."

She tilted her head slightly, giving me a rather seductive look. "You know, you're really handsome, and your accent is *sooo* sexy?" she said softly.

Oh no!

"This is extremely inappropriate of you, Miss Donovan, and I really must ask you to leave *now*."

"Oh, don't be like that, Mr Marshall," she reached out and placed a hand on my arm, running her fingers up and down, at which point I immediately stepped back.

"Step back, Bronwyn!" I snapped.

She glanced over to where my ward was, and my eyes followed hers. *Shit and double fuck*. She was gone, and so was the boy she was talking to. A grin crossed Bronwyn's face as she looked back at me.

"It was nice knowing you, loser."

She gave me the finger and turned away to rejoin the group on the beach. I was too busy scanning the beach for my ward to care.

She couldn't have gotten far, but I didn't even know which direction she'd gone in, and a mistake now would cost me dearly. There was no way I would lose my exceptionally good pay and benefits for this little brat. I looked over to where the small group of two remaining girls and a boy were looking over and laughing at me.

Those laughs quickly diminished as I strode towards them, and the boy jumped up. Seconds later, my hand was around his throat and slamming him down into the sand.

"Where the fuck's she gone, Bronwyn?" I demanded, staring up into the young girl's now terrified eyes. However, she was a loyal friend, and it would take much more to get her to say anything.

"Let him go, or I'm calling the police," she said icily.

I closed my hand around the boy's throat. He gagged and struggled under my weight as I knelt on his chest and continued to squeeze. As fear entered Bronwyn's eyes, I knew I was close to winning this fight. I didn't have long before I would start drawing attention from other beach dwellers.

"Let me be very clear with you, Bronwyn. You've heard of my boss, haven't you?" She nodded. "Then I'm quite sure you understand that I'm more afraid of her, than I'm of any police officer. Now I'm giving you one chance here, before I beat this little shit into a pulp, and then I'm going start on you until you eventually tell me where she's gone."

"You know who my dad is," Bronwyn snapped back at me. Sure I did, Kelvin Donavon, another rich guy with many companies, but he was insignificant next to my employer.

"He could be the president of Australia for all I care, Bron. So you can't scare me by invoking your Daddy's name. Now this guy is about to pass out, and only you can stop that from happening."

She looked down at the boy whose struggles were starting to diminish, then back up at me.

"The ice cream parlour on Main," she said quietly.

I didn't say another word as I released the boy and headed off at a brisk pace across the beach.

"Emily, give me directions to the ice cream parlour on Main."

It was less than two minutes away, and I looked through the window to see that she wasn't there. I considered that Bronwyn had possibly lied to me, but as I looked up the street, I could see the blonde hair of a girl dressed in a bikini with a wrap-around skirt. The boy from the beach was at her side, and both were enjoying their ice creams.

I headed briskly up the street towards them, coming up from behind. Without a word, I grabbed the boy by the back of the neck, spun him around, and slammed him against the wall. I muttered a curse as he dropped his ice cream onto the front of my trousers, not improving my mood. He stared back at me, afraid, as the girl turned around and punched me in the back, much harder than I thought was possible, and although it didn't have its desired effect of getting me to release him, it still hurt quite a bit. Holding the boy against the wall, I turned to her and shouted.

"Don't you fucking move!"

She stood frozen on the spot, totally surprised by how I had just spoken to her. I turned back to the boy, pulled him off the wall, and slammed him against it again so it hurt.

"Listen to me very carefully, arsewipe, because I will only say this once. If you so much as ever try this again, I will class it as an attempted abduction, and we won't be having a friendly chat. You'll be going to fucking jail. Do you understand me?"

"Yes!" he gasped out.

"Good. Now fuck off."

I released him. He didn't need to be told again as he raced off down the street back toward the beach. I then turned around to face the girl, who was red-faced with anger.

"Oh my God, you're such a shithead," she said aggressively. I stepped close to her and slapped that flawless face hard. She was more shocked than hurt as she brought her hand up to her cheek.

"Oh, you're one dead motherfucker," she said with quiet venom, pulling out her phone from the waistband of her skirt. I immediately slapped it out of her hand. It clattered to the ground, cracking the glass casing.

"Quit acting like you're some sort of royalty," I snapped.

"I'm the closest thing to royalty you'll ever know!" she snarled.

"What you're, *Duchess*, is a self-centred, selfish little bitch," I said, pushing my face just an inch from hers, and she stared back at me in utter shock. "You would destroy my career, just so you can go down on some guy in an alley?"

Her face instantly flushed a nice shade of pink.

"Wait! What? No!" she stammered out. "We were just having ice cream, for fuck's sake!"

She looked positively embarrassed by the suggestion I'd just made.

"I don't care what you were planning on doing. If you'd wanted to go and have ice cream with a boy, that would've been fine. You simply tell me, and I'll give you your space, but I will always have eyes on you. Try to lose me again, and your day will go really, really bad, really fast. Do you understand me?"

"But don't you have instructions to keep me away from boys?" she sulked, still sounding uneasy.

"How I interpret my responsibilities is up to me, and personally, I take it that I'm not to let you get yourself into any *trouble* with a boy. I don't see eating ice cream as problematic. Unless your mother tells me otherwise, it'll remain that way. I'm here to keep you safe and alive, and no-one will stop me from doing that. Not even you. Beyond that, I don't care what you do."

She looked down.

"I'm sorry," she said for the first and only time. Then she looked up at me with those large blue eyes. "You're not like the others. They made me feel like a dog on a lead. You have no idea how much I hate that."

My voice softened as I said, "If we work together, Hannah, we can make this as easy as possible. I don't want to get in your face, and I don't want to get into your business. But you really have to understand, you're at risk due to who your mother is. If you force me to not be in your face, then I have to be. You might be able to get rid of me like you have my predecessors, but your mother will still get security for you. You can continue making it as hard for them as possible, but wouldn't you like to make it easier for yourself?"

She pondered this a moment, then grinned and put her hand out to me. "Start over? Clean slate, Mr Marshall?"

I smiled back at her.

"Clean slate, Miss. Grant," I replied and shook her hand.

Now, I guess you're probably wondering how I, a former British Special Air Service member, came to be the security detail for a spoiled Australian teen. Simple, really. Pay and pensions.

Everyone has a story to tell about the fall of the Pacific Alliance and how it irrevocably changed their lives. I was born in London, and as soon as I turned eighteen, I joined the army. After a year of fighting in the back end of space, I joined the S.A.S., until a bullet wound to the back of my head almost killed me. Although I recovered, I started suffering migraines sufficiently bad enough to get myself medically discharged.

I didn't do particularly well at school, so I wasn't destined for college or anything. Being only qualified to kill people, I didn't exactly have transferable skills to put to use in the civilian arena. So, I worked in retail until an opportunity arose for an actual career. Grant Industries was the major employer in the country, and I found a recruitment pamphlet sitting in the cafeteria of the store I worked in. Grant Security Services. It offered double the wage I was working on, but most of all, it had an excellent pension, but still being in my twenties, I didn't really give a shit about that. The job was to simply be a security guard.

I submitted my application online that very day and was surprised to find an e-mail asking me for an interview waiting for me the following morning. I don't know whether I particularly impressed the bored-looking woman who interviewed me, or they were simply desperate for bodies to fill their vacancies, but I got the job.

Two weeks later, I was spending my nights wandering around a warehouse in East Ham, bored out of my life, but now, I had an income where I could rent myself a modest flat to move out of my parent's place.

I appeared to impress my bosses, as six months later, I was promoted to shift supervisor. It wasn't particularly hard to impress one's superiors in this job. You just had to turn up on time and keep your uniform clean. Just over a year later, I was called into my boss' office. She was looking at me with concern as she asked me to sit.

"I just received an instruction from Philip Crawford. Apparently, he wants me to send you to the corporate office for a meeting."

I had no clue who this was, despite the name sounding familiar. "Okay, I'll head over there."

"No, Liam, I'm not talking about the London head-quarters. I mean the actual headquarters in Melbourne, Australia."

My eyes widened in surprise. "Why?"

"That's what I'd like to know," she replied curtly.

I shrugged. "I have no idea. Who is this Philip Craw-ford?" (Aaron Note: American)

"Crawford is the Chief Executive of Grant Security Services. He answers only to Marcia Grant. You must've se-verely fucked something up to obtain her attention."

"How am I supposed to get there? I can't afford to fly to Australia."

"The company is paying," she replied.

And they did. The following day, I boarded a direct flight to Melbourne. First-class, even. It didn't really make sense if the corporate head of security was out to tear me a new one.

I felt quite important when I arrived at the terminal and a man was waiting to drive me to the Grant Industries

Tower. I was led inside and taken up almost a hundred and three stories, to the executive suite. I started becoming nervous, since I hadn't even remotely imagined my job would take me into the echelons of the company hierarchy.

That was when I first met Philip Crawford. He was a tall, handsome man, clearing me by a couple of inches. He had strong, hard features with a square jaw and piercing blue eyes.

"Good morning, Mr Marshall. Please take a seat," he said, indicating the chair opposite his desk. I complied, sitting in that awkward upright position that most people do when undergoing an interview. "Your managers speak very highly of you. Your performance reviews are quite outstanding," he spoke with a distinctly American accent.

"I endeavour to do my best, sir," I replied, trying to sound both modest, yet not undermining myself.

"You do know you're overqualified for your position?" he stated.

"I have no qualifications. I didn't even from graduate school."

Crawford gave me a wide smile. "I'm talking about your military experience in Britain's elite service. According to your records, you have a well above average proficiency in firearms."

"Indeed," I replied with some concern. "Sir, forgive me for saying so, but my records are sealed by the Ministry of Defence?"

He simply dismissed that with a wave of his hand. "I'm considering you for a position based in Melbourne, and you'll be expected to move here. Will you have a problem with that?"

I didn't, 'cause apart from my parents, I had no particular attachment to London.

"I've always wanted to broaden my horizons," I smiled, but he didn't return it, making me quite uncomfortable.

"We have a variety of openings that need your particular skill set, Mr Marshall. Ones that pay considerably more than you'll get as a warehouse guard."

"I can't see how. I really only have military service to offer."

"Exactly, Mr Marshall. Exactly."

I laughed. "You sound like you have your own military, which'd be highly illegal."

A slight smirk crossed Crawford's face as he replied. "Oh, Mr Marshall, we have incredibly expensive lawyers who work very hard to ensure that no-one ever says that."

My face fell, but he quickly moved on to talk some more about my experience and background. Nothing important to relate here, and then he wrapped up. The interview ended, and I returned home.

CHAPTER TWO

DUCHESS

O bviously, I got the job. Otherwise, there would be little point in telling you this.

I learned about it the next day, after receiving an e-mail and another ticket to Melbourne. My mum was understandably upset when I told my parents that I was moving, but they understood, and to be honest, I think they were pleased that I appeared to have a career, despite my poor academic record.

The instructions in the e-mail were to bring just one suitcase and leave a list of anything else I wanted shipped out, and Grant Logistics would pick them up. My parents saw me off at the airport, and thirty-five minutes later, I was landing in Australia.

I must admit that I was completely surprised when Crawford met me at the terminal. "Welcome to Australia, Mr Marshall."

"Delighted to be here, Mr Crawford."

I returned the smile and his handshake, before he led me out to where a Grant Industries car was sitting in a tow zone, ignored by the passing police. Grant Industries certainly had a lot of clout.

He opened the passenger door for me and then stepped around to the driver's side, and we both climbed in. He programmed the onboard auto-drive with the address, which didn't sound very much like Grant Industries' corporate headquarters to me. As it pulled away, he saw the curious look on my face.

"You have one final interview to go through, Mr Marshall," he smiled.

"Oh, really? I was informed that I had the position," I said, a little concerned that I'd gone through all this for nothing.

"You're absolutely guaranteed a position with us at our head office security services, but I have a rather special position that I want you to be considered for. And for this position, you need to be signed off by Marcia Grant herself."

My jaw almost dropped. Marcia Grant was the ipso facto God-like head of Grant Industries, descended directly from the original founder. What the hell had I just gotten myself into? What's more, Grant wasn't exactly renowned for being nice. To be a successful businessman, they say you need to be at least a little bit sociopathic, but, at least by reputation, Marcia Grant was full on.

Soon we entered the suburbs of Melbourne, and Crawford advised me that we were going to the Grant residence. I'm not usually a nervous person, but this, indeed, was making me a tad uneasy.

When we finally pulled through the gates of what I can only describe as an almost palatial estate and headed up the long driveway, my professional side couldn't help but notice the number of cameras facing us. There was no guard at the gate as everything was automated, and the cameras would have both recognised Crawford's car, and even scanned his face, just in case someone else was driving it. I found my door being opened by some form of antiquated footman, and I thanked him as I stepped out, and noticed Crawford was treated likewise from his side.

As we headed up the steps of the grand house, we were greeted by a pretty young girl with a smart business outfit, who I would later find out was Marcia Grant's personal assistant.

Rather than lead us through to any offices, I found myself taken into a living room. I instantly recognised the Grant Industries C.E.O. sitting at a small desk, writing with an old-fashioned pen and paper. Slouching on an overly large couch was a teen girl resting her head lazily in the palm of her hand as she watched the T.V.

Marcia Grant looked up at us and smiled. "I take it this is Mr Liam Marshall?" she said in her distinct Australian accent.

"It is indeed, ma'am," Crawford replied.

She rose from her seat and came and stood in front of me, looking me up and down, as one would a slave they had just purchased. I felt rather uncomfortable.

"Does he ever smile?"

Crawford smiled. "On occasion, ma'am."

Marcia Grant chuckled at this. "I assume you've done all his background checks?"

"Yes, Ma'am," Crawford sounded positively offended.

Marcia glanced at him with a knowing smile.

"Of course you have, my dear. My apologies." She then looked back at me. "This is quite a privileged position you're being considered for, Mr Marshall. We don't take just anybody, but if you're good enough for Crawford, you're good enough for me. However, I'll make it very clear that I expect absolute loyalty from you."

"That shouldn't be a problem, Ma'am," I replied, still clueless about my new position.

"Accommodation has been provided for you here, and at the city apartment. I'll have Williams show you to your room whenever you're ready."

I looked considerably confused and glanced toward Crawford, who coughed slightly to draw his boss's attention. "I haven't actually told Mr Marshall the nature of his position yet, ma'am. I thought it wiser to obtain your approval first."

"I see," Marcia said softly. She turned to the girl slouched on the couch, still watching the T.V. "Come over here," she instructed the girl.

"I'm watching the telly," she replied disinterestedly. Marcia simply used a voice command for the T.V. to be turned off. As it fell silent, the girl got up sulkily.

"Oh, for fuck's sake, Mum," she said, approaching us. To my surprise, Marcia's hand came up and slapped her hard around the face. The girl looked hardly fazed but glared angrily at her mother.

"Don't you ever let me hear that word come out of your mouth again, young lady."

Now, I can't let it pass without saying how unbelievably beautiful this young girl was, even though she was only sixteen. She had bright blue eyes, golden hair, and perfectly unblemished skin. She was clearly a GenMod. I'd worked with one before. A man called Jayson Plularian.

"Mr Marshall, this is my daughter, who you'll be responsible for keeping safe. Your schedule will operate around hers, and you'll be answerable to me directly," she gestured to her daughter. "Mr Marshall, please meet my daughter Hannah."

To say I was shocked and surprised would've been quite an understatement. Suddenly finding myself as the security for a member of what was known by the media as the first family of Australia was quite unexpected.

I didn't exactly get to speak to her that first day, as I was taken to be shown my quarters, and that was where I first met Kirsty Fillion. I admit that I was surprised that I would be sharing my accommodation with a young woman. It was a suite in the family's wing that had two rooms. Kirsty was about two years older than me and had served in the household for a couple of years as the security for Hannah's sister, Annabelle. She was Australian, an ex-cop, and had a very cheerful disposition.

"Welcome to bitch central," she told me once I was left alone with her.

"What exactly does that mean?" I asked, genuinely curious.

"You've just become security to one of the biggest divas in the solar system. Annabelle isn't so bad, but Hannah's a pain in the arse. I'm warning you right now."

"In what way do you mean?"

"She doesn't like having security around her and will do everything she can to ditch you. That's actually why you're replacing her last security officer. She let Hannah get away far too many times for Marcia Grant's liking."

"Well, that's certainly not going to make my job much easier, is it?" I said softly. "It's virtually impossible to protect someone who doesn't want to be protected."

"Yeah. To be honest with you, Hannah's security doesn't usually last more than three or four months."

"Well, let's see if I can break that record," I chuckled.

Kirsty grinned. "We'll see."

She then spent the next few hours reviewing my specific responsibilities and Hannah's itinerary with me. It seemed fairly simple, but it looked like I would have most of the day off, as I wasn't expected to stay with her at school. I would drop her off and pick her up, and should she remain in the house, I wasn't responsible for her to the degree that I'd have to stay with her. It was only the rare times she left the premises that I'd be expected to accompany her.

I wasn't expected to start work for another day, but I thought I'd take the opportunity to get to know her a little better. I found her once more in the living room, watching the T.V. again.

"Excuse me, ma'am, do you mind if we talk briefly?"

She didn't look up or appear to notice me in any way, but she said lazily, "Don't call me ma'am."

18

"Well, that's the protocol for someone in my position," I replied.

She turned her head slowly towards me and gave me one of those sighs of someone not wanting to use the energy to respond to me.

"Do I look like I give a fuck about what your protocol is? The name is Hannah or Han."

"As you wish, Hannah."

"Where is that accent from?" she frowned at me. "Scotland?"

"London," I replied simply.

"Same difference. It's all British," she frowned.

I took great offence at this. I didn't try to hide it. "Scotland hasn't been British for hundreds of years. Don't they teach you that in school?"

She simply shrugged. "Do I look like I give a fuck what they teach in school?"

"Well, you should. Education is very important." No, I wasn't being a hypocrite. My failure in the education system proved to me how important an education was.

She snorted at this. "*You* may need education to get a job, but it's pretty much guaranteed where my income will come from."

"Well, don't be too confident about that. There's a war on, and wars constantly change governments and companies. You can't rely on a silver spoon to see you through, and it's quite possible you could need a job. Even if you don't, you can hardly take over your mother's company if you're dumb."

"Oh, trust me, Mr Marshall, I have no interest in taking over Grant Industries. And I'm quite sure I can get a job, without a high school diploma."

What came out of my mouth next was wholly inappropriate and, to be honest, probably grounds for dismissal, but quite frequently, I spoke before I thought about it.

"Oh sure, you might suddenly care if you end up as a security officer taking care of a mouthy little brat."

Rather than get offended, she turned to look at me with a big wide grin across her face, lighting up those bright blue eyes, and she sat up.

"Nice one, mate. That was a good comeback. I might even like you, but don't let that go to your head."

"Oh, my dear Hannah, I don't require you to like me to carry out my duties. Although it would make them easier," I smiled back at her.

"Oh, my dear Mr Marshall," she replied sarcastically. "Even if I do like you, I won't make your job easy. I really don't want a fucking security guard following me around all day and getting into my business."

"You're not concerned about your safety?"

"Benjamin Franklin once said, 'Those who would give up essential liberty, to purchase a little temporary safety, deserve neither liberty, nor safety.'"

"And who exactly is Benjamin Franklin?" I asked.

Her eyes widened. "And you seek to lecture me on getting an education? Look, it's nothing personal, but I really don't want you around telling my mother everything I do."

"Well, I can honestly say that I've been given quite the list of instructions for your safety, but I haven't been instructed to inform your mother of everything you do."

"Maybe not, but that's not going to stop you. She'll ask you, and she's your boss, so you can't refuse to answer her."

"I'll do you a deal *if* you don't try to mess with me. I won't tell your mother anything about your actions even if she asks me. However, there's one exception to that. If you compromise your own safety, then I'll have no alternative."

Hannah grinned. "Oh my God, you're not going to last more than three days working for my mother."

I didn't pursue the issue and found the next few days relatively easy. I drove Hannah to school and picked her up, and I took her on trips into town to meet with her friends.

Things seemed to be going fine for just over a week, until I ultimately ended up outside the ice cream parlour.

I have no idea how Marcia Grant learned about the incident, but we weren't home for more than an hour, when I was summoned to her private quarters.

I knocked carefully on the door, entering when she permitted me to do so. Marcia Grant was an alluring woman, but that was mostly thanks to the excellent work of surgeons. As I entered her room, she sat before a vanity, applying makeup.

"I'm sorry. Would you like me to come back later?" I asked politely.

She glanced back at me through the vanity mirror with a raised eyebrow.

"If I wanted you to do that, Mr Marshall, I wouldn't have asked you to come here, now would I? Come in and shut the door." I did as instructed and patiently waited for her to continue speaking. "I just heard an interesting story about an incident at the beach."

"There was a minor incident, but it was resolved."

"You hit my daughter, Mr Marshall. Would you care to explain that?" She lay down her mascara and turned to face me.

Wow, there it was. I was about to lose my job. Oh well, I had nothing to lose by being honest with her. "There is clearly a problem with your daughter's respect for her security. She's managed to intimidate and get rid of most of her previous security officers. Am I not correct?"

There was a short pause. "Go on, Mr Marshall, you have my attention."

"The only way that could've possibly happened is if her previous security allowed your daughter to walk all over them. This has meant they've put her social class before her safety and behaved subserviently to her."

"Well, they are, in a way. You are employees," Marcia frowned, trying to work out what I was getting at.

"Yes, ma'am, but I don't work for Hannah. I work for you. I don't care what Hannah has to say or what she thinks or wants. She behaved in a manner that endangered herself, and I'm responsible for ensuring she's not in any danger. To achieve that, she clearly needs to understand that where her safety's concerned, I'm the boss, not her. And if you'll forgive me, not you."

She raised an eyebrow. "Well, that's certainly very forward of you, Mr Marshall."

"Not really, Ms. Grant. You pay me for my talents, experience, and expertise. You don't expect Hannah to tell your cooks how to prepare a meal, and Hannah shouldn't be able to tell me how to do my job. Nor should you."

"I take your point. But that doesn't explain hitting her."

"But that was unfortunate, but necessary," I said, doubling down. I wasn't going to apologise for something I wasn't sorry for. "Hannah displayed a disrespectful attitude and was about to create a scene that would have drawn attention to us."

"Hannah frequently makes a scene," Marcia shrugged it off. "But don't you think hitting her will draw attention?"

"To some degree, yes. But I'm sure you don't want negative attention. Specifically, towards Hannah."

Marcia tilted her head, looking almost accusingly at me. "Why Hannah especially?"

"Your daughter is getting older, and forgive me for saying so, becoming incredibly attractive."

"So?"

"Ma'am, she's becoming *too* attractive. Unnaturally so, and that's going draw attention."

Marcia positively stiffened and narrowed her eyes at me. "What exactly are you implying, Mr Marshall?"

"Ma'am. You want me to protect your daughter. If you hamstring me in a position where I can't discuss something that will clearly become subject to the media, that'll make it more difficult. I ask that you trust me and that I'm only bringing this up to fulfil that role. You need to be prepared for it, and so do I."

She didn't relax as she fixed that stare upon me. "Spit it out, Mr Marshall. Let me hear you say it."

"As you wish, Ma'am. The nature of Hannah's genetic modifications are going to become a matter of public interest. I assume you made sure you have all the records attesting to the fact that she is a naturally birthed person?"

"Mr Marshall, I'm sure you're very well aware that genetic modification is illegal in Australia. What you're saying, if it was true, could have both Hannah and myself incarcerated for a very long time. It's quite an accusation to make."

"Is it not better that I make that accusation than the general media, Ms. Grant?"

A thin smile crossed her lips. "Possibly. However, you've been my employee, at least directly, for a little over a week, and you're asking me to trust you with an aspect of my life that, if true, could cause me a considerable amount of embarrassment."

"Ma'am, you trust me with the life of your daughter, a responsibility that I take very seriously. It's not in her best interests that she gets stripped of her Australian citizenship, as required by law, for anyone discovered being genetically modified. I don't think it's in my job description to allow you, or Hannah, to be arrested by the authorities. Nor is it in *my* interest to allow that to happen. I'm merely saying that it's an issue that must be addressed and prepared for. The older Hannah gets, the more attention will be drawn to her. They call you the First Family of Australia, and the tabloid press would love nothing better than a juicy GenMod story. I ask that you trust me enough, or at least allow me to prove that you can, so we can work together to protect not only Hannah but yourself."

Marcia appeared to ponder this, then smiled. "I won't discuss this any further, but I'll take you at your word that you will prove to me that I can trust you. Then maybe we'll talk more on this subject. However, in the meantime, I give you the liberty to take any action you deem necessary to protect, not only my daughter's safety, but also her best interests, whether she approves or not. Am I understood?"

I nodded. "Completely understood, ma'am."

Chapter Three

A Little Too Perfect?

It happened just before Christmas. I'd been in my position for around two months, and the holiday was rapidly approaching. It was a Saturday morning, and Hannah wanted to go into town with Bronwyn for some Christmas shopping. Although the concept of shopping centres and malls had been long gone in favour of online purchasing, there were still some malls catering to the higher-end market. Melbourne had several of these, and Hannah frequently spent vast sums on her ever-expanding wardrobe. However, on this occasion, they were looking for gifts.

Hannah had recently passed her driving test, and there was no way in hell she was now going to accept rides from me anywhere. As a result, I would follow her in my car wherever she went. I was initially concerned that she would try to lose me occasionally, but that fear was baseless. In fact, I think she'd completely forgotten I was there whenever she was driving. In time, her mother would give her permission to drive to school without me doing even that.

Prior to this day, there hadn't been any incidents. However, as we pulled into the car park and I parked several cars down from her, I quickly grew concerned as I noticed someone was heading toward her car. A man in his fifties was watching as they got out. I moved faster, jumping out of my car as quickly as possible.

It was a hot December day, and Hannah had dressed for such an occasion, wearing cut-off jeans and a crop top exposing her midriff. At her side, Bronwyn was dressed in jeans and a T-shirt. However, the stranger wasn't interested in Bronwyn, as he was clearly looking straight at Hannah, who was still oblivious to his presence as she chatted away with her friend.

As they stepped out from the side of the vehicle, the man noticed me heading towards them and hurried his pace. I instantly took this as an aggressive sign.

"Hey!" I shouted, and both Hannah and Bronwyn turned to look at me. The man clearly ignored me. It was only then that Hannah noticed him, and the look of fear crossed her face as I broke into a run. He pulled a small device from his pocket and pointed it at her as I dove at the man, bringing him down to the ground and landing on top of him. "Don't move, or I'll break your neck," I growled softly as I noticed the feet of both Bronwyn and Hannah standing on either side of us.

"Get off me," he gasped. "I wasn't attacking her."

"Show me what's in your hand," I demanded, pulling him up. He held out his hand. I took the small camera and then looked at him suspiciously.

"I'm a journalist. I'm doing a story on Miss Grant here. If you don't let go of my collar, I'm calling the police."

"Go on then. Fuck off." I said as I let him go.

However, rather than leave, he turned to Hannah. "Would you be interested in being interviewed for a story I'm doing?"

"No, she won't." I stepped between them. "As I said, fuck off!"

"Hey, I can answer for myself!" Hannah said snippily as she pushed me aside with that genetically enhanced strength.

A grin crossed the journalist's face as he noticed how easily the slight girl had moved me. "You tell him, young lady."

I ignored both of them. "If you don't leave now, you won't be leaving at all."

"Is that a threat, Mr Marshall?" The use of my name startled me. It wasn't like I'd introduced myself to the scumbag, and it also made me think how in the hell he knew we'd be here. The only obvious answer was someone within Marcia Grant's household was a tattletale, but I'd have to worry about that later.

"She's not gonna answer any of your questions."

Thinking about it now, it was probably the wrong tack to take, as I was infuriating my young ward by making her think I was treating her like a child. Therefore, her reaction was to rebel against me.

"What is it you want to ask me?" she asked the journalist.

He grinned triumphantly at me. Then, looking back at her, he said, "Would you care to explain the nature of your genetic modifications?"

The smile on Hannah's face suddenly fell. She glared at him for a long moment.

"I'm not a GenMod," she said softly and turned to look at me. "Would it be inappropriate for me to ask you to break his kneecaps?"

His face went white as I grinned back at her. "If that's what you wish me to do, Miss Grant."

"It is, Mr Marshall, and I apologise for not listening to you in the first place."

"Oh, no need to apologise, Miss Grant. This sleaze was just taking advantage of your caring and gracious nature."

Hannah grinned at that comment. "Yes, I'm certainly too nice for my own good."

As she turned away, I punched the man hard in his solar plexus until he collapsed on the ground. The two girls started heading to the mall entrance, and I did exactly what she requested. With a couple of stomps of my heel on one of his knees, I left him screaming in pain. Working for Marcia Grant was like having diplomatic immunity. He could complain until he was blue in the face to the authorities, but nothing would happen. Fortunately, we had arrived early enough that no-one else was around, and as he writhed in pain, I dropped the little camera next to him and shattered it with my heel. However, he must've set it to automatic upload, 'cause a week later, the pictures of her appeared in a magazine with the headline, 'A Little Too Perfect.'

The story didn't specifically say that Hannah Grant was genetically modified. They got around a potential lawsuit by simply alleging that she 'appeared' to 'possibly be' genetically modified. Within an hour of learning this, I was seated at a boardroom desk with Marcia Grant and Philip Crawford.

"I'm not happy," Marcia Grant started the meeting.

"Understandable," I responded honestly.

"The current situation is completely unacceptable, and I really need it resolved."

"Well, surely, as long as the story can't be proved, eventually people will get bored of it, and it'll go away," I suggested.

"It's not really that easy, Liam," Crawford said with a long sigh. "If someone were to get Hannah's D.N.A. and analyse it, then they would have evidence."

"Then we have to find a way to compel them to lose interest in the story before it gets to that stage," I stated.

"Glad you see eye to eye with me," Marcia smiled. "I'll leave it to you to sort out the details and look forward to hearing of a resolution to this abominable situation."

And with that, she simply got up and left.

I looked questioningly at Crawford, who simply shrugged it off.

"Plausible deniability, Liam. She's given us the go-ahead to do whatever is necessary without specifying anything, and if she doesn't know what it is we're doing, she can't face any accusations. At least, not any she can't deny."

"Understood," I replied. Off-the-books operations weren't exactly new to me. I was involved in quite a few during my army service, and although this was now the private sector, it didn't exactly weigh on my conscience. "However, taking out journalists isn't likely to make the story go away. Simply give it an interesting twist for other journalists."

"I completely agree, Liam. However, I don't think we even need to go that far, unless it's absolutely necessary. This is only being picked up by one magazine, and we need to move quite swiftly to stop it becoming a viral story."

"I take it you have something in mind?"

"The editor of that rag is a man called Duncan Levine, and he needs to be *encouraged* to squash the story. I had my people run a psych evaluation on him. I had hoped that there was a possibility that we could set him up, but he's not likely to go for that. He's a holier-than-thou church-going man with very few vices, other than running stories on the private lives of celebrities."

"Everybody has a weakness," I responded.

"Indeed, he does. He has a daughter who he's extremely devoted to."

"And you plan to set her up somehow?" I frowned.

Crawford laughed. "Not exactly, Liam. She's only seven years old. We're going to make him fear for her welfare."

"I can't really say that I'm on board with harming a child," I protested.

"Oh, I don't think it will come to that. It simply needs to be implied."

So, two days later, I found myself parked outside a small suburban elementary school, waiting for the kids to come out. I can't say I was overly happy about it, but it wasn't like the Grants had started this affair. There was going to be absolutely no harm done to the kid, at least not from my side. I watched as parents began to arrive, and noted when Susan Levine's car was parked a little way up the road. That was my target's wife, who was here to pick up their precious little child. It was less than thirty yards, and that was the distance where I would have my only opportunity to intercept the young girl.

Somehow, Crawford managed to get me multiple photographs of the child, and I had memorised what she looked like. As they let out the kids, I started to scan each of their little faces until I found my mark. She was a cute little girl with pigtails and a freckled nose, and she came out gripping the straps of a little backpack as she started to walk to her mother's car. I pulled out of my parking spot and drove up beside her, opening the window.

"Hey, it's Alyssa, isn't it?" I called to the little girl, who turned around and looked nervously at me.

"Yes, it is," she said uneasily.

I had nothing particular to talk to her about. I just had to keep her there talking to me until her mother noticed. It's not exactly something hard to do because, although parents teach their kids not to talk to strangers, they also teach them not to be rude when they're out and a stranger says hello to them. It's a nice little conflict that'll make her look both nervous, and yet continue talking to me.

"How was school today?"

She shrugged. "It was fine."

"Do you have any plans for Christmas?"

She shrugged again. "No."

Yeah, I wasn't exactly good with kids. However, I noticed Mrs. Levine getting out of her car. A tall, glamorous woman in her thirties.

"Well, I hope you've been good because Santa only comes if you've been a good girl."

She rolled her eyes at me. "There's no such thing as Santa."

"Excuse me, Sir!" Mrs Levine ran up to the car and pulled her daughter behind her. "Just what do you think you're doing?"

I smiled at her and pulled my wallet out of my pocket. "You have a very beautiful and intelligent child, Mrs. Levine. I'm sure Duncan is very proud of her." She immediately looked confused by my recognition of her. I slipped one of my business cards out of my wallet and handed it to her.

She glanced at it and then looked up at me with a frown. "Grant Industries Security Services? What exactly does this have to do with my daughter?"

"Oh, just pass on my regards to your husband, Mrs. Levine." I then looked back at the child. "It's been exceptionally nice to meet you, Alyssa, but hopefully, we won't meet again." I smiled at the scared-looking woman. "Have a great day," I said and pulled my car out into the afternoon traffic.

I headed to the corporate building of Grant Industries, rather than go home as always, to meet Crawford to inform him how it went. I was pleasantly surprised to see that he was in a video conference with Duncan Levine as I walked in.

"I quite agree with you that it would've been very inappropriate if one of my officers had gone to your daughter's school, but I'm not aware of that event having ever taken place," Crawford was saying as his secretary let me in.

"Don't play games with me, Crawford! This is all about that GenMod freak of a daughter of Marcia Grant, isn't it?"

"Oh, that's quite a serious accusation, Mr Levine. The automatic assumption that someone has to be genetically modified to be as attractive as Hannah Grant is positively ludicrous," Crawford sounded personally offended.

"I'm not playing games, Crawford. I will be filing a report with the police about your intimidation."

"Oh, really, Mr Levine? Do you want to ruin your Christmas this way?"

"I'm certainly not giving in to your threats. In fact, you can expect to see Hannah Grant on the front cover of our next issue with a very interesting headline!"

"I'm very disappointed to hear that, Mr Levine. I wonder if your wife will support that decision?"

"The next time you send one of your lackeys anywhere near my daughter or my wife, I will have them arrested, and there will be a story about it. Good day, Mr Crawford."

I sighed regretfully. "Well, it appears that didn't work."

"Oh, don't give up that easily, Liam." Crawford turned his chair towards me and smiled. "We just have to move to phase two."

Phase Two involved me sitting outside the elementary school once again. This time, when Mrs. Levine arrived, she got out of her car to wait by the gate. She noticed me sitting there, and she looked uneasy. She didn't return my smile and wave. The moment her daughter came out, she virtually ran her back to her car, and I waited until she pulled out into traffic. I then followed her closely. Very closely. In fact, I clung to her rear end, leaving barely an inch between our two cars. I could even see her glancing at me in her rearview mirror. I followed her all the way home, but instead of stopping at the house, she just drove past it and continued on. I continued to follow until I noticed the flashing blue lights in my mirror and heard the sirens coming up behind me. I sighed, pulled over, and watched as Mrs. Levine disappeared down the road.

I put in a call to Crawford.

"I just got stopped by the boys in blue."

"No worries, let me make a call."

The cop got out of his car and started heading towards me as I watched him in my side-view mirror. Just as he reached the boot of my car, he stopped, and I saw him talking into his radio. He looked a little confused, and as he looked up, his eyes met mine via the mirror. He stood there momentarily, then turned, went back to his car, got in, and drove off.

There was no chance of me finding Mrs. Levine now, so instead, I turned the car around, drove back to her house, and parked outside. The look on her face was sheer terror when she saw me sitting there, but she drove into the driveway, hurried her daughter up to the house, and slammed the door hard enough that I could hear it even with my windows closed. I could see her watching me from the kitchen window, talking animatedly on the phone and clearly getting annoyed with someone. I stayed there for about an hour before driving home.

"Where have you been?" Hannah Grant greeted me in the doorway, which wasn't exactly something she usually did.

"I had some business to attend to, Duchess, that's all. Why? What's the problem?"

"I wanted to go out with Bron and Sarah, but I'm not allowed to leave unless I've got your dumb arse following me."

"We can go now if you like," I said with a shrug.

All she did was roll her eyes at me and storm off, muttering, "Oh, it's too late now, mate. You're ruining my life."

CHAPTER FOUR

TAKING A BULLET

There were no more reports.

Of course, this didn't end the rumours surrounding Hannah Grant. Nothing would achieve that, but it did curb overt scrutiny. Basically, everyone knew Hannah was a GenMod, but no-one would actually say so. Even if a teenage kid so much as stated it in a blog, they would quickly find themselves served with a cease-and-desist order, with the threat of a libel suit. It wasn't like the government would investigate Hannah's status. Marcia pretty much had far too much influence there for anyone to take an interest, but even that authority could falter under public pressure. So, we simply continued to manipulate that pressure to make it a non-news item.

Genetic modification was society's new bogeyman. It'd been seventy-odd years since the Prague Convention had outlawed all human genetic modification, with the exception of the correction of potential birth defects. This didn't mean there weren't illegally created GenMods. However, whilst most never aged and died, they could still be killed in accidents and other violent incidents. It was estimated that there were less than two hundred of them remaining in the entire solar system. They were allowed to live out their lives, albeit with severe restrictions on the positions they could hold. However, there was still a faction that wasn't satisfied with that and believed that GenMods should be entirely eliminated. Most established religions had proclaimed them to be 'non-human' as they were the creation of man and not God and, therefore, had no souls.

Personally, I had no particular opinion on it. Hannah Grant was only one of two GenMods I'd met, and apart from her appearance, she appeared no different than your average spoiled brat of a girl.

However, I developed an affection for the teenager. Despite that arrogant attitude, I liked her tough, no-nonsense outlook on life. She treated me somewhat respectfully, and although we maintained a professional distance, neither of us could say we disliked each other. However, something happened that would irrevocably change our relationship forever.

I remember the day as if it was yesterday, 'cause it's forever burned into my brain. There was a big sports event at her school, and she wanted to go. It was pretty routine, and normally, she would do school activities without my presence, but on this occasion, I thought it would be fun to watch an Australian Rules Football match, and she conceded that I could go with her. This was one of the rare times that I actually travelled in a car with her since she'd gotten her licence. Of course, she wasn't about to let me do the driving, being a little bit of a control freak that she was.

Hannah drove like she owned to the road, and in some ways, she actually did. Grant Transit Limited owned all of the toll-paying private expressways in Melbourne. I must admit I closed my eyes a few times as she weaved in and out of the traffic, ignoring my requests to put the vehicle in automatic. It was already getting dark by the time we arrived at Melbourne Grammar, and her friends, Sarah and Bronwyn, were already waiting for her. However, as she got out of the car, she was distracted by a young lad who came walking up to her.

"Oh my God!" she muttered irritably to me. "I will give you a million dollars if you keep that little shit away from me."

I glanced from her to the kid coming ever closer. He looked innocuous enough. "What's the big deal with him?"

Hannah rolled her eyes. "That's Joshua. The little shit is my own personal stalker. He's always following me around and staring at me."

I could hardly blame the kid for that. Most red-blooded straight men would stare at Hannah Grant, but I just smiled at her and told her to go on ahead, and she left to join Bronwyn and Sarah. I stepped between her and her admirer.

"Can I help you, son?" I asked as he reached me.

The boy looked at me uneasily. "I just wanted to say hello to Hannah," he said innocently.

"Sorry, son, but Hannah doesn't want to say hello to you."

He seemed almost confused by this, and staring at me for a few moments, he ultimately said, "Why not?"

I couldn't help but wonder if this kid was for real. Throughout history, there's always been a pecking order in the school hierarchy. Clearly, this nervous little kid was unaware that Hannah was way out of his league. "Don't know, don't care."

"Are you her father?"

I took offence at this but laughed, 'cause as I was barely eight years older than her.

"No."

"Then who're you to tell me that I can't talk to Hannah?"

"Oh, I'm the guy that will break both your kneecaps if you try to," I responded, now getting irritated with his attitude. "Go on. Turn around and piss off."

He stared at me with a vacant, almost lifeless expression before he turned around. I stood watching him go, making sure that he wasn't going to double back and go around me to try and catch up with Hannah. I then turned away and headed to the back of the school where the footy oval was. Although I was technically not on duty, it just felt uncomfortable not sitting somewhere where I could see my young ward. I made my way up the bleachers to sit a few rows behind her and her friends, but as I passed them, Bronwyn waved me over.

"You know you can come and join us, Mr Marshall," she said.

I looked towards Hannah, who just grinned at me as she glanced at her friend and just nodded to me. I couldn't help but wonder what amused her so much, So, I sat down next to Bronwyn to watch the game, and it was only later that Hannah would admit to me that her friend Bronwyn had a crush on me.

It was the semi-final match of some competition, and as a result, it was packed out. Some really fat guy sat next to me, and I found myself pushed up next to Bronwyn, who clearly didn't have any objections to it, but left me feeling quite awkward. Partway through the game, Hannah decided she was hungry and headed off to the concession stand. I made to get up and go with her, but she placed her hand on my shoulder as she stepped past me.

"I'm just going up there," she said, indicating the top of the stairs. "I'm sure I'll survive for a few minutes."

Reluctantly, I allowed her to go and watched her ascend the stairs and disappear from view.

"Do you have a girlfriend, Mr Marshall?" Bronwyn asked me, and at her side, Sarah giggled.

"No, Miss Donovan, I don't."

"Do you have a boyfriend?" Sarah asked, only to receive an elbow in the ribs from Bronwyn.

"No, I don't have one of those either."

Bronwyn started arguing with Sarah, but I paid no attention, for at that moment, my phone started to emit a high-pitched whistle. Hannah's phone was programmed with a panic button, and she'd clearly just set it off. I was out of my seat and running up those stairs before you could blink, pushing people out of my way who were coming in the opposite direction. Ignoring their protests, I reached the top, and my eyes scanned the concession stands, but there was no sign of her. I looked down at my phone, bringing up the small map that clearly showed her location was out in the car park.

What the fuck!

I turned and ran from the sports field, spoiling the evening for the few people who had the bad luck of being in my way. I looked at my phone again, and she wasn't moving, and that scared me more than anything. I slipped my hand into my jacket and withdrew my pistol.

I darted in and out between the parked cars, trying to get a visual on her. She was struggling between two men who appeared to be trying to force her into the back of a truck. When I was about two car lengths from them, I stopped running and took aim.

"Freeze motherfuckers."

To my complete astonishment, the only reaction was one of them turning swiftly, bringing up a gun, and firing. I felt a sharp, stinging pain in my shoulder, and I immediately dropped down behind the car just before a second bullet whizzed overhead. This wasn't just some random attack on a pretty girl. This was a professional hit.

Despite the pain in my left shoulder and the sensation of warm, sticky blood seeping into my shirt, the adrenaline held back the pain. I moved several car lengths away outside of their vision, peering up through the windows of the cars to make out their position. Hannah was not going quietly and was kicking and biting. Her job was now made a little easier when one of the men became more concerned about me, but not for long. I came up quickly and double-tapped two rounds into his face from several car lengths away. As he went down, his companions swung Hannah around so that she was now between me and him. I was a good shot, but even I wasn't going to risk firing toward the girl I was supposed to be protecting. This wasn't some movie where the hero saves the day with a magic bullet. However, I now stood up.

"You aren't going anywhere!" I shouted at him. "That is, if you don't count leaving in a body bag, if you harm her."

"Stay back, or we'll find out if GenMod necks break as easily as human ones," he replied with a slight accent that I couldn't quite make out.

"It'll be the last thing you ever do. I promise you that," I said, but I stopped moving forward. "Let her go, and I'll let you walk away from here."

He pondered this and glanced toward his vehicle. I felt sure that he was wondering if he could make a break for it. Then he looked back at me and carefully let her go. She didn't move at first, clearly terrified about what was going on. But the moment the man stepped towards his car, and was no longer behind her, I double-tapped again, bringing him to the ground. I then hurried over to her to check if she was alright, and promptly made an incredibly rookie mistake. I didn't take the time to check if anyone else was in the vehicle, and I suddenly saw a hand gripping a gun come out of the window, aimed at Hannah. They were too well hidden for me to take them out, so I dove forward, covering Hannah with my body as a shot rang out. As I brought her down to the ground, a sharp pain emanated from my back as I heard the squealing of tyres as the vehicle sped away. Silence fell all around as I lay on top of the young woman, unable to move. My head lay on her shoulder, and I could hear her breathing softly. I then heard the clip-clop of feminine shoes and heard the voices of Bronwyn and Sarah, who carefully rolled me off of Hannah. I lay on my side, struggling to breathe, realising the blood was filling one of my lungs. All I could see was the ground around me and the feet of the three girls as they stood over me. I heard Bronwyn on her phone calling for an ambulance and Sarah's anxious voice asking what the hell was going on. Hannah didn't reply, and her high-heeled, open-toe sandals suddenly came into view. She crouched down on her haunches until all I could see were her bare knees. I felt her hand gently brush my hair back.

"It's gonna be okay, Liam. We're gonna get you help," she said softly.

I just lay there, unable to speak. Unable to move. She stayed at my side until the police made her step away and started to question her. I then saw the white trainers of paramedics as they moved around me, and I was carefully lifted up onto a gurney. I was struggling to retain consciousness now, and as I lay there, I felt someone take my hand and hold it gently. I could just make out Hannah talking to someone, but the words didn't register. On the other side was Bronwyn, and both girls came with me as I was taken to the ambulance. Then, a medic shoved a stim into my arm, and within seconds, everything around me faded away.

I have vague memories of drifting in and out of consciousness over the next few hours. Visions of different doctors and nurses, occasionally Hannah or Bronwyn. At one stage, I even saw Marcia Grant, who was talking animatedly to one of the doctors. It turned out that once I'd been fixed up in the emergency room, my boss had had me transferred to a private Medical Centre owned by the family. When I woke to a level where I could comprehend what was going on around me, I found I was in a small room, and I could now breathe properly. The bullets had been removed, and both my back and shoulder had been healed. I felt like I'd just woken up from a very good sleep. I saw a nurse in a cute little uniform sitting at the edge of my bed, reading through some notes, unaware that I was awake.

I simply sat there silently, thinking through what had happened. Even during my military years, I'd never been shot before, and I cannot understate what an unpleasant experience it was. The vulnerability I felt as I lay on the ground at the mercy of some teenage girl's ability to get me help.

"Well, g'day. Good to see you awake," the nurse said softly, smiling at me as she rose from her seat.

"Hannah?" I asked, my mouth and throat quite dry.

"Apart from being quite concerned about you, she's doing perfectly fine," the nurse said, pouring a glass of water and handing it to me.

"How long have I been here?"

"Two days. You had surgery to remove the bullets and fix the collapsed lung, and your medical nanobots have been upgraded to the latest from Grant tech."

I looked a little concerned. "Does my insurance cover that?"

She chuckled lightly. "To be honest, Mr Marshall, I have no idea. But I can assure you Marcia Grant is picking up the bill on this one."

"Nice to know," I said, lifting my sheet slightly to see that I was wearing one of those unflattering hospital gowns. I looked back at the good-looking young nurse with dark hair and unnaturally long eyelashes. "Am I allowed to get up?"

"I don't see why not, Mr Marshall. However, I'm instructed to call Hannah Grant when you're ready to leave. I understand she wants to pick you up herself."

"I don't suppose you know anything about the incident the other night, like who it was?"

"I'm sorry, but I don't. All I know is what was said on the news, that there was some random sexual attack."

Now that, I knew to be a blatant lie. I clearly remembered the hand that came out of the car, and the slender fingers with highly polished nails that gripped the gun. Whilst it wasn't unheard of for a woman to be involved in a potential rape situation, it was extremely rare. On top of that, the professionalism with which I was shot wasn't conducive to a gang of perverts looking for an easy target, although once again, not impossible.

As I climbed out of bed, the nurse turned away, pulling her phone out of her pocket. I couldn't help but notice those long black stockinged legs, perfectly shaped, stretching up into her uniform.

"Please inform Miss Grant that the patient is awake and ready to leave." She then stepped over to the cupboard and pulled out a clean change of clothes for me, which someone must have brought from home. She made no sign to leave as I got changed but turned her back to me again.

"What's your name?" I asked.

"Skylar. But everyone just calls me Sky."

"Well, Sky, how d'you feel about coming out for a drink with me sometime?" I said as I pulled on my jeans.

She glanced back at me without actually looking at me.

"Mr Marshall, it would be quite unprofessional to go on a date with a patient." Despite her words, her tone was flirty and coquettish, which made it even more endearing.

"Well, that's really what the fun is," I replied with a laugh.

She didn't reply, at least not immediately. Instead, she pulled a small notepad out of her pocket. She jotted something down on a piece of paper, tore it off, and turned back to hand it to me. I looked down at the phone number.

"Call me," she said, then headed out of the room to sort out my discharge papers. Once ready, I headed out after her. I signed some paperwork, and she told me I was expected to wait until Hannah arrived.

I couldn't help but feel curious as to why she'd personally come and get me, as it was quite out of character. I waited by the nurse's station, flicking through my phone messages. Clearly, my family had been informed that I'd been involved in some sort of incident, but there were several stressed messages from my mother back in the UK. I quickly texted her, saying I was fine and I'd call her later.

About twenty minutes later, Hannah Grant stepped through the door to the ward. She was casually dressed in jeans, a T-shirt, and trainers, with her long blonde hair clearly having been hastily tied back in a ponytail. Again, this was out of character for a woman who spent positively hours getting ready for anything. Her look of concern towards me turned into a smile, a surprisingly affectionate one.

"Hey there, Duchess," I smiled at her.

"It's good to see you up and well, Liam." And before I realised what she was doing, she placed her arms around me and hugged me. She laughed at the startled look on my face. "Come on, let's get you out of here and home."

She frowned slightly when I turned back to Skylar, who was behind the counter. "I'll call you tomorrow."

"I look forward to it," she replied.

Surprising me yet again, Hannah took my hand and led me out into the corridor. A short elevator ride later and heading out to the car park, we didn't say much to each other beyond some small talk. I got into the passenger seat of her car, and she started up the engine.

"Why did you do it?" she asked, as we pulled into the nighttime traffic.

"Do what?" I asked, genuinely bewildered.

"You took a bullet for me," she said, glancing over at me.

I merely shrugged. "I was doing my job."

"Oh, I don't think so, Liam," she said, almost laughing. "It's not like you're some sort of government agent, and it's certainly not in your job description."

"Honest truth, Duchess. I couldn't have lived with myself if anything had happened to you. I'm responsible for your welfare and survival," I shrugged.

"You actually care about me?" she asked, looking a little confused.

"Of course I do. I guess, in a way, you're kind of like family now. However, it's also my professional responsibility. Don't read too much into it."

"Well, that's the stupidest thing you've ever said," she chuckled lightly, and she took the car off the freeway and headed through the neighbourhood where we lived. "That gun was pointed directly at my head. If you hadn't done what you did, I'd be dead now. That was loyalty above and beyond the call of duty, and even my mother agrees. She wants to afford you the Right of Patronage."

I looked at her with surprise. For a country that prided itself on the pretence that it was a classless society, the Right of Patronage had been around for about a hundred years. It had started in an era of great economic depression and high unemployment. It was basically the sponsorship of an individual by a wealthier member of society. To support and take care of someone unable to care for themselves. Over the years, it'd developed into a reward for outstanding service by the nation's elite. Accepting this would be like being adopted by the Grant family.

"Your mother wishes to become my patron?" I responded with complete surprise.

At this, Hannah looked somewhat uncomfortable and said a little sheepishly, "Not exactly."

Silence fell between us, and she was clearly reluctant to explain, leaving me to ask, "Then what exactly??"

"Well, I thought... um ... considering everything you've done for me ...that I ... um... well ... I would be your patron."

If I wasn't already completely in utter shock, I certainly was now. Another long silence hung between us as this idea ruminated in my head. This caused her to become even more uneasy until she turned to look at me square on.

"Never mind, it's okay. Perhaps it's a silly idea. I just thought...." but her voice trailed off. I could see the look of disappointment on her face as she turned back to look at the road.

"You're only seventeen. Would that even be legal?" I asked.

"To be honest, that's what I thought, but apparently, as long as my mother signs off on it, it's all perfectly above board, but seriously, you don't have to worry about it. It was just an idea."

It was both a crazy, and yet amazing idea, in the sense that I'd be set for life with no concerns. As long as Hannah was successful, I would receive an income from her. Yet, it also meant this teenager would, to a degree, become legally responsible for me. I mulled it over in my head as we pulled into the driveway of the house. As she turned off the engine, I looked over at her and said simply, "I'd be absolutely honoured, Duchess."

Her head snapped around to face me, and I noticed tears had welled in her eyes when she thought I was going to reject her, but now they eyes lit up. Unfastening her seat belt, she leaned over, gave me yet another hug, and kissed me on my cheek, causing me to chuckle. It was only when I went to bed later that night that it occurred to me that I'd just gone from a salaried job with the Grant family, into a lifetime commitment.

Chapter Five

Coming of Age

My actual duties hadn't changed with this new situation, but the dynamic between Hannah and me, had. As a result of that incident, she'd clearly developed a level of affection for me. However, it would be many years later before I knew the degree to which that affection fell.

In the immediate aftermath of the incident, I met once more with Marcia and the head of security. The head of Grant Industries was rather frustrated when it was discovered that there wasn't any identification of who the assailants were. This was of considerable concern, since hiding one's identity was something that only happened at a supreme government level. A medical examination of the bodies came back that one was American, and the other was German. This was particularly confusing because, on one side, it implied Peon activity, and on the other, it didn't. The investigation would continue, but that wasn't my responsibility.

I maintained a much higher alertness level during this time. And there was one thing I wanted to do that I knew Hannah was going to object to.

"I want to place a subcutaneous transponder in you," I told her simply one morning. It was a Monday, a time when we regularly met up for breakfast to go through her weekly itinerary. Which was usually when I raised concerns about anything she wanted to do, and for her to argue back with me. Whatever had changed in our relationship, it didn't take away the fact that Hannah was still an arrogant little rich kid.

"Exactly what the fuck is that?" she asked, frowning at me before stuffing a large forkful of bacon into her mouth.

"It's basically a tracking system," I said, trying to sound casual as if this was a simple routine matter. "It would allow me to know where you're at all times."

She looked a little confused as she responded. "But you already have that. You track my phone."

"That's all well and good, as long as you don't somehow get separated from your phone," I said, sitting down adjacent to her.

"So, you're looking to permanently tag me like a dog?" she asked with a sneer.

I was about to argue that point, but ultimately ended up simply shrugging and smiling. "I guess you could put it that way," I smirked.

She rolled her eyes at me but smiled. "Frankly, mate, if you think it's for the best, I'll agree."

Surprised she didn't put up a bigger fight, I picked up the small box that I'd brought to the table with me. I opened it up to reveal a small gun-like object that was similar to those used to pierce ears.

"You want to do it now?" Hannah asked, her eyes widening. Of course, I did. Hannah had a penchant for changing her mind and not sticking to agreements. However, I didn't say this.

"It'll only take a second," I smiled.

She rolled her eyes again as I got up out of my seat and moved behind her. She tossed her fork onto the plate and sat up straight, as I pulled her hair away from her neck and placed the little gun at the base of her skull. There was a light click, and she jumped slightly, more from being startled, than any pain.

"Happy?" She scowled at me as she rubbed the back of her neck.

I grinned back at her as I pulled my phone out of my pocket. "I'll tell you as soon as I check whether I'm receiving a clear signal or not."

She simply shrugged and went back to eating her breakfast as I activated this small application, which immediately brought up the floor plan of the house and the small red dot indicating Hannah sitting in the kitchen right in front of me.

"I'm happy now," I chuckled at her indignation. I then moved on to an important subject that was coming up. "We have to talk about your birthday. It's going to be a very high-profile affair, but your mother wants your security to remain discreet, and she's asked that I don't come with you, but follow behind. I'm not happy about it, but she's pretty insistent."

"Well, if you think about it, the only time anyone has ever approached me for various reasons has been when I've been alone, and I'm certainly not going to be alone at my birthday celebration."

"You have a point," I shrugged. "But all the same."

"Oh, you worry too much, Liam," she said with a mouthful of eggs. "I can't imagine there's going to be *constant* attempts on my life."

When the actual day of her birthday came, there was an altercation between her and her mother. Hannah had wanted a particular type of car for her birthday, but didn't get it, and was throwing one of her frequent tantrums. During these occasions, I kept out of the way, so as not to become embroiled in this clearly family matter.

I usually followed her to school, but on this occasion, it turned out that she stormed out to her new car and drove off without me. I made a mental note to give her a hard time about this, because it was almost thirty minutes before I became aware of it. There was no point in following her now, so I just monitored her transponder signal on my phone. She was driving extremely fast, and I thought it'd be just my luck that she wrapped herself around a lamp-post on the one day I wasn't with her. When she suddenly stopped on the highway and didn't move for about ten minutes, I logged into her car's computer to discover that police had detained her for speeding. I considered calling her to ask if she needed any help, but I thought, *'screw her'*. If she was going to run off without me, she could bloody well deal with the cops herself. She clearly did so as, eventually, she was driving off once more, and when she reached the school, and I followed her movements, walking into the building. I slipped my phone back into my pocket.

I didn't see her again until that evening, and it appeared that she was still in a foul mood. I usually avoided her on these occasions if I could help it, not because I was afraid of her or anything. It was simply I couldn't stand the brattiness of her moods.

I met with Crawford to make the final arrangements for the evening's events. The celebration of her eighteenth birthday was an incredibly high-profile event that was going to be attended by all the big names in business, as well as members of government from throughout the Pacific Alliance. As a result, we had to liaise with other people regarding security. When our business was concluded, Crawford looked at me.

"There is another matter we must discuss, Liam. Hannah is now eighteen, and technically, your contract has officially ended. You're no longer directly employed by the C.E.O. Both Marcia and I have discussed it with Hannah, and she wishes to retain your services, which, of course, wasn't unexpected. However, this means that we need to draw up a new contract, and Hannah Grant herself will become your boss. This comes with the difficulty that she'll make the decisions on her own security, and you're no longer going to be able to instruct her. Instead, you'll only be able to advise her. This is going to make your position a lot more complicated, especially as Hannah is quite hot-headed, and frequently responds emotionally, rather than logically. Now, you do have the option to decline. However, I should point out that, as she is now your patron, it would be very embarrassing for her, should you do so."

I didn't hesitate. "I've given a lot of thought to this situation because, obviously, I saw it coming. I'm more than happy to stay in the service of Hannah Grant, and I think I have a relationship where I can, let's say, curb her eccentricities."

He didn't look quite as sure as I did, but simply said, "Good luck, Mr Marshall."

That evening became the busiest of my life as I checked in with the various groups of security along the route that Hannah was going to be taking. The ballroom at the Crown Towers was also on high alert. However, all my preparations didn't prevent the paint incident from happening. She was gonna head there in a limo with her sister, Annabelle, and I was to follow behind as was the norm, and all appeared to be going exceptionally well. There were crowds outside the Crown Towers, along with the expected paparazzi. I pulled up in front of the red carpet about one car length behind her. My attention, however, was on the crowd, not her, as I stepped out of my vehicle.

Pearson, the chauffeur, opened the door, and the flashing lights of paparazzi cameras lit up, as she stepped out onto the red carpet, waving to the cameras and onlookers in a luxuriant dress that probably cost more than my annual salary. Annabelle stepped out behind her but was mostly ignored. Everyone wanted to see the girl that was known as Australia's Princess. And that was Hannah.

They stopped for the obligatory posing for photographs, and then it all went to shit. I saw someone in the crowd launch something at Hannah, and I was already running towards her as it hit her in the face and splattered. The red paint went into her eyes and mouth as someone shouted, "Hang the damn GenMod. It shouldn't be allowed to live."

Along with other security, I reached her, and she was hustled inside, where she burst into tears.

"Did they get whoever did this?" Marcia Grant snapped at her own security man.

"Yes, ma'am, the police have him in custody."

"Well, make sure he gets a damn good beating while in jail!" she snapped, and he stepped away to make a call on his radio. "Come on, Hannah, let's get you cleaned up."

"For fuck's sake, Mother, do you really think I'm going now?" she cried.

She slapped her hard on the arm. "You can cut out that language for a start, young lady!" she shouted at her. "And, of course, you're going. We will not let some protesters stop you from making this appearance. It would mean that they would get the better of us, and no-one gets the better of a Grant."

She sent Hannah into a room and turned to me. "We will be talking about this tomorrow, Marshall!" she growled venomously before following her daughter.

For the rest of the night, I maintained a low profile, and the ball appeared to go well, though the mood of my ward was such that she was best avoided anyway. The initial intention had been that she would depart in the limousine, just as she had arrived. But considering that everything that was now flying around the media, Hannah Grant getting assaulted with video footage to show, even the more serious news outlets started to run Hannah Grant stories. Hence, I took her out of a back door round the corner where I had my car waiting, and we slipped off unobserved into the night. She was quiet and solemn, and the journey home was in absolute silence.

We didn't return to the house but instead went to an apartment that Marcia maintained in the centre of Melbourne, for occasions when she didn't want to travel all the way back out to the suburbs to the official residence. As we headed up in the elevator again, we said nothing, and she acted like I wasn't even there. As soon as we entered the apartment, she headed off to the shower as I did my mandatory check for potential intruders. I should have been suspicious when she spent well over an hour in the shower, but eventually, she emerged, went straight to her bedroom, and slammed the door behind her.

I headed over to the bar at this point, poured myself a large whiskey, and wondered exactly how much Marcia was going to tear me a new one the following day. Although I technically now worked for Hannah, I knew full well that if Marcia wanted me gone, I would be gone. I downed the drink, poured another, downed that, and headed off to the guest room, unaware that I would never see Marcia Grant again.

At least, not alive.

CHAPTER SIX

ARMAGEDDON

"You're late," Skylar gently chided me as I met outside the restaurant for a lunch date. It was the day after Hannah's coming-of-age event. Although I'd been dating the young nurse for several weeks now, I hadn't seen much of her due to my intense responsibilities in preparing for that event. I now had time to make up for that and was looking forward to getting to know her a little better.

I glanced at my watch.

"Only by ten minutes," I responded to her.

"A gentleman should never keep a lady waiting, even for a minute," she said teasingly.

"Then I humbly beg my lady's forgiveness," I chuckled before informing the maître de that I wanted a table for two.

He led us over to a small alcove, where we took our seats opposite each other and handed us each a menu. I laid mine down on the table and reached over to pick up the wine list.

"Do you have a preference for red or white?" I asked her.

"Personally, I always find red a little bitter. I prefer white regardless of what we're eating," she replied, and I ordered a rather pricey bottle, hoping to impress her. Coincidentally, it came from Grant Vineyards, but to be totally honest, it was hard to purchase anything that didn't have some association with Grant Industries.

As we placed our food order, she looked at me with a slight smile. "It's really nice you can actually find some time for me."

I sighed softly, noting the sarcasm in her voice. "It's not like I work a nine-to-five job, Sky. I'm paid a lot of money for what I do, and as a consequence, I sometimes have to put in long hours."

"Oh, I understand it's really nice to have a man in your life who puts another woman first."

I have to be honest and say I found this a little annoying. "It's my job, Sky. If you can't accept that, perhaps we're wasting our time here."

She narrowed her eyes at me.

"For fuck's sake, Liam, I'm just teasing you," she said with a sigh. "I thought you Brits had a sense of humour."

I sighed and shrugged it off, unsure whether she was really joking or not. "I'm sorry, it's been a tiring week."

"I hope you're not too tired," she said, reaching out and running her finger over my hand. "I thought maybe we could go back to my place after this."

Now, that instantly made me give my full attention to her.

"Well, that certainly does sound interesting," I smiled. Indeed, I had spent the last several weeks fantasizing about

what I'd discover beneath her clothing. Although not exactly a GenMod like Hannah, Skylar was an exceedingly
good-looking woman with all the curves in all the right
places.

She grinned at my reaction, but our starters arrived before she could say anything. It was the sort of place where
one is expected to taste the wine before it's poured, and we
went through that routine before being left alone again.
However, at that moment, the sirens began to blare. Silence fell in the restaurant, and suddenly, everyone was
getting up out of their seats. There hadn't been an air raid
in the two years I'd been in Australia, and it was rather
unexpected.

"Fuck!" Skylar muttered, putting down her glass as I
pulled out my phone.

"You need to get yourself to an air raid shelter," I said as
we got out of our seats.

"You're just going to leave me?" she said with considerable consternation.

I was too busy looking at my phone to really notice as I
saw the transponder blip showing Hannah was at school.

"I need to get to Hannah," I replied, slipping the phone
back into my pocket.

"Fuck you, Liam."

She slapped me hard around the face, and before I could
react, she was heading out of the restaurant. I hurried out
to my car, looking up and hearing the drone of hundreds
of aircraft. This was no simple air raid. This was positively Armageddon. All around me, people panicked, and I
found myself getting blocked off as I tried to drive out of

the car park. Suddenly, my passenger door opened, and Skylar jumped in, and I looked at her with surprise.

"There are too many people trying to get into the shelters. There's no way I can get in before the bombs drop."

"No worries, hang tight." I pulled the car off the pavement and went through the shrubbery surrounding the car park and onto the road. Traffic all around was at a virtual standstill, due to people abandoning their cars and thus, blocking the way. I slammed my hands frustratedly against the steering wheel. "We're gonna have to walk."

She simply nodded and climbed out at the same time as me. I pulled out my phone again and quickly checked the way to Melbourne Grammar on foot. It'd take me at least twenty to thirty minutes. *Fuck!*

Taking Skylar by the hand, I slipped on my glasses and had Emily give me directions for the fastest route, but she didn't respond. We ran through alleys and side streets, the sounds of distant explosions coming ever closer. Looking up, I could see the towers of Melbourne exploding into flame, as we pushed past panicking people.

"Liam, we are not going to make it!" Skylar shouted, and I couldn't disagree. I stopped running and looked about, but we couldn't find cover. I brought her into a nearby department store, knowing they would have a basement where we could hunker down. Others had the same idea, and a rather brave staff member was standing there giving directions to where we could go. Minutes later, we found ourselves in some sort of boiler room with several other people and sat on the floor, pressed against each other. I placed my arm around her shoulders, and she rested her head on mine. I pulled my phone out again, but I no longer had a signal and thus had no idea what the situation was with Hannah.

Deep down in the bowels of the department store, the explosions outside sounded dim and distant, and it did occur to me that the building could collapse above us, trapping us here. No-one spoke.

An hour passed, then two. The attack was relentless, and during the entire time, we could hear the sounds of explosions and the collapse of buildings. I couldn't help but wonder if there would still be a Melbourne to go up to when it was over. I checked my phone occasionally, but there was no service or connection to Hannah. My first objective, when I got out of there, would be to head over to her school to find her, and then find a way to get her out of the city.

Eventually, it stopped, but it was a while before anyone moved as we awaited the all-clear siren. That siren never came. Eventually, I got up, and Skylar followed me to the entrance and the stairs leading up to the ground floor. It was blocked with fallen masonry, but there was just enough room for us to squeeze through. The store around us was in devastation, collapsing walls revealing sunlight and the roof hanging down in parts. I stayed to help others get out despite the risk of it coming down on us. There was just something about walking away that would've made me feel sick. When Skylar and I eventually headed out of the building, I desperately hoped my car had been spared, but when I saw the devastation, I realised how stupid the hope had been. Skylar must've been in shock because she was silent at my side. I stared out at the ruin. I looked up at towers of flame. In the distance, I could hear screams, gunfire, and the fires burning unchecked. I tried to get my bearings to work out which way to go, but the streets weren't recognisable as streets anymore, and even if you could find one, it wouldn't go too far before debris from a collapsed building would block the way.

However, I'd been trained for such an event during my army career, although I'd never experienced it. Everything was lit in a dull orange twilight smoke blocking the sun, yet fires lit the way. I reached into my holster and pulled out my pistol. It held twelve rounds, and I had a spare clip. Not exactly the same as a Peon assault rifle, but it would have to do. It was unlikely the Peons caused this devastation and just left, and it started to dawn on me that this was a full-scale invasion of Australia.

"Where are we going?" Skylar asked me at last as she gripped tightly to my hand and jogged to keep up with me.

"I need to get to Hannah's school and find out if she's alright," I replied, expecting her to argue with me, but she didn't.

"Then, can we go find my mother?"

My first responsibility would've been to get Hannah out of there safely, but I could hardly say no to this woman who was clearly willing to wait until I completed my task before finding a member of her family.

"Of course, we will," I said, squeezing her hand tightly.

Although I couldn't see the sun behind the blanket of black smoking clouds, I could work out where it was, by seeing where the dark sky was at its lightest. Had this been winter, I would've been completely lost. A walk that should have taken an hour took three as periodically, we had to climb over rubble, or even go through precariously toppled buildings in order to get to my destination. We'd barely spoken as we passed the bodies and people wandering around aimlessly in shock at what'd just happened.

Eventually, we arrived where Melbourne Grammar should have stood, but nothing was left except a pile of rubble. I tried to gauge where the school's air raid shelter entrance was. Obviously, I'd made sure I knew where she could go to be safe if such an occurrence took place, even though I never expected it to happen.

The doors were open, and I was immediately concerned to see the body of a Peon soldier in the entranceway. As I stepped inside, I saw another enemy body, and next to him, a civilian. A portly man who I assumed to be one of the teachers. Of course, by this time, I had my gun in my hand. I told Skylar to wait by the entrance. As I turned into a corridor, a girl let out a scream as she saw me with the gun, which I immediately lowered, then raised my other hand to indicate I meant no harm. There was another person's body in the corridor, but I kept my concentration on the girl.

"It's okay. I'm one of the good guys. Are there any other Peons in here?" The girl simply shook her head, and I holstered my weapon. "I'm looking for Hannah Grant. Is she here?" Again, she shook her head, and at that moment, an elderly woman came around the corner looking incredibly nervous.

"Mr Marshall?" she inquired, and only then did I recognise her. I frequently liaised with school staff over security issues, and this was one of Hannah's teachers.

"Where is Hannah?" I asked.

"She left several hours ago with Bronwyn, Joshua, and Sarah. Sah-rah I didn't know they were going. It was only after they'd left that I found out."

"Shit!" I muttered. She could be anywhere by now, and any hope I would be able to find her disappeared at that moment. Other students appeared in the corridor, and I asked the teacher, "What's your protocol to follow now?"

"We're to wait until the authorities come."

Shit and double damn. There would be no authorities coming, but if I said something, they would more than likely look to me to help them. Fuck if I knew what to do.

"Are any of you injured?" I turned to see Skylar walking up behind me, having heard us talking and realising it was safe to do so.

"No, everyone's perfectly fine, although I must admit our nerves are rather rattled, especially after Joshua shot the Peons."

I felt that I recognised the reference to someone called Joshua as someone Hannah had spoken to me about it, but I couldn't place it at that moment. It was only later I realised it was her creepy little stalker.

"We have to get them out of here," Skylar said, looking up at me.

"And take them where exactly?" I replied. I turned back to the teacher. "How long do you have supplies for?"

"Oh, at least six months. This bunker was designed to withstand a nuclear attack."

Now, that was an extreme level of paranoia. It'd been well over a hundred years since mankind had realised the stupidity of nuclear weaponry and mutually assured destruction. Nukes had long since been eradicated, but the paranoia hadn't.

"Then you're better off staying here. However, get some of your kids to come and help me clear the rubble from the doorway so that you can lock yourselves in."

We knew there were about twenty to thirty kids. I wasn't not completely sure because I didn't exactly take a head count. It didn't take us long to move the debris that had collapsed into the main entrance when the door had opened, and then I had the morbid task of moving the bodies of the dead outside, one of which, apparently, was indeed, one of their teachers.

I then turned back to the old lady. "I don't know what's going on out there right now, but clearly, there are Peons on the ground. Seriously, do not open this door to anybody."

"Would you stay with us, Mr Marshall? We could do with a man around here."

"No, I have to look for Hannah. I assume she's still alive, and I have to find her whilst that situation still holds true." I turned to Skylar. "You should probably stay here. It would be a lot safer."

She shook her head. "You said you'd help me find my mother."

The teacher headed back inside, and I bid her farewell, as I went back out of the exit and helped her shut the door behind me. Skylar suddenly grabbed my shoulder and gasped with fright. I spun around with my hand going up towards my shoulder holster, but I stopped when I saw a familiar-looking girl standing at the top of the steps, dirty and dishevelled. Her face was covered in black soot. It took me a moment to recognise her.

"Sarah?" I asked just to make sure.

"They're all dead, Mr Marshall," she said weakly. At my questioning look, she added, "My home isn't there anymore. There's just a crater."

I approached her and put an arm around her. "It's okay. Everything's gonna be okay. You're gonna be safe here. You don't know for sure that your family were at home, do you?"

She shook her head. "It was always my father's plan that we go to the house in the event of an air raid. I'm fairly certain everyone was there."

I turned back towards the door and was about to bang on it to get the teacher to open it again when Sarah said something that changed everything.

"If you're looking for Hannah, she's heading out of the city."

I turned and looked back at her. "You know where she's going?"

"The general direction. I was with them for some time, but I decided to go looking for my parents, and they refused to come with me."

"Would you be willing to take me in that direction?" I asked.

She shrugged. "Will you let me stay with you?"

"Yes," I replied immediately, not thinking about the responsibility I was undertaking.

"You promised you would help me find my mother," Skylar said softly, a slight tremble in her voice.

Damn it to hell! I had a lead as to where Hannah had gone, but yes, I'd given her my word that I would help her find her mother. I would lose valuable time trying to catch up with Hannah, not that I truly believed that I would ever find her amid this chaos. I just knew I was duty-bound to try.

So it was that I found myself escorting Skylar and Sarah to the area where Skylar lived and wasted several precious hours searching debris for someone I was certain was already dead. I refused to stop until Skylar conceded it was hopeless. However, this time wasn't so wasted as it occurred to me why my phone didn't work. The Peons had probably taken out the Australian satellite system. However, I worked for Grant Security and realised that getting my hands on some of their equipment would make my life a lot easier. So, the three of us headed out towards the suburbs, and once we had cleared the main metropolis, roads became clearer, and that pace quickened. It was almost night by the time we arrived at the Grant residence. The West Wing had been completely demolished, but ironically, the electronic gate at the front remained intact.

I had both women wait outside while I climbed over the wall and made my way into the house. There was almost total darkness, but I'd lived there long enough to work out how to get to the kitchen, and in one of the drawers, I pulled out a torch. I suddenly screamed as I was startled by a body slumped over the table. I moved to where I could see the face. Annabelle Grant was dead, but initially, it made no sense. The house hadn't been hit that bad, and she'd clearly been able to make her way into the undamaged kitchen and sit down. I moved closer and saw that on the other side of her head, there was a bloody wound that appeared to be from a gunshot. This confused me even further as I couldn't imagine who would possibly harm Annabelle, who was actually quite a sweet girl. However, looking around the body, I found my answer. Her right hand hung down, and a gun lay on the floor beneath it. Rather than face the aftermath of this attack, Annabelle had taken her own life, for reasons I would never know, but could only guess. I took the gun as a backup and slipped it into the back of my trousers. I then headed out with my flashlight to find the security officers. At this time, I wondered where Kirsty had gone, considering she was responsible for the welfare of Annabelle, but I didn't encounter her body.

I picked up extra clips for my gun and one of our secure security communicators. They worked off of private Grant satellites, and it was pretty unlikely the Peons had taken out all of those. No, they wouldn't have really needed to since Grant Industries didn't even allow government access to them. This was Marcia Grant's private international corporate network. I worked my way around the offices, picking up any equipment I thought would be useful and stuffing them into a backpack with the Grant Industries logo on the back. I then made to head back to the girls, but something occurred to me. I should at least check the damaged wing for survivors who may be trapped. I headed over there and climbed through various fallen beams and carefully passed walls that were leaning in the stairway. I was still nervous about my safety as I headed up, but most of the second floor was gone. However, I came across the bodies of both Kirsty and Marcia Grant. A wave of panic came over me as I realised had I not had a date with Skylar, I'd have probably been here with them. I then went to the garage. Fortunately, every car the Grants owned was keyed to my thumbprint, and I could not only open them, but also start them up. Hotwiring a car had long been impossible. As the engine came on silently, I was pleased to see it had a full charge. I drove down to the gates, and to my surprise, they opened upon detecting my vehicle, and I pulled out of the Grant estate for the last time. Skylar climbed in beside me, and Sarah jumped into the back.

Technically, to go the way Sarah told us that Hannah had gone, we'd have had to drive back through the city if we wanted to take the shortest route. However, I now needed roads, and we spent several hours navigating around the suburbs to go round the city, rather than through it. This all happened in silence as we drove. We still encountered obstacles, because the ordinance had indeed been dropped in the suburbs either by mistake or to take out utilities. My two companions stared in disbelief at the devastation around them. Burnt out cars, bodies lying in the street, fires burning unchecked. Sarah was able to give a surprisingly detailed account of the direction they went in. However, as we reached the north side of Melbourne, I started spotting Peon troops on the ground, and effectively, it turned us onto an even longer route to avoid them. I could only hope and pray that we could escape Melbourne without being stopped.

CHAPTER SEVEN

ONE STEP BEHIND

As we reached the outskirts of Melbourne, I was relieved that we didn't encounter any Peons, and I pulled over into a quiet neighbourhood.

"What's going on?" I don't remember if it was Skylar or Sarah who asked, but it didn't really matter.

"I honestly have no clue where we go from here," I replied. "I'm going to see if I can make contact with Grant Security Services." I leaned over into the back and had Sarah pass me up the bag that I'd brought from the estate. "Maybe they can help us out. We need to find Hannah, then we need to get out of Australia."

"Leave Australia?" Sarah asked, somewhat surprised. "Are you serious?"

"Very serious. This is seriously a bloody invasion, and it clearly looks like it's not going Australia's way."

"I'm not leaving Australia," she stated defiantly.

"That's up to you," I replied as I searched through the bag. "You're not my problem."

"Well, she sort of is," said Skylar at my side. "You stopped her from going into the bunker, where she would have been safe, so you could get her to help you find Hannah."

I sighed but didn't reply. I guess she had a point, but I was in full military mode. My mission was to protect Hannah Grant at all costs. I pulled out the large brick-sized radio and turned it to the G.S.S. frequencies.

"This is Angel Two to security command. Do you read me?" I said, using my established call sign. There was a pause before a rather broken reply came.

"We read you, Angel Two. Alpha Leader Seven wants to talk to you."

An alpha leader was a high-ranking member of the security department.

There was a short pause, and then a thick South African accented woman came on.

"This is Alpha Leader Seven. We have been trying to contact you. Can you give me a sitrep on the first family?"

"I can, and it's not good news. Mama Bear is down and out, and First Baby Bear is also down and out. Second Baby Bear has gone walkabout, and I'm trying to locate her. Last known to be heading north out of Melbourne."

"Can you confirm? Are you certain Mama Bear is down and out?"

"I can confirm. I saw the bodies myself."

There was another pause before the South African said, "Updating call signs. Second Baby Bear is now Mama Bear and must be located at any cost. Your callsign is now Protector One. Please confirm your understanding."

"Understood," I replied.

"What are your intentions now, Protector One?"

"I'm going to go north. I hope that I can pick up her transponder signal. Any assistance you can give will be greatly appreciated."

"Oh, trust me on that. The entire security division is now devoted to one cause only, and that is finding Hannah Grant."

"Will do, and you do the same. Angel Seven out."

"What was all that about?" Skylar asked me.

"I informed them that Marcia and Annabelle Grant were dead, and that we're looking for Hannah. She then upgraded Hannah's status to the new head of Grant Industries."

"Hannah is the head of Grant Industries?" Sarah chuckled in the back.

"Technically, yes, but honestly, I don't know the legalities of it," I replied, as I tossed the bag back to her and headed north once more.

"Surely that means she's not your responsibility anymore. Someone more senior will fill that role," Skylar said.

"And they just put me into that senior position, making me Protector One. I'm now the most senior member of Grant Security Services that's responsible for her life."

At that moment, my phone started to bleep. Although I'd not been getting any signal, it hadn't occurred to me to turn it off. The battery could literally last for weeks. I slipped it out of my pocket, and the front screen had changed with some sort of update. The G.S.S. logo I'd gotten when I joined the security services now appeared, and I had phone service again. I pulled up the tracking application, but there was no sign of the little blip indicating Hannah's location. I slotted the phone into the car's holder so that I could keep an eye on it, and then we just drove. I didn't know where we were going. For all I knew, Hannah could have been travelling faster or slower than me. She could have even changed her mind and headed off in a different direction. Eventually, I got too tired to drive. Unable to connect the car to the satellite systems, I couldn't switch on the auto and had no choice but to stop. I pulled into a small motel situated in the middle of what appeared to be nowhere.

It'd been abandoned, but one broken window in the reception later, I had a set of keys to one of the rooms. Sarah said something about getting her own room, but I advised her that it was best if we were stuck together for safety's sake.

I got some snacks out of a vending machine, which would have to be our meal for the night.

As we stepped into the modest room, Sarah went straight to the T.V. and turned it on, and Skylar flopped down onto the bed as I went to the little table to sort out my equipment. There was nothing on the television appearing that all broadcasts were apparently offline. She then tried to pick up an Internet signal but was unable to. I stepped over to the bed and pulled out the little bunk from underneath, turning the double bed into a triple bed.

"Get some sleep. We're not going to stay here all night. I just want to get in a few hours' rest before we continue on."

"Are you expecting us to sleep in the same bed, Liam?" Skylar asked me irritably as I lay down next to her.

"I don't care where you sleep, but I'm sleeping right here," I said patronisingly. Then, turning my back to her, I found myself fast asleep within seconds.

"Mr Marshall, Mr Marshall." There was an urgent voice, and a hand shook me roughly. I opened my eyes and looked up at Sarah, who was looking scared.

I sat up immediately. "What's happening?"

"Some sort of shuttle has landed out in the car park. Soldiers got out and searched the rooms. I think it's the Peons."

I jumped out of bed and headed over to the window. Lifting the edge of the curtain, I looked out. She was right. A small shuttle that could probably hold no more than a half dozen troops had landed. I could see one or two soldiers in the light blue uniforms of the French military walking around, but there would certainly be more of them.

"Fuck!" I muttered as I went over and gently woke Skylar. I had them both get dressed as I went through to the back of the rooms and looked for an alternate exit. There was a small window that looked out on the back of the facility. All I could see through that way was the relative desolation of the Bush. Going that way would mean abandoning our car, but I thought we could at least hide out until they left. There was also another drawback in the fact that the window wasn't designed to be opened. I went back into the bedroom area and grabbed some tools out of my Grant Industries security kit.

It wasn't like I could simply smash the window. That would immediately draw the attention of the Peons. But

I would have to work fast as eventually they would come and search this room.

"Sarah, keep a look out and let me know when any Peons start heading in our direction." She nodded and went and stood by the edge of the curtain as I headed back into the bathroom. I carefully and quietly broke away the seals around the window until I was able to see the screws. Not wanting the noise of an electric screwdriver, I had to manually unscrew each one, until very carefully, I was able to push the window out of its frame, and, gently, I lowered it to the ground outside before calling to the girls in a loud whisper to come on in.

We almost made it. Sarah went out first, followed by Skylar, and just as I was about to climb through, the front door of the room was kicked open. I froze, slipping my gun out of my holster, and stood behind the door as a Peon came in. He looked a little confused as he saw the hole in the wall and stepped over to it. I was hoping the girls had moved out of sight, but when he suddenly started and called out to them, I realised they hadn't. Stepping out from behind the door, I quickly moved behind him. In a quick move, I had my arm around his neck, closing off his ability to either breathe or cry out, and with a knee in his back, I brought him down and twisted his neck until it snapped. I quickly checked the bedroom to see if he had a partner, but clearly, he didn't. And then, in a swift movement, I pulled myself out through the window, taking the soldier's rifle with me.

We were hunkered down behind the wall as we worked out what to do next. The soldier would be missed, and we would be searched for. It wouldn't be like we'd be hard to find with the various infrared and light-intensifying equipment the Peons undoubtedly had with them. If we headed off on foot, we would quickly be hunted down, and the chances of them taking us prisoner after we had just killed one of their buddies was highly unlikely.

"Stay here. I'm going to check out the situation," I said to the girls, who looked positively terrified. I headed to the corner of the building and peered around the side. Seeing the way clear, I headed forward, and I peered into the darkness. I pulled my glasses out once more and put them on.

"Emily, give me night vision."

Everything around me appeared to light up in a black and white daylight. I could see bored-looking Peons walking around checking rooms and couldn't help but think that this particular group was quite unprofessional. Good.

I looked at where our car was parked. There was no way in hell we'd ever get to it without being discovered. Not that that would be any use since the shuttle would merely take off and hunt us down. No, from the position where we were, we were pretty much trapped, unless we wandered off like idiots into the Bush. I pondered turning ourselves in, rather than being in a shoot-first-ask-questions-later situation when they encountered us.

However, I had left the dead body of one of their buddies on the bathroom floor, and I didn't relish their reaction to that. I headed back to where the girls were and reaching into my Grant Industries duffel bag, I pulled out my radio.

"Mayday, mayday," I muttered, albeit with a sense of urgency. "This is Protector One. I'm pinned down at the Golden Hills Motel, somewhere between Kangaroo Flats and Bendigo. I'm not engaging the enemy, but in imminent danger of discovery. Unable to move from current position."

"I'm reading you, Protector One. Have you located Mama Bear?" The South African woman replied.

"Negative."

"Understood, Protector One. We can't perform an extraction at this time, but we'll be sending automatic assistance drones. Do you have security pins?" I did indeed, but my two companions didn't, and I quickly searched the bag and pulled a couple out.

"Can confirm we do," I said as I handed out the pins, indicating they should put them behind the collars of their shirts.

"We? Please identify your companions, Protector One."

"Skylar Richards and Sarah Monroe-Jenson," I responded.

"We have Skylar Richards listed as an employee of Grant Industries Medical Division, but no identity on Sarah Monroe-Jenson. Can you provide more information?"

"For fuck's sake, is now really the time?" I responded.

"The quicker you answer my questions, the quicker we will get you your support, Protector One."

"Sarah Monroe-Jenson is an eighteen-year-old high school student and friend of Mama Bear. She has been assisting me in locating Mama Bear."

"Thank you, Protector One. I have found her record. Hang tight. Help is on the way."

As the line went dead, Skylar looked at me and said, "What do we do now?"

I shrugged. "I guess we hang tight."

Oh, if life was just that easy. A voice from the empty window frame suddenly shouted to us in French, and as I looked up, I saw a Peon soldier bringing his rifle up to point at us. Slowly, I started to raise my hands, and the two girls followed my lead. However, the soldier made a big mistake as he turned his head back to talk to someone. In that time, I managed to pull out my handgun and fire a neat headshot. We broke into a run down the back of the motel rooms. Another shot rang out, missing Sarah by less than an inch. I pulled her down and spun upon my back so that I was facing our attacker, but he'd clearly gone from the window and most likely coming round to the back of the building. I now heard shouts going up, and lights flared brightly, which I could only assume was coming from their shuttle. I could hear someone shouting orders in French as we scrambled to our feet and continued to run. However, Peons aren't stupid, and soldiers came around from both ends. As soon as we saw one come around the corner, he immediately opened fire, and in his haste, he didn't take care of his aim, and his shot went wide, missing me. A double tap later on my own handgun, and he was down. It took a moment for Skylar to fall to her knees. I could see the blood soaking into her shirt. She looked up at me in wide-eyed shock. The bullet meant for me had hit her, piercing her heart. She was dead before her nanobots had time to respond. By this time, there were Peons in front and behind us, and I tossed my gun onto the floor and raised my hands, ignoring Sarah's screams as she looked at Skylar's body.

We were roughly pushed round to the front of the motel, and an officer started talking to his soldiers and then looking at us, but I had no idea what was going on. I was just praying they weren't going to shoot me for having killed one of their number. Whether that was their intent or not, I would never know, for in the distance, we could hear a faint whining hum. Grant Industries hadn't let me down. The officer was no fool, clearly recognised what it was, and started barking orders to his men.

It was almost like we ceased to exist as they began to scatter, looking for cover. I remained standing there, and Sarah looked up at me nervously. "Shouldn't we run?"

"No, as long as you have that security pin I gave you, the drones'll ignore you. Just don't get too close to a Peon."

And that was when we saw them coming over the building. It seemed like the sky was full of them, but if I were to put a number on it, there were only about twenty or thirty of them. They were small drones, about the size of a raven, clearly marked with the letters G.S.S. for Grant Security Services. The gunfire began, and a couple of the Peons went down, but most had already found cover, either within the rooms or the administrative area. However, Grant Industries doesn't produce dumb drones. The drones began shooting out windows and going in actually searching for the enemy. I grabbed Sarah by the arm, and we started to run towards the car. I barked out an order for it to start up and unlock, hoping that its voice recognition would understand me amidst the noise of gunfire. Fortunately, it did, and I pushed Sarah towards the passenger side as I ran around and jumped into the driver's seat. I heard a couple of stray bullets hit the side of the vehicle. They didn't appear to do much damage as I reversed out of the parking space, spun the vehicle, and put it into forward gear. I slammed down so hard on the accelerator that there was a squeal of the tyres as we shot out of the parking lot and back onto the highway.

CHAPTER EIGHT

TWILIGHT WANDERER

I was probably about five miles away from the motel when I was able to switch out of military mode and bring down my adrenaline levels. It was only then that I could think about what happened to Skylar. I'd seen many people that I cared about get killed in this war. It was hard to feel true grief. You simply get used to it.

At my side, Sarah just stared ahead with a vacant expression, clearly overwhelmed with everything that had been happening.

"Don't worry, Miss Jensen. I'll get you out of here as soon as we find Hannah."

"Call me Sarah," she said apathetically. "And just exactly where are we gonna go?"

That was a very good question. "I'm not sure yet. It all depends on the state of the war. We're going need to assess if Australia's going to beat these bastards back, or if the Peons are going to have success in this invasion."

"And if they do succeed?"

I shrugged. "Then we head out to either Japan or the United States. Anywhere we have allies."

"How is it that Grant Industries could fight the Peons, but the Australian government and all its military, couldn't?" Sarah seemed to think I knew everything, and it was getting a little annoying.

"Quite simply because Grant Industries isn't fighting back, beyond protecting its own. Grant Security Services is pretty powerful, but it doesn't have the resources of the Australian military. Back there was just an attack of a half dozen troops."

"How could a company legally have that sort of firepower?" she asked, apparently unaware of the frustration building in my tone.

"Grant Defence Services is the largest provider of military hardware in the world. Legally, it probably can't do what they did back there, but let's face it, who gives a fuck about legalities when we're fighting for our lives?"

She didn't respond to this, and thankfully, we fell silent for the next few miles. I didn't care about the fate of Australia as I did the fate of Hannah. Australia wasn't my responsibility, but she was. I had failed her and myself, and it wasn't sitting well with me.

The next time I looked at Sarah, she was fast asleep. I desperately wanted to do that too, for I'd only had an hour's rest in the last day. However, without a satellite system, putting the car into automatic wouldn't work, even if I was willing to take my eyes off the road and not watch out for potential danger. Finally, when my radio started beeping, I pulled it out. "This is Protector One. Go ahead."

"Well, thanks for letting us know you got out of there safely, mate." The voice came back irritably. It wasn't the same as before—a man, young and Aussie.

"My apologies," I said with a little embarrassment. "I've been running on one hour's sleep since all this started."

"You got an hour's sleep?" The voice came back patronisingly. "You lucky bastard. Anyway, we got a location on Mama Bear. Her phone was activated briefly, and we managed to pinpoint it. She's way out in the Outback, and it looks like she's heading towards Alice Springs."

I looked at the small mapping device on my phone as the signal came up. She was many miles ahead of us. More than a day. Control told me she hadn't moved for thirty minutes. In order to have gotten that far, she must be driving, so the fear was now that she'd broken down somewhere on a stretch of road heading through the Outback. I don't know what supplies she had with her. From that point on, I just drove, stopping only for a couple of hours of sleep. It'd make sense that if she were on the move again, she'd head for Alice Springs, because it was virtually the only thing ahead of her, unless she continued on several more days to the coast.

I continued on, hoping the power cells in my car wouldn't need recharging, and as the gauge dropped over the next few hours, I grew more concerned. I was about twelve hours away from Alice when control radioed through to me. "Protector One. We have located Mama Bear. She's in the custody of the Peons in Alice Springs. How far out are you?"

"I'm still twelve hours down the line, Control. Can you perform an extraction of Mama Bear?"

"This isn't the army, Protector One. We couldn't pull that many people together in this short amount of time. We're just going to have to do it the old-fashioned way. A little bit of bribery and corruption, in the hope they won't care enough about a little rich Aussie girl. We're going to send transport to pick you up. All senior ground personnel are evacuating Australia."

At that, Sarah looked up at me with great concern in her eyes but didn't say anything.

"I'm not alone. I have a young girl here with me. Will you take her too?"

"She a relative of yours?"

"No."

"She worked for Grant Industries at an executive level?"

"No."

"I'm sorry, mate, we can barely get everything together in time to get our people off of here. You're gonna have to leave her behind."

The look of concern on Sarah's face now turned to terror. I saw it and said softly, "Then I won't be coming."

"You got no choice, mate. This is a direct order from the C.E.O. You're a major employee of the family."

"I'm not going to leave an eighteen-year-old girl on the sidewalk," I said irritably.

"Okay, mate, let's do this. If she gets on the shuttle with you, there's pretty much gonna be fuck all they can do about it when you reach your destination. I just can't officially authorise it."

"Understood," I said, and the line went dead.

"I really appreciate this, Mr Marshall," Sarah said softly, hugging my arm and resting her head upon my shoulder.

I took her hand and squeezed it reassuringly.

"No worries." And with that, I pulled the car over to the side of the road.

"Where are they gonna take us?" she asked quietly.

I actually chuckled at this. "You know, I totally forgot to ask. Probably either Japan or the U.S.A., and then we'll see what we'll see."

As it would turn out, I was completely wrong. It wasn't a simple intercontinental shuttle, but an interplanetary one. At least one that was designed for near-earth orbit and docking with another ship. I took her by the hand almost instinctively, and we walked up to the craft as the boarding ramp came down, and a uniformed member of Grant Security Services met us. He held a device towards my eyes, scanning my retina together, confirmed I.D. on me, and then he looked at Sarah, then back at me. "I'm only to pick you up. The girl can't come aboard."

"I'm Protector One, and Marcia Grant herself has authorised me to take Miss Jensen with me." It was a lie, but one he could hardly confirm, beyond my identity.

"What the fuck, sir," he said in a dejected voice of resignation. "I have no clue what the chain of command is anymore. Everything's falling to bits. Come on in, go through the cabin and find a seat."

We stepped past him and walked through to the passenger cabin. There were various executives, some I recognised and some I didn't, in various states of condition. Some were still in their business suits, others dressed casually. In one case, a woman was clearly still wearing her pyjamas. It was a silent, dispirited group of people who mostly appeared in a state of shock. Sarah and I found seats, and as we took our places, I found we were still gripping each other's hands. Part of me felt a sense of relief as the ramp closed, and we slowly started to drift into the air on the dark energy compensators. Another part of me regretted that it wasn't me that found Hannah.

Sarah then drew me from my thoughts with a slight nudge and indicated towards the window. We were still going up and up, and daylight turned into night as I realised we weren't going to America or Japan, but we were headed into space. I'd never left Earth before, and I felt a slight, very brief lurch at what seemed like turbulence but was, in fact, the shuttle switching from actual gravity to artificial gravity. It was an expensive use of resources for a shuttle. But hey, this was Grant Industries, after all.

The craft was eerily quiet as no-one spoke and simply stared out of the windows. We couldn't see ahead, so I had no idea where we were going, and there was no shuttle-craft crew in the passenger cabin for us to ask. However, I noticed there were dozens of shuttles coming up from the Australian mainland, as probably the greatest exodus of refugees began. Only thirty minutes passed before we entered a vast docking bay, and I wondered where the hell I was. It landed, and everyone began to disembark. As we went down the ramp, I saw a gleaming sign that covered most of the wall: 'Welcome aboard, the Twilight Wanderer, where it's our pleasure to bring you pleasure."

I couldn't help but be surprised. There probably wasn't a human alive that didn't know of the luxury cruise liner known as the Twilight Wanderer. A mile-long behemoth of a ship that took exorbitantly wealthy tourists up on tours of the solar system. It will take you across the rings of Saturn, and park in orbit over the Red Spot of Jupiter. And whilst getting to these places, the individual could enjoy the vast resources of entertainment aboard the ship. From casinos, five-star restaurants, the gaming arcades, you name it. If it could be bought for an exorbitant price, then it was available on the Twilight Wanderer. Various people were waiting to give directions to the refugees departing the shuttle, and I made for two uniformed Grant Security Services individuals. As I approached, a short, blonde, gorgeous woman turned and looked up at me. (Aaron Note: Canadian)

"Mr Marshall?" she asked, and I nodded.

She turned to bid her companion farewell as he was apparently to wait for someone else. Looking back at me, she said, "Would you come with me?"

She made no comment in reference to Sarah, which surprised me, and I'd been prepared for an argument about bringing her aboard. We both followed her.

"Any news about Hannah Grant?" I asked.

"Yes, Sir," she replied. "She's been extracted from Peon custody and is en route to the moon."

I frowned at this. "Why the moon?"

"It was decided not to bring her to where we were evacuating everybody else, as it could become a target of a Peon attack."

"Correct me if I'm wrong, Miss, but the Twilight Wanderer is a civilian vessel. Under the Galle Convention, it would be a war crime to attack us."

"Unless that is, they consider us to be assisting in the military efforts. The powers that be decided that it wasn't worth the risk of bringing her here."

"Understood. Do you know who's with her?"

"I'm sorry. I'm not privy to that information," the officer advised me.

"What's your name, captain?"

"Robinson, Sir. Kennedy Robinson," she said as we got into an elevator.

"American?"

She shot me a quick glare.

"Canadian," she said with great afront.

"My apologies."

"No worries, Sir, I'm used to it," she said in a tone indicating that she clearly wasn't.

We were clearly on a residential level as we exited the elevator, and she led us to a suite. "My apologies, Sir, but considering your companion is an unauthorised passenger, she has to stay with you, and you're supposed to take responsibility for her."

"Understood," I replied, and she led us into a rather luxurious set of rooms.

"You're expected to stay here until called for by the Vice Executive Officer, who will want to talk to you. However, is there anything you immediately need?"

"Something to eat would be good," Sarah said.

"There's 24-hour room service available," she stated. "Would there be anything else?"

"Not right now. Thank you, Captain Robinson," I smiled.

She didn't reciprocate the smile, simply giving me a nod, then a glance at Sarah, and then she departed the room.

"So, what's gonna happen now?" Sarah asked.

"I have no clue. Hopefully, I'll be able to find some way to rendezvous with Hannah," I replied as I noticed there was a small bar complete with help-yourself drinks.

"Hannah! Hannah! Hannah!" Sarah said irritably as she dropped herself down in one of the rather luxurious armchairs. "Why do you even care what happens to Hannah? It's not like this is business as usual."

I glanced over at her as I poured myself a scotch and offered her one. After all, she was eighteen. She nodded.

"You may well have a point, but it's not like I've got anything better to do. Quitting my job seems to be a lot of trouble to go through. But most of all, it's pride. I was responsible for her, and I lost her. I've never failed a mission, yet here I'm."

"A mission?" Sarah replied as she down the drink in one go, clearly indicating she wasn't exactly alien up to the consumption of Scotch. "You talk like you're military, and your actions back there were certainly not your typical abilities of a common or garden security officer. You're clearly military."

"Everybody's military at some stage in their life," I chuckled at this as I took a seat opposite her.

"Oh, you clearly did more than just your average conscript. You were career, weren't you?"

"Well, I was conscripted at eighteen like anyone else, but I applied for the Special Air Service."

Her eyes widened, and she got out of her seat and walked over to the bar to pour herself another drink. "You're S. A.S.?"

"I was," I said modestly.

"Who Dares Wins, and all that." She didn't pour herself a single shot but filled the glass half-full.

"Go easy on that stuff."

She looked back at me, quite bemused. "I'm over eighteen, mate, and I can't think of a better reason than my country getting fucking annihilated to get well and truly munted."

"To be honest, Miss Jensen, I honestly don't care how old you are. We're in a situation where we don't know what's gonna happen, and we need to keep clear heads."

"Do you not think we're safe here?" She sat back down with her drink, but this time, she lifted her legs, resting them on the arm of my chair and crossing her ankles. I acted indifferent to this action, but I must admit I felt uncomfortable.

"Safe is relative," I replied. "We're on board a passenger liner, but I really don't think it's gonna take us out to see the Rings of Saturn. I have no idea where we're going to go and how long we're gonna be aboard this ship. I'm not even sure if we're gonna to be able to remain together."

She looked very concerned with this. "I can hardly say that I know you particularly well, Mr Marshall, but at least I know you, and honestly, I'd rather we weren't separated."

"Understood, and I'll do whatever I can to ensure we remain together, but right now, I have no idea what the next thirty minutes hold for us, let alone beyond that."

"Perhaps we can find out what's going on down on Oz."

She reached over to a small coffee table and picked up the remote control, turning on the large widescreen T.V. She flicked through the more common Australian channels. Nothing was broadcasting, and eventually, she switched over to an American news channel. Images of destruction from all around Australia appeared before our eyes. Cities aflame...Melbourne, Canberra Adelaide, the list went on.

"It is unknown how the European Union managed to get through undetected by the Australian defence systems. The country was taken by complete surprise by the greatest amphibious landing of any country in history. How they managed to pull this off is a major concern for the defence of the United States. The president has adopted a 'wait-and-see' policy before responding to the incident. It is believed that, being an election year, she's being cautious about committing American troops."

"Fuck the Americans," Sarah said, and as I looked over at her, I saw a tear running down her cheek.

Although I'd been there for two years, Australia was never really my home, and whilst, of course, I was concerned and somewhat distressed by what'd happened, it certainly wasn't to the level Sarah was. A native-born

Aussie. She lost her home, her family, and her country in a matter of hours, and it wasn't like she'd really had time to grieve.

The news that the Americans were not going to retaliate did cause me considerable concern, however. There could only be one tactical reason for this. However, it was politically dressed up. The Americans no longer had the resources to counter the attack. Though America was still militarily one of the most powerful countries in the world, it had long seen its heyday, and a strong pacifist movement over the generations had severely degenerated its capabilities.

The two most powerful countries in the Pacific Alliance were Australia and Japan. Economically, Australia had become a powerhouse. With its massive land resources, it was the primary import and export location for almost everything coming in and out of the solar system. This was in no small part to Grant Industries, which had its fingers in almost every pie, owning most major corporations to have ever existed. A company so powerful that it could thwart any monopoly laws of any country. Rumours had it that Marcia Grant held over five per cent of all finances in the entire world, but considering she owned most of the banks, no-one truly knew exactly how much money she had. However, she wasn't the outright owner of the company, holding only 49% of the stock and the rest being floated on the stock exchanges of the U.S.A., the U.K., Japan, and Australia. The last being where the largest number of shares were floated. A single share in the company was valued at more than the average person's annual wage.

This also meant she had most of the politicians in her back pocket, and not just in Australia. Despite laws preventing donations from foreign sources, it was generally believed Marcia bankrolled most of the campaigns in the United States, ensuring that the majority of people elected were sympathetic to her endeavours.

Sitting there, I couldn't help but wonder how this would affect the company. My own life was invested in it. It was where my pension was eventually going to come from to supplement my measly military one. Australia was the heart of Grant Industries, and with its loss also came the fact the controlling interest of the company was now owned by a spoiled little eighteen-year-old who technically couldn't own shares in the company due to the fact that she was genetically modified. The future wasn't looking very bright.

Chapter Nine

The Blink of an Eye

Eventually, unable to take it anymore, I turned off the T.V. Sarah was still trying to fight back the tears that wanted to flow freely, and I got up out of my seat and sat next to her, slipping my arm around her shoulder. She rested her head against me and sobbed quietly. We just sat that way in silence for about thirty minutes until I said, "We should try and get some sleep. I'm operating on fumes. I don't know about you." She nodded, but as we got up, she looked at me uncomfortably.

"I know this is an extremely weird request, Mr Marshall, but I really don't want to sleep on my own."

It *was* a weird request, but these were weird times, and I simply nodded. As a result, I didn't get undressed, and the two of us climbed into the same bed, and very uncomfortably for me, she hugged herself up against me. However, I was too tired to let it bother me too much, and I almost fell instantly asleep.

It was almost ten hours later when I woke up, and even then, it was by someone standing in the doorway of the bedroom, giving one of those attention getting coughs.

Instinctively, I sat bolt upright, and Sarah stirred next to me, having turned over to face the other way during the night. Kennedy Robinson was standing in the doorway.

"I did knock," she said uncomfortably, and when I didn't immediately reply, she added, "Several times."

Again, I didn't respond, glancing awkwardly at Sarah, who was now sitting up and rubbing her eyes.

"It's not what you think," I found myself saying.

Kennedy just shrugged. "It's not my business to think anything, Mr Marshall," in that 'I'm not judging you, but yes, I am' tone of voice. "Drake Tanner wants to see you."

The name sounded familiar, and it took me a moment before it registered. Drake Tanner was the chief operating officer who oversaw the daily running of the business. Basically, he was the highest-ranking member of the company, after Marcia Grant herself.

"Lead the way," I said, indicating the door as Sarah got up to join me.

"I'm sorry, Miss, but you're gonna have to wait here," Kennedy advised Sarah, who looked up at me with concern.

"Don't worry, sweetheart. I'll be back in a bit," I said in my best reassuring voice, and she simply nodded and sat back down as I left.

"What's going on?" I asked once I was following her in the corridor.

"We've left our space and are on course for Venus."

"I need to get to the moon. It's gonna take us months to get to Venus," I said with urgent frustration.

Kennedy just shrugged. "Sorry, I can't help you with that. It's not my call."

"I have a responsibility to locate Hannah Grant," I insisted futilely.

"Talk to Tanner about it. I *really* can't help you," she said, growing impatient with me.

We entered an area where the décor changed to that of corporate offices. It was rather bizarre seeing people acting like it was business as usual as they went about their daily jobs. I was led down the corridor to a suite where the receptionist announced me to the Chief Operating Officer, Drake Tanner.

He looked like your stereotypical corporate executive in an expensive business suit with an arrogant demeanour. "Oh, come in, Mr Marshall. Please take a seat."

I did as asked.

"I wanted to talk to you about Hannah Grant. We're in a very awkward position here, after you failed to protect her."

The hackles raised on the back of my neck.

"Now, you just wait a goddamn minute," I said aggressively, getting ready to rise from my seat. "There's absolutely no way I could've foreseen a Peon invasion of Australia. The girl was at school with the usual security that such an exclusive establishment provides, just as she had been for the last two years that I've been responsible for her."

"Be that as it may," Tanner responded so calmly, it was patronizing. "You were responsible for her. However, we can get back to that later. We've lost Hannah Grant again."

"What the fuck are you talking about?" I said, actually rising from my seat and causing his security guard by the door to tense.

"Please curb the profanity, Mr Marshall. Let's act professionally here," Tanner said quite calmly, waving me back down with a hand. "Her arrival on the moon didn't quite go as planned. Somehow, the authorities discovered that she's genetically modified, and it's illegal for Gen-Mods to be on the moon. She managed to escape with the help of your department, but we lost contact with the vessel whilst it was en route to Mars. It may be just a simple communications failure, but we're working on the possibility that her ship is lost."

"You should be working on the possibility that she's still alive and doing everything you possibly can to find her!" I screamed at him, banging my fists hard on his desk. "She is, after all, the new head of this company."

His guard took a step towards me, but Tanner raised a hand to stop him.

"Do you really think that?" He actually had the audacity to grin at me. "Hannah Grant is an illegal GenMod, and she's not allowed to own jack shit. All I need you to do is sign off on a statement that you witnessed that Marcia Grant was dead and leave everything else to us."

"Why do you need me to do that?" I scowled, managing to calm the rage welling within me.

"Without the positive identification from a recognised source, her estate remains intestate."

"It's only been a day since your country surrendered, and you're worried about some corporate bullshit?" I snapped.

"It's exactly why I have to worry about this corporate bullshit. We have to re-establish the company headquarters and our leadership structure now that it's gone. Grant Industries employs almost fourteen million individuals, and I have those people to think about," he said in his best altruistic voice. "We're not just an Australian company. We are established in every country in the Pacific Alliance and the colonies. We need to move quickly before confidence is entirely lost. Our share prices have plummeted by almost seventy-five per cent in the last couple of days, and I need to maintain that confidence to avoid us going under."

"You son of a bitch. I'm not stupid." He casually pulled out a handkerchief from his pocket to wipe the spittle from his desk as I berated him. "Is the status of Hannah Grant complicated enough that you'd be better off if she didn't survive, either? No doubt Marcia Grant has left her shares to her daughter, believing that no-one would ever find out about her genetic nature."

He sat back calmly in his chair and arched his fingers like the villain from an old Bond movie. All he needed was a Persian cat to complete the picture. "I couldn't really care less if Hannah Grant was alive or dead. Although I readily admit that if she were dead, it would make things a lot smoother for us, but if you're implying that I had anything to do with her disappearance, trust me, I will not take that lightly."

"Then give me a damn shuttle which it is capable of interplanetary flight, and I'll go looking for her."

He shook his head and sighed dismissively. "She is no longer your responsibility. Due to your failure to protect her, I'm terminating your contract. Now, if you're unwilling to sign the documentation I have asked for, I can promise you that I will make your retirement very uncomfortable."

"Bring it on motherfucker," I said softly. "Unless you actively help me try to find Hannah Grant, I'm not doing jack shit. I have the Right of Patronage, and you can't touch me."

He simply smiled in response and said, "Hannah Grant was your patron, Marshall. I'm fairly certain she's dead. You can't hide behind her overly expensive skirts now." He didn't wait for me to respond. "You brought aboard an unauthorized passenger, did you not? Miss Jensen is effectively a stowaway. Would you like me to have her arrested and thrown into jail?"

I glared at him. "I hardly believe that a passenger liner would even have a jail, but I get your point," I sighed and sat back down, realising I was as responsible for Sarah as I was Hannah now. I let out a long, weary sigh. "You win, Tanner. I'll sign your documents in exchange for documents that would indemnify me from any sort of civil legalities you decide to throw at me or Sarah. Considering you're trying to pass the blame on me for the loss of Hannah Grant, that's the least I can expect."

He smiled triumphantly. "A pleasure doing business with you, Marshall."

I was escorted back to my suite by one of the civilian corporate people. I didn't tell Sarah about what'd happened, saying simply that it was business stuff. I'd been provided with a tablet in order to receive the documentation they sent over, but as I sat down to read it, I heard a quiet voice coming from a chair by the bar. I looked up to see where I'd hung my jacket, and I stepped over to it, realising it was Emily. I pulled out the glasses and slipped them on.

"You have an incoming call. Do you wish to accept?" she repeated.

"Who is it?"

"The caller is not identifying themselves," Emily replied.

"Well, let's find out who this mysterious person is. Put them through, please, Emily."

The voice that came on the line was familiar, but I couldn't immediately place it. "Operation Funnel-Web is go."

"Huh?" was all I replied.

"I said 'Operation Funnel-Web is go.'"

"Oh, I heard you. I just have no clue what you're talking about."

"I'm talking to Protector One, am I not?" I finally realised it was Kennedy on the line.

"Well, technically, I just got fired, but I guess so," I replied.

"He's bluffing. Drake can't fire you. Your contract is directly with Hannah Grant, not the company, but he can dispose of you permanently if you sign that documentation. As long as Marcia and Hannah Grant are not legally dead, then you're pretty much safe, no matter what he claims. But are you really telling me you know nothing about Operation Funnel-Web?"

"I have absolutely no clue what you're talking about," I replied.

"Stay where you are. I'll come to you."

"Where exactly do you think I'm gonna go?"

But there came no reply as she disconnected.

"What's going on now?" Sarah asked.

"Honestly, I have no clue," I said, slipping my holster back on, followed by my jacket. A few minutes later, there came a knock at the door. Kennedy didn't wait for an answer as she rushed in.

"So, you've never been told about Operation Funnel-Web?" she asked, looking confused.

"Never heard of it."

"Okay, come with me. I'll explain on the way, but we've gotta move fast."

I glanced at Sarah, who just simply shrugged, and for lack of a better response, we followed Kennedy out of the corridor.

"Marcia Grant set up Operation Funnel-Web to come into play when there was a hostile intent to take over the corporation. Drake Tanner is trying to do that right now. If you sign off on the death of Marcia Grant and he reveals that Hannah is a GenMod, then he can do that immediately. Under no circumstances can you be allowed to sign off on that."

"But Marcia Grant *is* dead."

"Not legally. It could take years for him to get that through the court system. However, the longer we can delay that, the more chance we have from stopping it from happening altogether."

"I don't understand. What's in this for you?" I asked suspiciously.

"Grant Security Services has a lot of influence within the company, and we want to maintain that position. All of us involved with Operation Funnel-Web have devoted ourselves to the family, and it's our responsibility to ensure that the company remains within the family, no matter what it takes."

"Hannah Grant is the sole surviving member of the family. But if she is a GenMod, as Tanner claims, she couldn't hold the position anyway," I said, taking Sarah's hand as she struggled to keep up with our pace.

"Oh, you should know how the rules don't apply to the Grant family, Mr Marshall," Kennedy smirked. "Everybody in the entire world knows that Hannah Grant is genetically modified, and yet no-one has ever investigated it or tried to arrest her. That was, however, until she arrived at the moon. Drake has seen to it that the lunar authorities became aware of her status. He was hoping they would terminate her, but we stayed one step ahead, and she's on her way to Mars."

"But Drake has lost contact with the ship and believes it's been lost?"

"Yes, there is that possibility, but we're hoping that the security services with her have simply decommissioned the ship's transponders to avoid being picked up."

"This is all well and good," Sarah said. "But what exactly are you doing with us?"

"We need to make sure that Drake doesn't get his hands on you," Kennedy stated. "It's my job to see that he doesn't."

At that, I released Sarah's hand, and my gun came out and I placed it on the back of Kennedy's neck. "You plan to kill us?"

Kennedy stopped walking and raised her hands slowly. "Don't be a fool, Marshall. We are well aware of your relationship with Hannah Grant, and she's not going to thank us for putting you out of an airlock. If I was going to kill you, it would already be done, and I wouldn't be explaining to you about Operation Funnel-Web. We have a hidden M.E.T. system set up in a cargo hold that only we know about it. We plan to upload you and the girl until such a time that we have Hannah secured, and in a position to defend herself and the company."

"You can't be serious?" I said, slowly lowering my weapon, not entirely convinced.

"I'm deadly serious, Liam. The moment you sign those forms, Tanner will make sure that you can't argue that it was done under duress or any other such legal manoeuvre. You're as good as dead," she slowly turned around. "You can shoot me right now if you want to, but what are you going to do next? Maybe I'm lying, and I'm here to kill you? However, maybe I'm not, and I'm actually your only chance of surviving this. Drake wants to take control of Grant Industries, making him possibly the most powerful individual in the solar system. Do you really think he's going to hesitate not to skin you alive?"

If I pondered this a moment, then holstered my weapon. "I guess I have no alternative but to trust you."

"Gee, how magnanimous of you," she rolled her eyes at me. "Come on, we've wasted enough time."

We hurried through the corridors and down several elevator rides until we came out in the cargo area. She weaved in and out of the thirty-foot-high stacked containers until she appeared to go down a dead end. She then tapped her ear to activate some sort of communication device. "Banshee to base control, I have Protector One and a companion. Password: Wonderwall."

The entire wall slid open. A nervous-looking technician greeted us as we stepped into a small, cramped area. It was barely the size of a cargo container, containing nothing more than a compact M.E.T. system. The wall slid closed behind us, and we were in a dimly lit environment. The technician started powering up the device as Kennedy started removing her clothing. She looked up at us and said with a frown, "I take it you've never used an M.E.T. before?"

"I don't think either of us has ever been off-world before," I replied. "But my understanding was that these M.E.T. devices were experimental only. Even the military doesn't use them yet."

"Government paranoia! Grant Industries have been installing them in all their major craft for the last year or two. Even some of the smaller vessels have been upgraded with them. However, we can discuss this all day, but you need to be naked to go into the M.E.T."

I stared at her for a few moments, then started slipping off my jacket. Sarah looked positively horrified, but I simply shrugged at her, and she started to undress. Once the three of us were naked, Kennedy indicated for me to stand in a small circle underneath the device.

"No, I wanna make sure you upload Sarah too. Too many people have questioned her being with me to trust anyone with her safety."

"Fine," Kennedy said irritably. "Go ahead, Sarah, stand with your legs apart, and your arms outstretched."

Nervously, she stepped into the circle and did as she was told. I smiled at her and nodded to her reassuringly, and she smiled weakly back at me before there was a flash of light, and she disappeared. The brightness of it blinded me, and I let out a curse. "You could have fucking warned me!"

"Sorry!" Kennedy said sheepishly. "Anyway, it's your turn."

"Why are you coming with us?" I said as I stepped into the circle.

"It's not going to take a tactical genius to work out that I was the one that got you out of there. I really don't want to die today."

"Well, they're certainly gonna search for me. Where are they gonna think I've gone?"

"Of course they will," Kennedy said as she tossed her trousers aside. "However, we're going to release several escape pods with security personnel on board. They're going to assume that you've left the ship."

"You seem to have this all planned perfectly. Too perfectly. So perfectly that I'm certain something's going to go wrong."

She smiled at this. "Grant Security Services are better at this shit than the bloody military. You really have nothing to worry about, Liam. But can you please hurry up, before our technician here is missed?"

I lifted my arms and parted my feet, and there was a bright flash of light once more.

It appeared like nothing had happened, and I had no memory of the passing of time. All I could see was the lights in front of my eyes, but it appeared that the room had brightened.

"What the fuck!" came a familiar, incredibly astounded voice. "Liam! I thought you died back in Oz."

As my vision cleared, I found myself looking into the eyes of Hannah Grant.

"Hello, Duchess," I said, immediately stepping towards her, delighted to see her safe and alive, but she took a step back.

"Yeah, let's get you in some clothes before we do the huggy stuff, mate," she grinned at me. A tall woman at her side, dressed in an all-white business suit, handed me some clothing. Just some basic jeans, and a t-shirt. As I dressed, I stared at Hannah. She looked different, and I couldn't quite work it out. However, I couldn't help but feel glad that she was apparently extremely pleased to see me. I pulled on my final item of clothing, and to my surprise, she stepped up, threw her arms around me, and pulled me to her with a tight embrace. "I really thought you were dead, you fucker."

I laughed lightly. "It's against company regulations to die on the job."

I stepped back to look at her again, and it started to dawn on me that she looked older. Gone was that teenage look, but now before me stood a woman in her mid-twenties. A cold chill went down my spine.

"How long was I in that damn thing?" I asked nervously.

She turned to a young technician. A different one from the individual that had uploaded me. At her questioning look, he replied. "According to the records, for five years, seven months, and nineteen days."

CHAPTER TEN

AN UNUSUAL CHANGE IN STATUS

"Are you serious?" I stared at her open-mouthed, causing her to laugh.

"Yeah, well, it can be very disorientating," Hannah said sympathetically. "The same thing happened to Bron and me en route to Mars when the cabin depressurized. I was stuck in that bloody thing for two years. You're damn lucky we found you. It's only because this entire cargo bay has been converted into a medical facility, and they wanted to take this wall down to expand into the next cargo bay, that we found you."

"How did you end up in here?" The woman with her spoke with a South African accent, and I realised it was the woman I had initially had contact with when on the run. Alpha Leader.

I looked questioningly at Hannah.

"Oh, introductions!" she said as she realised what I was silently asking. "Liam, this is Emberlynn Stepanchikov. Stepanchikov, this is Liam Marshall. He was my security back in Australia before you took over the role."

I shook her hand and acknowledged her with a nod. "How did you end up in here, Mr Marshall. Last time we spoke, you were driving out to Alice Springs."

"A Grant Security Services captain called Kennedy Robinson instigated something called 'Operation Funnel-Web'. Some sort of plan to ensure no-one takes over the corporation in the absence of a Grant. She's uploaded in there." I nodded to the M.E.T.

"They activated Funnel-Web?" Surprised, Stepanchikov smiled and turned to Hannah. "That's why your mother has never been reported as dead. At least, not until recently."

Hannah looked at her questioningly. "What exactly is Operation Funnel-Web?"

"Basically, it's a group of highly loyal and trusted members of security services. I was part of it, but obviously, I was in the M.E.T. with you when they instigated it. Thus, I never knew anything about its activation." She then looked suspiciously at me. "That doesn't explain why they hid you away as part of that operation?"

"So that I couldn't confirm that Marcia Grant was dead," I replied.

Stepanchikov smiled. "Well, that makes sense."

"You know that my mother is dead?" Hannah frowned at me.

"Yeah. I saw her body myself," I said as caringly as circumstances permitted. "So is Annabelle."

She smiled lightly. "Oh, don't concern yourself, Liam. I've come to terms with it. If she wasn't dead, I would have heard from her by now. It's just kind of a shock hearing it for a certainty."

"The readouts are saying there are two people uploaded in that device," Stepanchikov said. "Who are the others?"

"One, I assume, is Captain Kennedy Robinson," I advised. "And the other is Sarah Jensen."

Hannah's eyes widened.

"Well fuck me! I thought she was dead, too!" She turned to the tech. "Download her. Download her now!" she said excitedly.

I moved away from the device and turned to face it, and to my surprise, Hannah slipped her hand in mine and smiled at me, before eagerly looking toward the M.E.T.

I cursed, as once more I completely forgot to shield my eyes from the flash of light, and before my vision cleared, Hannah had released my hand and was hugging her friend tightly.

"Oh my God, Sarah! Oh my God! Oh my God!"

Sarah looked bewildered, but I was no longer paying attention to their conversation as my mind was a complete clusterfuck, as it tried to adjust to the sudden unexpected circumstances. Six years. What the hell had been going on?

Hannah wanted to take us back to her quarters. But Stepanchikov stopped her. "If you don't mind, Miss Grant, I need to debrief Marshall and Robinson, but I'll bring them straight up to you as soon as I'm done."

Hannah looked quite put out but agreed.

Robinson was downloaded, and being more professional than me, she immediately saluted Stepanchikov, clearly recognising her.

"Good to have you back, Robinson. Please, will you both come with me? I'm sure you have more catching up to do than I do."

So, much to my disappointment, I was separated from Hannah once more as we went through the docking bay, which now looked completely different from how I had seen it minutes before. It certainly had been turned into a medical centre with rows of beds, most of them empty. It would turn out that it had been set up during the Battle of Deep Space, which was one of many events I had missed.

As we made our way to Stepanchikov's offices, she gave us a rundown of events, but it was all too much to take in. The news that the Pacific Alliance had surrendered wasn't as much of a surprise as you may think. Anyone with a brain knew that we were losing the war. However, the news that some woman called Jenna Plural had united the fleets, was.

"So I take it that returning to Earth is not an option?" Kennedy asked the question we were both thinking as Stepanchikov led us into her office, telling her assistant to get us some coffee.

"It's not outside the realms of possibility, but returning to your respective countries would mean capitulating to Union rule," Stepanchikov said as she took her seat. "It may even be an option you might consider, considering you're still both of conscription age."

"Grant Industries has been listed as providing essential civilian services, and I can't be conscripted," Kennedy advised, although she looked concerned.

"And I've completed a year beyond my national service requirement," I added.

Stepanchikov just smiled. "You're in the Solar Confederation now, not the Pacific Alliance. Jenna Plural has torn up the rulebook. However, Miss Grant has a fairly cordial relationship with the Admiral, and it'll be up to her how she wants to proceed with this."

"Jenna Plural?" I asked, never having heard the name before.

"That's a long story I'm not going to go into, but basically, she is now ipso facto ruler of the fleet and the new Solar Confederation."

"How does Grant Industries fit into all of this?" Kennedy asked.

"Now, that is quite a complicated situation, Miss Robinson," Stepanchikov replied. "Drake Tanner owns 53% of the company. Miss Grant owns 5%, and the rest are regular shareholders. The company was floated on Wall Street after the decline of Australia, and it still is, but it is also under the auspices of the European Union now. However, there was also a European wing of the company that was separate, but now the Europeans are running America. Drake has managed to reunite the two halves of the company. Once that merger goes through, Miss Grant's share of the company would drop to 2.5%, and she won't even be the second largest shareholder."

"That's double damn," Kennedy muttered. "That was precisely what Operational Funnel-Web was designed to stop happening."

"Indeed, Miss Robinson, that was the case. However, Drake quickly got rid of any opposition, with the exception of Hannah, who has proved most resilient. He must have eliminated Funnel-Web in the early days of his takeover. That is why no-one was aware you were stored in a hidden M.E.T. device until construction workers found you this morning."

"Is there any way you can let my parents know that I'm still alive?" I asked.

Stepanchikov sighed. "Since the destruction of the Phobos communications base, there has been a technical warfare of jamming and counter-jamming communications. It is extremely difficult to communicate with anyone on Earth, but we will try." She paused for a moment and looked at each of us in turn. "I know you have a lot to take on board, having been out of the loop for some time, but you're in quite a unique position. You are legally dead and will not show up on anyone's records. That could be quite useful to us."

"Well, personally, I'd just like to return to my duties as Protector One," I said, knowing full well that someone else probably fulfilled that role.

Stepanchikov smiled. "That privilege is now mine, Mr Marshall, and let me be quite honest, I don't plan to retire for a very long time. Both of you have proven loyal to the company and Miss Grant and will hold significant positions. So significant that they would have to be signed off by Miss Grant herself. However, I personally want to transfer you both to Grant Special Services."

"I've never heard of it," I responded.

Stepanchikov chuckled. "I should certainly hope not, as that defeats its purpose." However, before she could elaborate on that, she lifted her hand to her ear, clearly receiving an incoming message. The smile quickly faded to look at frustration. "As you wish, Miss Grant. I will send him along right now." She then looked back up at me and, with a weary sigh, said, "It appears our illustrious leader is getting impatient to spend time with you, Mr Marshall. I will have my assistant take you up to her quarters whilst I get Miss Robinson here acclimatised."

Hannah Grant's quarters were well beyond opulent. Styled upon the seventeenth-century Palace of Versailles, it was like stepping through a time warp. Screens even covered windows that made it look like you were looking out onto the palace's grounds. It was only the appearance of modern tech, such as monitors and other computer equipment, which were decorated in the style of the rest of the room, but clearly didn't fit.

As I walked in, it was bizarre to see Hannah sitting on a couch with her legs crossed, drinking a glass of wine, and laughing at a joke her companion made. The companion startled me in more ways than one. I distinctly recognised the voice of Bronwyn Donovan, but when the woman turned around, I couldn't hide my shock. I saw that half of her face was covered in a metal plate, and an artificial red eye was staring out at me like something out of a science fiction horror movie. She looked irritated by my reaction but then appeared to shrug it off, and she said, "Good to see you, Mr Marshall. Welcome back."

Both she and Hannah got out of their seats and came over to me. Hannah handed Bronwyn her glass and embraced me once again.

"I really thought you were dead, you arsehole. I can't believe you're here right now!" She stood squeezing me tightly. It didn't feel appropriate for me to reciprocate the tight hug, and I awkwardly patted her gently on the back, much to Bron's amusement.

"Where's Sarah?" I asked as she released me.

"She's having a lie-down. She's exhausted," Bronwyn told me.

"So what happened to you after Last Day?" I asked. "I tracked you as far as Alice Springs but then was informed the G.S.S. got you out and that you were en route to Mars before they lost contact with your vessel."

"There was a decompression on the ship we were on," Hannah told me as she returned to her seat, pulling me to sit down beside her. "Like you, I was trapped in the M.E.T. but only for two years as we took a quick jaunt around the sun and were picked up on our return. Fortunately, we were returned to this ship, and we've been here ever since."

I found that quite disconcerting as I realised that Hannah had aged almost three years whilst I remained at the same age. She was now legally twenty-three, and I was …. what the fuck, I was now *thirty*! Realistically, I was still twenty-six, and she was twenty-one. The gap in our ages had dropped by years. M.E.T. transit really screws up your head.

Hannah's whole demeanour was different. The look of that bratty, stroppy teen who was dominated by her mother was clearly long gone.

There was a light in her eye that I had never seen before. She was happy. She continued to tell me her story just as she recounted it in her autobiography, *Awakening of Hannah Grant*. Her smile lit up the room as she looked over at Bronwyn, who was now telling part of the tale. I couldn't help but let a smile cross my face. Hannah noticed this, and she looked at me quizzically but said nothing. I simply grinned back at her with a shrug and smiled wider. She returned it, shook her head, and rolled her sparkling, deep blue eyes.

Then, it became my turn to tell my story. It was very disorientating to evaluate all the differences. The fall of Australia was five years ago. For Hannah and Bronwyn, it was three years ago, and for me, it was yesterday. The fall of the Alliance was almost a year ago and the first anniversary of the Battle of Deep Space was coming up.

"I'm hungry," Bronwyn suddenly said, standing up. "What say you to getting out of here and going down to one of the restaurants for dinner?"

Hannah smiled, clearly liking that idea, but she looked at me. "You up for it, Liam?"

It may sound odd, but in the two years I had known Hannah, I had never sat down with her for a meal, other than occasional light lunches whilst on shopping trips or other similar activities.

"Sure, why not," I responded, getting up.

Sarah was woken, and we headed out to one of the Twilight Wanderer's many luxurious five-star restaurants. Sarah remained subdued for a while, but when the conversation got around to reminiscing about various high school shenanigans they got up to, she seemed to relax a little bit and show some cheerfulness.

"You know what I'm never gonna get used to?" she eventually said as we started on the dessert course. "Yesterday, we were all the same age, but today, you're now both three years older than me."

"I hope to God I never have to go into the M.E.T. again, mate," Bronwyn said but with a dry chuckle.

As Hannah laid down her fork, I suggested that I ask the waiter for the bill, but she just chuckled at that. "I own the damn place, mate. I don't get bills."

Now, that was the hardest thing to sink in for me. Hannah was now the boss, and not just the daughter of the boss. In my befuddled brain, I'd only seen her three days ago as that spoiled eighteen-year-old, but in the blink of an eye, three years had passed in her life, and she was an experienced corporate mogul.

Her eyes met mine again, and she stared ponderously at me as I tried to work out what was going through her mind. She then interrupted Bronwyn and Sarah, who were chatting about some boy they once knew at high school.

"Hey, why don't the two of you go find something to do this evening? I wanna spend some time catching up with Liam."

There was a pause. Then, a coarse grin crossed Bronwyn's face. "Sure, whatever you want, Han."

Sarah giggled, glancing over at me. Call me dense, but I had no idea what was going on between them. Hannah rolled her eyes at the pair and flipped them off as she slipped out of her seat. She then looked at me and held out her hand. "Come on."

I got out of my seat and nodded to Bronwyn and Sarah. "Goodnight, ladies," I frowned as they grinned gormlessly at me.

Back in Hannah's quarters, I took a seat whilst Hannah went to the small bar to get a couple of drinks.

"I missed you, you know," she said quietly.

"Well, I'd like to say I missed you too, but it's really only been a couple of days for me, and most of that time, I was running for my life while trying to find you."

"I wish you had," she said as she handed me a glass and sat down next to me. "Found me, I mean. I think the last couple of years would have been better with you with me." She crossed her legs, and the split down the length of her dress fell away, revealing those long, perfectly shaped legs. Being professional, I made sure that my eyes didn't fall in that direction.

"You know you should have waited for me," I told her.

She laughed. "I spent several days in a state of shock. It didn't even occur to me that you would come looking for me."

"Why wouldn't I? It's my job to look out for you."

She raised her eyebrows at me and said, "I think when the apocalypse happens, your day job isn't really a concern anymore." She uncrossed her legs and crossed them again the other way, but this time, her leg brushed against mine.

I started to think about the British Prime Minister and other ugly bastards as I found myself getting a bit turned on by this. "No, Liam, you came after me because you actually care about me."

"And that surprises you?"

"To be honest, yes, it does." She tilted her head at me. "Aren't you supposed to have a professional detachment?"

"Yes, and I do. However, when you spend virtually two years living in someone's presence, you either grow to care about them or grow to hate them."

"Can I assume that I don't fall into the hate category?" Hannah grinned.

I laughed, feeling rather hot under the collar as she gently ran the back of her finger up and down my arm and sipped her drink.

"Yes, I can quite assure you that you definitely don't fall into the hate category."

She leaned in closer to me, and it was getting incredibly uncomfortable. "You know I always had a bit of a crush on you?"

"Actually, no, I didn't," I replied honestly.

Her face came so close to mine that I could feel her breath and smell the late-night remnants of exceptionally expensive perfume. I immediately found myself becoming aroused, but rather than respond, I stood up quickly. Hannah sat back and glared up at me.

"What the fuck?" she said, sitting back.

It was one of those difficult situations where I felt confident that she was trying to seduce me, but not enough that I could accuse her of it.

"I probably think it's time I went to bed," I said uneasily.

Hannah grinned. "Well, that is precisely what I was working on, darling."

I don't know if I actually flushed, but I certainly felt like I had. "Hannah, this is just too weird. The last time I saw you were a high school kid."

She shrugged. "So? We're now only a few years apart in age."

Putting her glass down, she stood up and sauntered towards me. She reached out and took my hand, pulling herself closer. I tried some mental relaxation techniques and thought of everything I could, other than what I really wanted to do right now.

Hardening my resolve, I took a step back and gently pulled my hand away from hers. A flash of anger lit up in her eyes.

"Oh my God, Liam, what's your problem? I don't want to sound arrogant, but I know you want to fuck me."

I raised an eyebrow, and whilst it was true, I replied, "That's quite an assertion, Duchess. How can you be so sure that's true?"

She rolled her eyes at me yet again. "Because society deems that my almost billion-dollar D.N.A. makes me one of the hottest bitches in the solar system. Unless you're either gay or a eunuch, then you wanna fuck me." The charming look on her face suddenly dissipated. She looked at me quizzically, tilting her head slightly. "You're not gay, are you?"

I laughed at this. It didn't stop my feeling of discomfort, but it did amuse me. "No, I can assure you, Duchess, I'm not gay."

"And I'm assuming you didn't have your nuts blown off when Melbourne blew up on Last Day?"

"I, fortunately, remained perfectly intact in that department."

To my utter surprise, her expression turned pouty. "Then why don't you wanna fuck me? You find religion or something?"

I laughed again but then said seriously, "No."

Her face grew serious again, and she fixed me with a determined and rather aggressive look. "I want an answer, Liam," she demanded coldly.

"It would be unprofessional of me, Duchess. I'm your security, and you're my boss," I responded.

Hannah looked at me quizzically again. "Your employment with Grant Industries ended the day you were listed as dead. Your position has been replaced by Stepanchikov."

"That might be so, but she did offer me another position today, so I'm once again an employee of your company."

She pondered this a moment, then took a step back.

"Do me a favour, Liam. Just take a seat for a minute."

A little confused, I did as she asked or rather instructed. She stepped over to the desk and picked up a remote control. The T.V. screen lit up, and Hannah said, "Hannah to Stepanchikov." There was a long pause, and I started to think that she was about to try to get me fired in order to have her way with me.

The bleary-eyed image of Stepanchikov appeared on the screen, and added to that, the fact that she was dressed in night attire meant Hannah had just woken her up.

"Miss Grant. What can I *possibly* do for you at this late hour."

Hannah didn't even seem to notice her Chief of Securities jibe at being woken up. "Did you offer Liam Marshall a job?"

"Yes, I did," Stepanchikov frowned. "Do you wish me to withdraw that offer?"

"No, no. I just want to know if the paperwork has been completed yet?"

"No," Stepanchikov responded with a little bit of confusion. "I only put it through to personnel a couple of hours ago."

"So tell me, would I be correct in saying that Liam Marshall is, at this moment, currently not employed by Grant Industries?"

Stepanchikov looked bewildered by the odd question. "Well, technically, no, he is not."

Before she could finish the sentence, Hannah simply said, "Thank you, Emberlynn. That's all I wanted to know." She immediately turned off the screen. She tossed the control onto the desk and made her way back to me.

"What's your excuse now, motherfucker?" she purred sweetly, as she lowered herself onto my lap with her knees on either side of my hips. Then, leaning down, Hannah Grant kissed me.

I did not resist.

CHAPTER ELEVEN

CROSSING PROFESSIONAL LINES

Her lips were soft and warm, the taste of the alcohol we had consumed at dinner still fresh upon them. My hands fell to her thighs, pushing away the opening of her dress so I could place a hand on each. They were soft like silk, and unlike any other woman I had ever touched. Flawless. As her tongue entered my mouth and intertwined with mine, I felt my arousal straining through my pants and pressing against her. From this point on, I couldn't care less about the rights and the wrongs of it. That male passion that destroys any sense of guilt or appropriateness was now in control of my brain.

She sat back and started unfastening the buttons on my shirt as I slipped my hand around her back and pulled down the zip of her dress. As it fell from her shoulders, I carefully unfastened the clasp of her bra, being careful to ensure it didn't snap back and ruin the moment. As everything fell down to her waist, my eyes followed, looking at those firm, pert, and exquisite breasts. She got tired of unfastening my buttons and ripped the rest of my shirt off in quite an aggressive manner. I reached up to cup one of those breasts as she leaned in to kiss me again. This time, it was harder and more intense as her hand slipped down to my belt and tugged at it impatiently. I reached down and helped her unfasten it. She left that job to me, bringing her hands up, wrapping her arms around the back of my neck, and pressing her breasts against my chest, as the kissing grew even more intense. The belt now dealt with, I slipped my arms around her back and backside and lifted her up as I stood up, taking her with me. She wrapped her legs around me, and we didn't break the kiss. I turned her around and gently placed her down, so she was lying on the couch. I broke contact with her to finish removing my pants and shirt, and she lifted her buttocks up and let me slip the dress from underneath her. I pulled it over her ankles after letting my shirt fall away and stepping out of my trousers. She reached out and caressed me through my underwear as I leaned down and hooked two fingers around her panties, and simultaneously, we tugged them off each other. Already at full mast, I took a seat at the end of the couch and lifted one of her legs over my head. Gently lowering myself, I buried my face between her legs, and she moaned softly, gripping my hair, and pulling my face harder against her as I did my best to pleasure her. She enjoyed this for several minutes before she told me to turn around, and realising what she wanted to do, I moved into a position where we could both orally pleasure each other. They say a man should not kiss and tell, but I have to say Hannah Grant's art of fellatio was beyond anything I had ever experienced. It wasn't long before I had to stop her for fear of ending the night prematurely. She grinned at me as

I turned around, but she pushed me away and sat up. I was momentarily confused until she pulled me down on the seat beside her, and then she swung her legs back into the position over my lap, but this time she guided me into her. I went deep, and her muscles clenched, gripping me hard. She began to pulse rhythmically as I gently pinched one of her nipples, causing her to let out a pleasurable moan.

Again, I had to get her to pause to stop me from finishing before her. We sat still for a good minute. She looked down at me and ran her fingers through my hair. Then, when she saw my expression start to relax, she slowly started moving up and down again, grinning down at the ecstasy on my face. Slowly but surely, she started to move faster, and I couldn't hold back a groan. Soon, she let her head fall back, that golden blonde hair cascading all around as she bit her lip and whimpered softly for a moment. She then cried out with orgasmic joy. That was the sign that I could release all my frustration. Our bodies tensed as we came together, and as I exploded inside her, logic swiftly returned, and a sudden concern crossed my mind that almost ruined the event. We had not used any protection, and I was now praying that she was on the pill.

She allowed herself to fall against me with her head over my shoulder. She panted softly and allowed her tense body to relax. "Damn, you're good," she muttered softly in my ear, doing wonders for my ego. After giving me one last kiss, she allowed herself to flop down beside me. I slipped my arm around her, and she lay her head on my shoulder, resting her hand on my chest. We just lay there quietly for a few minutes.

Eventually, she got up and said, "I need to take a shower." She headed towards the bathroom and then looked back at me teasingly. "Care to join me?" She laughed as I didn't hesitate and followed her in. She leaned into the shower and turned it on, and then she waited for the water to get hot. She turned back and pressed herself up against me once more, kissing me.

I pulled back after a while and looked at her quite seriously.

"We didn't use any..." My voice trailed off, uncomfortable with this subject, hoping that she would get what I was referring to. She didn't. She looked at me questioningly and waited. "We didn't use any protection."

She grinned at me and turned away to check the temperature of the water with her hand. "Oh, you don't need to worry about that, Liam. My genetically modified antibodies will see your inferior semen as a foreign body, like a virus, and will kill anything off." She turned back and, when she saw my frown, looked confused. "What's the matter?"

"While it's good that I can't get you pregnant, I'm kind of insulted by the idea that my semen is inferior."

She laughed at this, reached up, and bit me gently on the lower lip. "Hey, it could be so much worse. Unlike me, you didn't have to fuck a genetically inferior person," she giggled, taking my hand in hers.

"Fuck you, Duchess," I laughed.

"Well, if you insist, Liam," she smirked, and she pulled me into the shower with her.

About thirty minutes later, I was lying in the bed next to her. She was pushed up against me, her leg resting over my thigh and her head upon my shoulder, snoring softly. I had managed to perform for a second round in the shower, but there was no way I was gonna go for a third, despite her trying.

This was when the guilt came.

The dynamic between myself and Hannah had changed irrevocably. I had difficulty sleeping as I fretted about what the morning would bring, but after an hour or two, I managed to drift off, and when I woke, Hannah was no longer at my side. This didn't surprise me because I was well aware that GenMods didn't need more than two or three hours of sleep, and there have been many times when Hannah had got me up in the early hours of the morning because she wanted to go out somewhere before the sun had even come up. As I climbed out of bed, I had the uncomfortable realisation that I had left all my clothes on the floor of the lounge. As I approached the door, I could hear voices outside. Hannah, Bronwyn and Sarah. *Fuck! Fuck! Fuck!* I looked around for something to wear, but there was nothing except a fluffy pink bathrobe. I grabbed it up and pulled it on. It barely covered my privates, and as I went to the door, I hesitated. Did Hannah want her friends to know about what we just did? Did *I* want her friends to know what we just did? I turned away from the door and sat on the edge of the bed, resting my elbows on my knees and pondered the situation.

I don't know how long passed, but eventually, the bedroom door swung open, and Hannah stepped in to see me there in the pink bathrobe. She suddenly stopped and burst out laughing.

"Oh my God, girls, you gotta see this." She called back to her friends, and I jumped up with extreme embarrassment as the two girls came to the doorway and joined in with Hannah's humour.

"Any chance I can get my clothes?" I asked, irritated.

"Oh, don't be such a grouch," Hannah said, moving towards me and kissing me on the cheek, clearly not having a problem with her friends being aware of what was going on.

Bronwyn grinned at me. "Oh, but you look so cute like that."

I looked imploringly at Hannah, who rolled her eyes with a chuckle.

"Grab his clothes, would you, Bron?" A few seconds later, Bronwyn returned with a pile of well-used clothing. She and Sarah stood there looking at me with amused grins, acting as if I was going to get changed in front of them.

Hannah laughed at this. "Go on, get out. We'll be out in a minute."

Bronwyn shot me one last grin. "Nice legs, Mr Marshall," she said, closing the door behind her.

I looked at Hannah. "Did you enjoy embarrassing me like that?" I said curtly.

Hannah shrugged, still grinning.

"Yeah, I kind of did." She then looked at the clothes in my hand and scrunched up her nose. "Don't put those on. I'll order you something new."

I tossed the clothes down and sat back down on the bed. "So, what happens now?" I asked her as she went over to her wardrobe.

"What do you mean?" she asked as she went through picking out an outfit for the day.

"Well, doesn't this situation complicate my working for you?"

She glanced over her shoulder at me, but immediately returned to looking at her outfits. "Only if you let it."

"Won't you be uncomfortable?"

Pulling out an outfit, she turned back to me.

"Why should I?" she asked casually, as she slipped out of her pyjamas. She glanced up at me with a grin. "And, hey, you get bragging rights that you fucked the boss."

"Something tells me that you aren't completely joking there," I frowned.

"What do you mean?"

"It doesn't bother you for anyone to know about this?" I asked, bewildered.

She frowned slightly and then laughed again.

"Again. Why should it?" she shrugged as she pulled on a pair of underwear.

"Well, you're very high profile. You're the leading member of the Grant family now."

"Oh, my dear Liam, it's precisely because I'm Hannah Grant that I do whatever I like," she said with the weirdest grin. "And I don't give a fuck what anyone thinks. If you wanna tell the world you fucked the boss, then go for it. I *seriously* don't care."

I didn't honestly know how to respond to that and found myself saying sheepishly, "I'd rather say I was fucking the boss, than I fucked the boss."

She chuckled at me as she tucked her silk blouse into her formal business-like skirt. "I guess that's a possibility. Let's just see how it goes."

Now, that bothered me more than I care to admit.

Hannah had some temporary clothes delivered to me, and I got changed. She had to go into some board meeting, which Bronwyn was crying off. So it was with Hannah's best mate that I headed down to a rather exclusive shipboard mall. Bronwyn clearly didn't like my choices for my new wardrobe and took over. It all felt a little weird as she picked out my clothes and paid the bill, charging it to Hannah's account. I'd gone from wearing off-the-peg department store clothes to the latest in designer wear for men. I say the latest, but it wasn't like they'd been supplied since the fall of the Pacific Alliance, but it was modern to me.

"Unfortunately, there are two seasons out of date," Bronwyn said disappointedly. "It's not like we can get the latest fashions now. To be honest, I don't know what the latest fashions are. We're so out of touch up here."

It was still early, and she took me for breakfast and paid for it, which again was odd, and I was starting to feel uncomfortable. She noticed this and smiled softly at me.

"I know it must be really bizarre for you to come out of the M.E.T. after five years. I felt the same, and it was only two for me."

"Oh, it's not just that, Bron. I'm feeling incredibly uncomfortable about what happened last night."

"Why?" Bron snorted. "You wanted it. Hannah wanted it. What's the problem?" she said, sounding genuinely confused.

"Well, it changes the whole dynamic of our relationship," I said uneasily. "And I really don't know where I stand in that."

"Why should it change anything?" She shrugged.

"It shouldn't, but it's on my mind about where we stand now."

"Liam," Bronwyn said quietly, looking down at her plate. "If I tell you something, do you swear on your life you won't repeat it to Hannah?"

I looked at her curiously, wondering if I could make such a promise, but I really wanted to know what she was going to say. "My lips are sealed."

"Even back in the day, Hannah had a crush on you."

"Now, that surprises me," I responded, "However, a teenage crush is exactly that, a teenage crush."

"Oh, for fucks sake, Liam, open your eyes. Hannah is in love with you. She has been since she was sixteen years old, and you had that incident at the ice cream parlour back in Melbourne. She was always comparing her boyfriends to you, and to be honest, it seriously screwed up her relationships. I did think she was finally getting over you when she was with Pat, but any feelings she had for him were killed on Last Day, when he went batshit crazy with fear. She doesn't like weak men."

I sat there in stunned silence, her words ruminating in my head. "This is all too much too fast. You have to understand, Bronwyn. It is only three or four days since I saw her as this eighteen-year-old kid."

Her eyes widened at me. "Yet it wasn't too much to stop you from fucking her last night?"

I flushed slightly. "That was a mistake. I was wrapped up in all the emotions of everything that's been going on, and she was rather insistent."

This didn't appear to go down too well with Bronwyn, and she glared at me with her one visible eye and growled softly. "If you're fucking with her, I will seriously fuck you up."

"She doesn't seem to care about anything," I said dismissively "So I hardly think that I could cause her any harm."

"I can assure you, mate, there's one thing she really does care about, and that's not to be made to look like an idiot by anyone. Trust me on this. Hannah Grant can make her mother look like an elderly charity worker if you cross her." She sat back with a sigh. "My suggestion is you just play it cool. She'll let you know if she wants more from you, but if you don't want more from her, you need to make that very clear early on." Before I could say anything in response, her phone went off, and rather than pick it up, she just hit the speaker button. "Hey, Han, what's up? You having fun in there?"

"No! I'm fucking not!" Hannah's angry reply came. "You better get in here before I get Stepanchikov to go Jenna Plural on these motherfuckers."

A grin crossed Bronwyn's face.

"I'm on my way, Han. Don't go busting a genetically perfect blood vessel or anything." She disconnected the call and stood up, then looking back at me, she said softly, "Hannah really isn't the girl you once knew. Be really careful before you mess with her."

Chapter Twelve

Corporate Manoeuvres

After Bronwyn left me, I finished my coffee and wondered what I was going to do with myself. I didn't have my own quarters and wasn't sure if I was supposed to return to Hannah's. I called it Hannah's, but it was a suite she shared. Being the size of a house even rivalling the wealthier districts of the Melbourne suburbs, it had plenty of rooms. Both Bronwyn and Stepanchikov lived there, and there was no doubt that Sarah would probably move in, too. I spent the morning walking around the mall, but since none of them took Pacific Alliance credit or debit cards, and as I was fairly certain I no longer had a bank account, I couldn't exactly purchase anything. For the first time in my life, I felt like a homeless man. I didn't even know if I had a family, for there was no news about my parents or my sister back in the U.K.

It was bewildering to me that this whole community was run by Grant Industries. Even the public services. Instead of police, I noticed members of Grant Security Services patrolling the areas like they were cops. The uniforms hadn't changed much since my early days of wearing one myself. Most notably underneath the G.S.S. for Grant Security Services were the words, 'Division Five'. I couldn't help but wonder what that meant. One of the guards noticed me staring and looked at me suspiciously before walking over to me.

"Is there something I can help you with, sir?" she inquired in an unfriendly tone.

"No, but thanks for asking," I replied with a smile.

She apparently thought I was being sarcastic, and her eyes narrowed at me. "Let's see some I.D.?"

I pulled out my wallet and slipped the I.D. out to hand it to her. She stared at it, and then she stared at me.

"Are you fucking joking?" she asked, with me now realising that her accent was American.

I looked at her, confused. "I'm not sure what you mean?"

"This is an Australian I.D., sir. It hasn't been valid for over five years, and even if it was judging by the date, it expired two years ago."

"Oh, right," I said with a smile. "Now, that's a long story."

"Great," she said with a patronising smile. "You can tell my Sergeant all about it." She slipped the handcuffs from her belt and, smiling sweetly at me, she said, "Turn around and put your hands behind your back, if you please."

"No! Wait a minute, let me explain!" I protested.

Her other hand reached down towards the taser strapped to her waist, and I guess I should have been relieved it wasn't to her gun.

"Only two ways of doing this, sir," she said most politely but with a hint of a threat.

I turned and placed my hands behind my back and felt the cuffs click into place. "Spread your legs." Again, I complied, and she frisked me for weapons before stepping around to face me. When she checked under my jacket, her eyes narrowed as she saw my firearm in its holster under my arm.

"Do you have a permit for this?" she asked curtly as she removed the weapon.

"Yes, I do. It's in my wallet."

She tilted her head to one side. "A Solar Confederation-issued permit?"

I swallowed. "Well, no. It's also Australian and probably expired."

"Well, Mr Marshall, I'm sorry to say you're under arrest." I wondered for a moment how she knew my name before I realised that she must have read it from my outdated I.D. "Under the emergency procedures of the Solar Confederation, you're advised that any rights you considered yourself to have in your country of origin do not apply. During the emergency situation, you're subject to the security necessities covered by the rules of martial law." She spoke like she'd said this a hundred times, and I guess this was some cock-eyed Solar Confederation version of Miranda rights or, rather, the absolute reverse.

"Look, this could easily be sorted out," I stated.

"Hey, just consider yourself lucky that Michael Phelkar has come up with a penal system. A couple of months ago, you could have even gotten thrown out of an airlock. There were no resources for criminals."

"I'm not a criminal," I said softly.

"Yeah, well, like I said, you can tell it to my Sergeant," she said disinterestedly and pushed me ahead of her.

Thirty minutes later, I was formally charged with failure to produce a valid I.D. and possession of an illegal firearm. They took my pictures and the whole arrest routine before I was taken and locked into a cell. I wasn't permitted to call anyone, not even a lawyer. I wasn't even sure if such a thing existed in this new society.

With all my electronic devices taken from me, I had no idea of the passing of time, but I'm sure it was several hours before the door unlocked again. I was hoping it was Hannah, having heard what was happening and coming to get me. However, I wasn't even sure if she had the power to override an arrest because, truth be told, I *had* broken the law walking around without an I.D. and an unlicensed firearm, regardless of the reasons. It was the same cop who opened the door, but my eyes alighted on the tall, alluring woman in a black business suit, large glasses, and ridiculously high heels.

I thought for a moment that she might be some appointed lawyer. She stepped in and smiled at me, offering me her hand. "Nice to meet you, Mr Marshall. My name is Charlotte Kensett."

"You're with the company?" I asked hopefully.

She shook her head. "No, Mr Marshall, I'm with the government. I work for Jenna Plural as the First Minister of Internal Affairs."

I took from her demeanour that the name Jenna Plural was supposed to impress me, but although I'd heard it and that she was the admiral of the fleet, I didn't know anything else about her. "Why on Earth would a government minister want to see me?" I asked uneasily.

"When anyone is arrested for not having a legal I.D., police and security services are obligated to inform my department. We are rather concerned about espionage, you know." Her accent was British, like mine. However, she was distinctly upper-class and almost sounded like royalty.

I raised an eyebrow. "And the head of the department personally investigates?" I said disbelievingly.

She chuckled at this. "Only when we discover that that someone is closely associated with someone such as Hannah Grant. I called Stepanchikov, and she told me about your situation. She had already submitted your credentials to be updated in their records. You should get an appropriate I.D. in the next day or two, and then you can reapply for your firearms permit provided you're in a position where you're required to have one, and it's legal."

"So, I'm free to go?"

"Yes, you are. However, Stepanchikov is sending someone down here to escort you back, so I'd appreciate it if you waited for a bit."

"Okay, thank you very much. I do appreciate your help." I offered her my hand.

"Oh, Mr Marshall, public service is my sheer delight," she smiled, taking my hand and shaking it firmly. "I did happen to look into your background when your files came up. You have a most interesting career. A former S.A.S. soldier. You must be highly skilled."

"I get by," I shrugged modestly.

"It also says in your records that you're currently un-employed," she commented enthusiastically. "I could use someone like you."

"For what?" I asked curiously.

"For what you do best, of course, Mr Marshall," she beamed.

"You can't have him, Charlie," a familiar voice said with a weary sigh. We both turned to see Hannah standing in the doorway, looking at her disparagingly. "He's mine."

However, Charlotte simply grinned at her.

"Oh, that is such a pity, Miss Grant." She then looked back at me. "Welcome to the Solar Confederation, Mr Marshall. I'm sure we shall meet again," she said, and with a clip-clop of those high heels, she stepped out of the door-way and passed Hannah. Hannah briefly looked at me and then at the cop at her side.

"Who was the arresting officer?"

The formerly confident security officer looked up at her sheepishly. "I was, ma'am."

"Clear your desk out. You're fired." Hannah said coldly. "You have twenty-four hours to transfer off the Twilight Wanderer to a refugee ship. You also have a life ban from ever applying for a position with Grant Industries again."

"Now, wait a minute," I said, stepping towards her and seeing the sheer terror on the officer's face. "She was just doing her job, Hannah."

Hannah shot me a cold look. "Did I ask you for your opinion, Mr Marshall?"

I hesitated. "Well, No. No, you didn't."

"Then let's go, shall we?" She turned on her heel and strode out as I looked weakly at the young cop, and tears were streaming down her face.

"I'm sorry," I said weakly before following Hannah. I couldn't help but wonder what it was like on a refugee ship, if such a fate instilled such a reaction from such a tough member of Grant Security Services. Hannah didn't wait for me, and when I eventually caught up with her, she clearly didn't want to talk. That was until we were back in the apartment, and the door closed behind us.

"Was that absolutely necessary, Duchess? The girl was just doing her job," I said irritably to her.

Stepanchikov looked up at us as we came in. To my complete surprise, Hannah spun around and slapped me hard across the face.

"Don't you ever question me in front of anyone again. Do you understand me?"

As I lifted my hand to my face, I stared at her incredulously.

"What the fuck, Duchess?" I was ready to block her as she went to slap me again, but even with my training, I wasn't fast enough for her genetically modified reflexes. The slap was harder this time, and I wasn't sure what had hurt more, the strike or the indignation of it.

"Cut that out. You fired a girl for doing her job, and that's just not fair."

"And if you have a problem with that, you tell me in private, not in front of the hired help, or anyone for that matter!" Hannah shouted at me so vehemently that spittle hit my face.

"Mr Marshall."

During this altercation, Stepanchikov got up and walked over to us. "The officer in question failed to do her due diligence. Had she or her superiors checked the records effectively, your association with the company executive would have become apparent. Instead, they brought in the Ministry of Internal Security. No company likes government oversight, and this could have been resolved without bringing you to the attention of the likes of Charlotte Kensett. You are our asset and our asset alone, and we wanted to keep it that way. However, we now run the risk of the government trying to conscript you, thanks to your experience."

"What exactly is the damage that's been done?" Hannah said, calming herself down, walking over to the bar

Stepanchikov shrugged. "The ball is in Kensett's side of the court. We just have to wait and see where she lobs it."

Hannah raised a glass towards me, indicating if I wanted one, and I simply nodded. She poured me out a large one and then another for Stepanchikov.

"Sit down, Liam. We need to talk," she said as she handed me the drink. I did as she asked, but this time, rather than sit next to me, she sat in a chair adjacent to me. Stepanchikov did likewise. "I was gonna give you a few days to settle in before we talked about this stuff. I know everything is confusing for you right now, but the company is in a rather...precarious situation at the moment." She sat back and crossed her legs, not quite so seductively this time.

"When I came out of the M.E.T., I'd been listed as dead, just like you. In my absence, a man called Drake Tanner, has taken over the company."

"Your mother's former C.E.O. I met him on this ship when we left Australia," I advised.

"Well, I can assure you he's not on this ship now and hasn't been for a very long time. He's based on Venus, where he currently runs my company, while I run a lousy five per cent that he begrudgingly gave back to me to avoid the protracted legal battle in the American courts, where the company is now registered. Or rather, that was before the surrender," she sighed.

I couldn't help but smile. Five per cent was still multi-billions of dollars. "Is he doing a bad job?" I asked.

She shook her head. "No. He's actually doing a phenomenal job. But that's not the point. It's my company," she growled. "He took control of the Venusian communities and declared independence at the same time as the Pacific Alliance ceased to be. He's even in the process of reintegrating our former European assets that we lost over twenty years ago."

"One of the problems is that he has refused to recognise the Solar Confederation," Stepanchikov added. "He exclusively works contracts with the Europeans. We don't like this, and more to the point, Jenna Plural does not like this."

"I have an exceptionally good arrangement going with Jenna Plural," Hannah stated. "She will virtually give me a monopoly on all trade within this new, for want of a better word, nation. However, if the majority of the company is supplying her enemies, she's not gonna be particularly happy about it."

"I take it this Jenna Plural was a bit of a hard ass?" I asked.

Both Hannah and Stepanchikov grinned. "Combine my bitchiness with that of my mother's and then double it, and that's Jenna Plural," Hannah said.

"Oh fuck!" I said deliberately, sounding like that was a horror from beyond.

Hannah grinned at that. "There is a clause in my contract with Drake that I intend to exploit. A part of the agreement was, that in the event of his death, I inherit his shares of the company."

"How on earth did you convince him to do that?" I asked, surprised.

She shrugged and grinned. "I simply pointed out to him that being genetically modified and someone who is never going to age, I'm going to severely outlive him, and he was so desperate to get me off his back that he agreed, but no doubt regrets it."

"So what you're telling me, is that in the event of his death, you have complete control of the company."

"You got it in one, mate." Then her eyes narrowed with an intensity that surprised me. "This is my company, Liam, my birthright, and I'll be honest with you, I don't care who I have to fuck over to make sure I get it back."

"Well, you're quite a wealthy person," I pointed out. "Can't you take a contract out on him? I'm sure there are mercenaries out there that would jump at the opportunity."

"It's not quite that easy, Mr Marshall," said Stepanchikov.

"Please call me Liam."

"The problem is, Liam, that since he is now contracting with the European Union," Stepanchikov continued. "He's receiving European Union protection. You couldn't even get to him without a large-scale assault. Instead, we hope to infiltrate the rings of Venus and take him out in a tactical operation."

"I'm guessing that I fit into this somewhere," I questioned uneasily.

"I want you to lead that assault, Liam," Hannah said uneasily, clearly wondering what my reaction would be.

Even though I felt sure this was coming, I still couldn't help but react. "I was a soldier for the United Kingdom and the Pacific Alliance, Hannah. I'm not a mercenary, and I'm certainly not a murderer."

Hannah's face fell, looking more disappointed than annoyed.

"Liam, there are only three people I completely trust in this entire solar system. Bronwyn, Stepanchikov here, and you. Bronwyn was certainly ruled out from the start, and whilst Stepanchikov could possibly lead the assault, she doesn't have your experience in tactical matters."

"I will supply you with our finest people and equipment," Stepanchikov said.

I shook my head. "You said there's a possibility that Kensett could conscript me. That implies that the government has already done that to any members of your staff who even remotely have experience in such matters. Everyone you would have been left with is probably second grade, am I right?" Hannah looked at Stepanchikov for the answer.

Stepanchikov sighed. "You would be correct."

"You also said that Jenna Plural wants your resources. Correct?"

Hannah nodded but looked at me questioningly, wondering where I was going with this.

"We need her military. We need her best. It's clearly in her interests to take out this Drake, and unless it's changed significantly in the last five years, Venus has an incredibly low population. They only have those orbital communities that hang in the sky, like rings around the planet. If we were gonna do something like this and Plural could supply an elite team, we won't just take out Drake, but we'll take out the entire operations on Venus, or rather, bring them under her control."

"Well, I'd rather it be under *my* control," Hannah said cooly, clearly deep in thought about what I said. A silence hung in the room as she mulled it over. "What do you think, Ember? I wanted to keep this in the family and not involve Jenna, but perhaps if that's what it would take, we should do it?"

"It all comes down to whether you trust Jenna not to take over instead of you," Stepanchikov replied.

"When we negotiated the privatization of public services and for us to run all nonmilitary activity, it was pretty clear that Jenna wasn't interested in that side of things. The only person we could possibly have an issue with is Phelkar. As Minister of Civil Affairs, he may throw a spanner in the works."

"He is becoming rather a pain," Stepanchikov responded. "We may have to come up with some way of getting him removed from office."

"Yes, but we can worry about that another day." Hannah then looked back at me. "So! If I can get Jenna onside, then you're in?"

I hesitated before replying, wondering whether I really wanted to convince myself to do this. "If you make this a purely military affair, then I don't have a problem with it. It changes from being outright murder to a tactical decision."

Hannah grinned. "Yeah, I really need to work on that dumb attitude of yours." But then the smile faded, and she let out a long sigh before shrugging. "Fine!" she said with sudden determination. "I'll put in a call to Jenna and arrange a meeting with her."

Chapter Thirteen

Jenna Plural

In all the years I've come to know Hannah, there are only two people I know of who would dare to keep her waiting. One was that asshole Michael Phelkar, and the other was Jenna Plural. With regards to Michael Phelkar, I had no clue as to the animosity between them, and it was only later, when I read Hannah's memoir, *Awakening of Hannah Grant*, that I became aware of the reasons. However, I was more pissed off that she hadn't mentioned me once in the entire chronicle. She later explained that believing me dead, it hurt too much to talk about me.

In regards to Jenna Plural, it was never an intended slight, simply that there were a lot of calls on her time, just as they were on Hannah's. They didn't have a direct line to each other, but it was as close as you could get, going straight through to each other's personal assistants.

Hannah put in the request to meet her that evening, but it wouldn't be till the next day that she received a reply. I don't believe Hannah intended us necessarily to be alone that evening, but clearly, Bronwyn and Sarah had better things to do, and they didn't return to the quarters till late into the night. Stepanchikov eventually left us with other duties she needed to attend to.

"Are you hungry?" Hannah asked me as she left.

"I could do with a bite. I haven't eaten since breakfast."

She summoned the steward and gave him a food order. I couldn't help but notice she didn't even think of asking me what I wanted.

"How do I go about finding myself some quarters?" I asked as he left.

She looked surprised by the question, and uncomfortably, she said, "Well, I kind of assumed you were going to be staying here."

There was an awkward silence as I wasn't sure if she meant with her or in my own room. She suddenly realised why I wasn't responding. "We have plenty of rooms, Liam," she said with a grin.

I wasn't sure if I was relieved or disappointed. As we ate our meal, we chatted about nothing important. She told me more about the coming together of the fleet under the guidance of Jenna Plural. It became quite clear to me that, although Hannah had some respect for her, something had happened to cause tension between them. I knew nothing of her issues with her sister, Stacey, and she had never mentioned anything about her trip to Earth to find Michael Phelkar.

Stacey Grant was one subject Hannah was never willing to discuss. They'd met for the first time only a year before I came back, and from what I could gather at that time, they had some falling out. Although I know the whole story now, at the time, I barely knew Stacey Grant existed beyond some reference to estranged siblings. As we finished the meal, she called the steward back, who she had show me to a very nice room. As I saw the purchases that I had made with Bronwyn were already delivered and hanging in the closet, I realised Hannah had already established that I was going to be staying here.

I was very tired, and I started to get changed when, to my surprise, someone came through the door. It turned out to be a maid who came to turn down my bed. I almost laughed at this as if I was staying in a five-star hotel. I told her that I didn't need such services, and she left. A more masculine robe was awaiting me, and I slipped it on and went out to inform Hannah that I was going to retire early. She wasn't in the lounge, and after a quick check in her bedroom, I found she wasn't there either. I thought nothing of it and went to bed.

As would become the norm, Hannah was up before me due to her lack of a need to sleep and was having breakfast with Bron and Sarah as I stepped into the room.

"Well, that suits you better," Sarah said with a grin, referring to my gown. "Although it's not nearly as cute." I was about to slip into a vacant seat at the table when Stepanchikov came in.

"If you have a moment, Liam," she said to me as she walked over to the bar and placed the bag on top of it. I headed over to her as she opened it. I watched with curiosity as she pulled out a phone. "Your old one won't work on the new Solar Confederation network, so here's a new one," she said as she handed it to me. She then pulled out a glasses case. "The same goes for your glasses. The Emily model is quite obsolete now." I opened the case to see a rather fashionable pair of glasses. I had been lost without Emily, which had totally failed to work after leaving the range of the networks of Earth. And, finally, she pulled out a gun. "It normally takes several weeks to get a gun permit, but Kensett made sure an exception was made in your case."

"Why?" I asked, taking the Glock into my hand and feeling the weight of it.

"We mutually support each other in many ways," Stepanchikov said mysteriously. I placed the gun on the counter since I hardly wore my holster to bed. "You have unrestricted carry and conceal."

"What do you mean by unrestricted?" I asked.

"If you see any signs that say weapons are forbidden, you can ignore it." She then reached into her pocket, pulled out a plastic card, and handed it to me. "Your new I.D."

I looked down at it, emblazoned with the emblem of the new Solar Confederation. It stated my name and date of birth, and listed my profession as simply, 'Special Services."

"You got time for breakfast, Em?" Hannah called over to her.

"Unfortunately not. I have to go over the security detail for the shuttle taking you over to the Spirit of Freedom."

That was the flagship of the fleet and residence of the famous Jenna Plural. A behemoth of a ship that was formally owned by the United States and named the U.S.S. Constitution.

"Let me get Martin to pack you a to go," Hannah said and called for the steward. I could see in Stepanchikov's eyes that she really wanted to just leave, but stayed to placate her boss.

"Actually, can I come with you?" I asked Stepanchikov. "I'd like to see your security measures for myself."

Stepanchikov seemed to take offence at this in front of me. "Are you suggesting that I don't know my job?"

I smiled at her.

"No, it's simply professional curiosity." I looked back at Hannah. "If that's okay with you?"

Hannah merely shrugged without looking up, and I couldn't help wondering if I had done something to upset her. I hadn't, and I realised eventually that it was simply her way of responding to something she wasn't the least bit interested in. I went and changed quickly and came out just as the steward was handing a neatly packed breakfast to Stepanchikov.

"You lead a complicated life, Mr Marshall," Stepanchikov said as we got into the elevator.

"I wholeheartedly agree, Miss Stepanchikov, but are you referring to something specific?"

"Entering into a relationship with Hannah Grant is a life change you should really give some thought to," she said conspiratorially.

"Is there anyone that doesn't know about that? But anyway, I hardly call one night a relationship."

"Miss Grant is not the woman you probably knew back in Australia. Even in her time with me, she's changed."

"So everyone keeps telling me. However, I've spent more time with Hannah than probably anyone in the solar system, except for maybe Bronwyn Donovan."

"Sleeping with the boss never turns out well," she said as we stepped off the elevator and started making our way towards one of the many docking bays.

"Have you said this to Hannah?" I asked her, already knowing the answer.

Stepanchikov snorted. "Just giving you some friendly advice, Liam."

"Nothing personal," I said snippily. "But it really is none of your business."

She glanced at me as we stepped into the docking bay. "As someone who used to be Miss Grant's personal security, I'm assuming you're joking now?"

I looked at her quizzically. "What do you mean?"

"Hannah Grant *is* my business. *Everything* she does. *Everywhere* she goes. And *even* everyone she fucks."

I frowned. "You said that last part like she does it a lot."

"A simple turn of phrase, Liam. As far as I'm aware, you're the only person she's been intimate with since leaving Earth." She clearly didn't know about the Phelkar incident any more than I did at the time.

The conversation ended as we approached the shuttle, and I was once more reunited with Kennedy Robinson, who was standing outside the entrance, writing some sort of report on her tablet as we approached. She was no longer in uniform and dressed in a suit somewhat similar to that of Stepanchikov. She looked up at Stepanchikov with a smile. "Everything is in order, Ma'am."

Stepanchikov looked at her with a nod and a smile. "Very good, Captain Robinson. Wait here while I go aboard and do my inspection."

Robinson frowned behind Stepanchikov's back, and she went up the ramp. "Well, thanks for the trust that I can do my job," she muttered barely audibly to herself.

Stepanchikov turned back to her with a raised eyebrow. "It is not about trust, Captain Robinson. Everyone can make mistakes, and when it comes to the safety of our boss, the responsibility lies squarely with me."

"Of course, ma'am," Robinson said, flushing slightly as we both glanced at each other, wondering how the hell Stepanchikov heard her. I shrugged and followed Stepanchikov aboard.

I consider myself a thorough man when it comes to the security of my subject, but that was nothing to Stepanchikov, who went through nearly everything with a fine-tooth comb, pulling out various instruments and scanning for devices that could either blow us up or listen to us. She had barely concluded when Hannah actually arrived. Another Grant Security Services officer had escorted her and left her outside with Robinson. She clearly knew the routine and didn't attempt to board until Stepanchikov told her it was okay to do so. She was finally able to board and take her seat, whilst Stepanchikov went up to the cockpit to speak to the pilot. Robinson followed on behind, closing the door and checking the seals. I went to the main cabin and took a seat next to Hannah.

This wasn't a common event for her. Literally, anyone other than Jenna Plural was expected to come to the Twilight Wanderer if they were going to meet with Hannah. Transferring from one ship to another wasn't like you see in some sort of sci-fi movie. It took several hours. The distance between the ships was much larger than it appeared. Added to that, there was so much traffic between the ships that speeds were limited, and safety protocols when docking were severe.

It was three hours later that we found ourselves in the offices of Jenna Plural, which lay next to the bridge of the Spirit of Freedom. I was surprised when Stepanchikov didn't come in with us.

It's said that one doesn't forget their first meeting with Jenna Plural, and that is certainly true in my case. I was expecting some old wizard in general, not this twenty-five-year-old-looking cheerleader in a uniform. Jenna Plural was beyond beautiful, rivalling even Hannah, and it didn't take a genius to realise that she, too, was a Gen-Mod. She was quite pleasant, although she remained quite formal as she shook my hand and indicated to the seats in front of her desk.

"So, for what do I owe the honour of this meeting?" she said as she returned to her seat.

"Oh, I think it's probably better if I let Liam explain," Hannah stated. "He probably knows all the military mumbo jumbo for what we have in mind."

This hit me with a curveball, since at no time had it been remotely suggested that I would lead this meeting. I looked at her for a moment, and she just looked back at me, waiting patiently. I turned back to face Jenna. "The Solar Confederation has strongly been relying on Grant Industries' resources. At least Hannah's division. However, things are not moving in a direction that is... well, let's say, convenient for us as the company C.E.O. is now doing deals with the Europeans."

Jenna sighed. "Yes, I have to say that I'm quite annoyed with Miss Grant's reassurances that she can supply demand but now can't fulfil."

Hannah visibly tensed at my side but didn't say anything as I continued. "Be that as it may, Admiral Plural, you don't really have a viable alternative to Grant Industries. However, we can offer you an alternative to this to this situation, but we'll need assistance from you."

Plural raised an eyebrow. "Consider me interested, Mr Marshall. Let's hear it."

"It is our intention to remove the C.E.O. from office and replace him with Miss Grant here."

Jenna looked disappointed. "Oh, I thought for a moment you were gonna offer me a viable solution."

"Taking out Drake Tanner is the only solution," I said insistently.

"Drake Tanner is ensconced within the rings of Venus and has a Peon flotilla in orbit to protect him."

"Yes, but we have an advantage over the Peons," Hannah said. "What if we were able to get an assault team into the rings of Venus unseen?

Jenna narrowed her eyes at her but couldn't hide the look of intrigue. "I'm listening."

"You give us access to Mahoney's personal M.E.T. devices, and we can smuggle a whole bloody unit on board those rings," Hannah said impatiently.

Jenna's eyes narrowed further. "How'd you know about that?"

"Get real, Jenna. Where do you think Mahoney is getting the resources to develop her invention further?"

A slight smile crossed Jenna's face. "Good point. Do go on."

"The point is, Ma'am," I continued. "I believe this is also a chance for the expansion of the Solar Confederation. If we take control of the rings, we effectively take control of Venus. We'll have control of Grant Industries and you, one of the most strategically valuable planets in the solar system."

"That would be most beneficial to us," Jenna said softly. "What do you need?"

"A team of your best people. An assault team, small but effective."

"A small team to take out multiple bases that are overrun with Peons?"

"But it's not," Hannah sighed. "The *only* defences they have are corporate security services once you get on board the base."

"Venus is neutral, and even someone like Drake Tanner knows, but if he invites the Peons in, the Peons will stay," I said with a shrug. "The flotilla around Venus is simply there to stop you from getting there. Of course, I don't know what'll happen once we take the Rings of Venus. For all I know, they could turn their guns around on us."

"Not if we keep them distracted," Jenna commented clearly, liking what I had to tell her. "If we bring in a couple of frigates just after you take the rings, there's a strong possibility the Peons will move to intercept. They're still unaware of our new M.E.T. technology, and they won't be expecting what you're doing. They should conclude that the only reason we're in the neighbourhood is for an assault. The Peons lost most of their fleet in the Battle of Deep Space and still haven't recovered. If you can broadcast the taking of Venus, chances are they'll bug out."

"I bow to your superior knowledge on that front, Ma'am," I said. "I know little of interplanetary conflict, having done all my duty on the ground."

"Well, Jenna," Hannah interceded. "What do you think?"

"I think it's a good idea," Jenna replied. "However, I don't think Grant Industries even needs to be involved in this. This is a military matter."

"Wow, why don't you butt fuck me while you're about it," Hannah said snarkily.

Jenna grinned. "Now you sound like your sister."

"No need to get offensive, mate," Hannah growled. "If I could take out Drake, I gain control of the entire company. The resources that we'll bring to the Solar Confederation will be almost immeasurable. Added to that, the fact that he has reintegrated the company with the European counterpart, I gain access to all the Peon military contracts with the company."

"Why can't you do that anyway, even if you weren't present on Venus?"

"It's all about confidence. I don't just need to take control. I need to be *seen* to take control," Hannah said insistently. "Power is perception, Admiral Plural, not reality. Venus is the ipso facto headquarters of the umbrella corporation."

"Surely, knowing your allegiance to the Solar Confeder-ation, any European operations will immediately be shut down, should you take control," Plural replied, looking unconvinced.

"One of the benefits of running a virtual monopoly is your customers pretty much put themselves in a position where if they fuck with you, they fuck with themselves," Hannah shrugged. "Let's say you're right, and they do shut down all of our European operations. Where are they go-ing to go to buy their little guns and build their little space-ships? Sure, in time, they can take over our Earth-based plants, our supply chains, or whatever, but that will take a year or two, during which time the Europeans stop getting supplied."

"Are you seriously telling me that if you take over here, you'll continue supplying arms and equipment to the Pe-ons?" Jenna looked at her incredulously.

"Of course," Hannah said quite seriously. "If we were to stop, then they would absolutely have to retaliate and take out our operations on Venus. They'd have no choice."

"So let me get this right," Jenna laughed, but it was certainly without humour. "You want me to invest our manpower in taking over Grant Industries for you to con-tinue supplying the enemy?"

"Exactly. The Peons are gonna get their weapons one way or another. If they shut us down, it will slow them down, sure, but eventually, they will create their own sup-ply chain. This way, you know exactly what they're getting, when they're getting it, and how they're getting it."

"You have no idea how fucking crazy that sounds!" Jenna snapped, and to be honest, I was on the Admiral's side on this one. "If it was to get out that I was supplying ordinance via you to the enemy in order for them to attack our people, there would be a lynch mob outside this cabin."

Hannah snorted. "Bullshit. Countries throughout history have supplied the enemy with weaponry during times of war. Arms manufacturing is not the most salubrious of business activities. It's as simple as this, Jenna. Not only will you get the massive resources of Grant Industries, which Drake is now holding back from you, but you also get Venus. That would be a massive propaganda coup."

"Not to mention that it will also be one of the best strategic locations in the inner planetary system," I added. I may have doubted Hannah, but I was still on her side.

Jenna stared at us for a long time before saying, "And I thought it was your sister that was the crazy one." She sighed and tapped the desk a couple of times as she thought about that, then looked up at Hannah. "Okay, let's do this."

Chapter Fourteen

Relationship Problems

"It's going to be a combined team of Confederation military and Grant Security Services," I told Stepanchikov once we got back on board the Twilight Wanderer. I wasn't sure how she was going to react to that, but she didn't appear at all phased by it.

"Who will be in overall command?" she asked.

"We will," Hannah responded. "Liam will take the lead, although the Confederation troops will be led by one of Plural's officers."

"Do we have a name yet?" Stepanchikov asked.

"Plural named a woman called Emma Dodgson, although she'll be answerable to me."

Stepanchikov looked down at her terminal and typed in the name a few seconds later. She looked up with a frown. "A rather odd choice as less than a year ago, she was a private." She carried on reading, and her face relaxed a little. "Ah, I see. She was the leader that successfully took Enceladus."

"Yes, well, that's a problem for the two of you. Personally, I find this military bullshit is making me hungry," Hannah said actually yawning. "Let's call it a night, and the two of you can meet up to talk about this shit tomorrow."

Back in the quarters, we had dinner with Bronwyn and Sarah. It turned out that Hannah had given Sarah an executive position in the company's textiles wing. She told me that she was probably one of the most fashion-conscious people she knew, and her new job was to coordinate with designers. With no clothes being imported from Earth, Grant Industries had expanded to enter the market of creating high-end fashion. She seemed quite happy with this, and whilst it took longer than me over the coming weeks, she seemed to adjust quite well.

The following day, I received a memo from Stepanchikov asking if there was anyone, in particular, I wanted as part of my team. Well, I didn't know anybody, so I was about to say no when a couple of thoughts occurred to me. I typed out my reply.

"I would like Kennedy Robinson and that cop that arrested me."

Yeah, I still wasn't happy with what Hannah had done to her.

The reply came back instantly. "Approved, but I suggest you get an armoured codpiece because Hannah's gonna rip your balls off when she hears about this."

"You're an asshole," Hannah said to me the following day when she heard about my choice. The one thing you really had to be aware of around Hannah is only to bring up things when she's in the right mood for it. She happened to be quite pleasant when she heard about it and was more willing to brush it off. Her words to me were almost whimsical.

"You got a thing for the little cop?" she asked me. "Did she get you going when she wrestled you to the ground when she arrested you.?"

"Very funny. I just felt bad for her. She made a mistake, and I'd like to give her a second chance."

"I'll let it slide this time because you bring out a soft spot in me," she said with a wry smile. "But you know if you cheat on me, I will cut off your balls."

She said it jokingly, but there was something in her eyes that made me feel she was deadly serious. However, there was something else in that statement that drew my attention.

"So, are you considering us to be in a relationship?" I asked with raised eyebrows.

"Meh!" she shrugged. "I'm not really sure, but I do want you to remain exclusive to me when I think about it."

"Well, isn't that precisely what a relationship is?" I chuckled.

She shrugged. "I never said anything about remaining exclusive to you."

I laughed at this, but again, that look in her eye gave me doubts that she was joking. "Are you serious?"

She shrugged. "Do you have a problem with that?"

"Of course I do?" This time, my laugh was with incredulity.

"Then I suggest you get over it," she said in a voice that sounded like it was me who was being unreasonable.

I looked at her incredulously. "If that's the way it is, but I'm sorry, Hannah, I'm not interested."

Her reaction to that was to simply shrug and say, "That's up to you. I'll get Stepanchikov to find you some new quarters, and you can move out. However, just know this, I will be making sure that no other woman looks at you twice," she said determinedly.

"Please tell me this is a joke."

"Liam." She now sounded like a mother scolding a small child. "You probably know me better than most people. Maybe only Bronwyn knows me better than you. Do you honestly think I'm joking?"

"Do you have any idea how seriously fucked up this is?" I snapped.

"Liam, I've become accustomed to getting what I want, and I'm not about to let that change. I want you, but I want you on my terms," she shrugged dismissively. "It's really as simple as that."

"Yes, well, we'll just see about that," I said, getting out of my seat and walking away.

"Liam, don't push me," she said softly, but I didn't look back as I strolled out the door.

As far as I was concerned, any relationship between Hannah and me was well and truly over. Any mission to Venus was over. Everything was over. I didn't know if I was more hurt or angry, because I had really developed serious feelings for the woman. But come on, who was seriously going to put up with that shit?

I went straight to Stepanchikov in a seriously pissed-off mood.

"I need you to arrange separate accommodation for me," I said, barely giving her time to say hello when I entered her office.

"I take it all is not harmonious with our leader?" She sighed.

"I'd rather not talk about it, Emberlynn."

She rolled her eyes and sat back in her chair, folding her arms. "I'm afraid I must insist I'm talking about it."

I frowned. "Matters of my personal life really aren't your concern, even if you're my superior officer."

"Absolutely, that is the case, but matters of Hannah Grant's personal life are my concern. What's happened?"

I sighed, sat down in the chair opposite her desk, and reluctantly told her the story, but I saw no reaction on her face as she listened to me, and when I reached an end, there was a long silence.

"How long did you actually live with the Grants?" she eventually asked me.

"Just over two years, why?" I replied irritably.

"That's about the same time I have, and yet I clearly know Hannah Grant far better than you do. Liam, Hannah clearly is really into you, but there's one thing that she loves more than anything in this world."

"And what do you think that is?" I snapped back at her.

"Her power." She said it like it was normal. "She's the daughter of Marcia Grant, and you know Marcia Grant better than I do, considering I only met her once."

"You can say what you like about this situation, but she just talked to me like I was property, and there's no way I'm gonna put up with that," I argued.

"What do you exactly expect to do about it?" She raised her eyebrows at me like I was being ridiculous.

"Exactly why I'm here. I want to get my own quarters as far away from her as humanly possible."

She gave me an almost pitiful look. "But Liam, Hannah doesn't want that."

I was starting to get infuriated now. "I don't really give a fuck what she wants."

"Well, you better start to," she said with growing irritation. "I can assure you she can make your life very, very uncomfortable."

"Are you seriously telling me that I don't have any say in this matter?"

"Yes." Was all she simply replied.

"Do you have any idea how fucking crazy that is?!" I shouted.

Stepanchikov simply shrugged again. "Well, perhaps you should have thought of that before you put your dick in her. You knew *exactly* who you were getting involved with here."

"I knew she was a spoiled brat, but I never knew that she was a vindictive spoiled brat."

Stepanchikov smiled at that. "Well, now you do." There was a silence that hung between us once more before she eventually continued. "If you require new quarters, fine, but to be honest, I'm not willing to do it without her authorization. Unlike you, I'm not willing to piss her off."

I stared at her long and hard. "I resign."

Her eyes widened. "Are you serious?"

"Never have I been more so."

"Oh, my dear Liam, you really *are* a clueless little fuck, aren't you?" she sighed, tapped something into her tablet, and slid it over the table. "If you really wanna quit, just sign this, but know this. No-one is allowed to be unemployed on the Twilight Wanderer. If you can't pay your way, you have to leave the ship for one of the refugee ships, and trust me, they're not a pleasant place to be."

I didn't respond and simply placed my finger on the screen.

Following protocol, she summoned two guards. "Do you need to collect anything from your quarters?" she said coldly.

"No," I said with equal chill. "I will ask you just one favour, and please don't tell Hannah about this until I've left the ship."

Her eyes widened, and she laughed. "Oh, Liam, do you really think I'm as stupid as you? The first place I'm going upon your leaving this room is to tell Hannah about what has transpired here."

"You're as much as a bitch that she is," I muttered.

"No-one is as much of a bitch as she is," Stepanchikov replied quietly.

Less than thirty minutes later, I was sitting in the docking bay waiting for the next available transport to take me off the Twilight Wanderer to a refugee ship. I had to admit I was uneasy since I saw the reaction of that cop back at the station.

No longer having any authority under Grant Industries, there was no way of using my position to speed up my departure, and I literally had to wait hours for a space aboard a shuttle. When I eventually boarded one, I didn't even know where it was going to go. I sat in economy class with about thirty other people, and about an hour into our journey, the captain came online. "I apologise for the inconvenience, ladies and gentlemen, but we have just received instructions to change course and dock with the Spirit of Freedom by the orders of Admiral Jenna Plural. I'm afraid I don't know the reason for this nor how long we will be delayed, but Grant Transit appreciates your patience during this situation."

At the close of this message, the typical chatter of irritated people went up, but I remained silent because I had a nagging feeling this had something to do with me.

My fears were confirmed when one of the flight attendants came up to me as we were docking and said to me quietly, "We will be asking you to disembark first, Mr Marshall."

"Why?" I asked,

"No idea. We have orders from the Office of Jenna Plural."

Docking took a further forty minutes, and it wasn't in one of the docking bays, and it was clear that the shuttle wasn't going to wait for me. As I got out of my seat, I felt the eyes of everyone upon me as I walked to the airlock. Another flight assistant placed the D.E. belt around my waist to enable me to walk across the umbilical tube and board the Spirit of Freedom. A familiar face was awaiting me on the other side. The beautiful, yet intense Charlotte Kensett waited patiently in her designer suit and high heels. "Good to see you again, Mr Marshall. Now some-one's been a naughty boy, haven't they?"

"I have no idea what you mean, Miss Kensett."

"Nor do I exactly, but I do know you've seriously pissed off Admiral Plural. Come on, she wants to meet with you."

With the clip-clop of those heels, she led me from the docking bay and across the ship to the office I'd only been in the day before. We stepped straight past the receptionist without a word and into Plural's office. She looked up from the tablet she was reading and simply pointed to the seat in front of her. To my surprise, Charlotte remained and sat next to me. Plural lay her tablet down on the table and sat back.

"I've been informed that you have withdrawn from the mission we only discussed yesterday. I would like to know your reasoning," she fixed her gaze upon me.

"It's a personal matter, Admiral. I'm quite sure I can be easily replaced."

"Logistically, that's not a problem; however, this plan relies on the goodwill of your boss."

"I have tendered my resignation with Grant Industries. I don't have a boss," I said dismissively.

"I have no clue what the issue is between you and Miss Grant, and I really don't want to know. However, I really would consider it a personal favour and be very grateful if you reconsidered." While the wording was most polite, the tone wasn't, and it was clear it was a demand, not really a request for a favour.

"With all due respect, Admiral Plural, as a private civil-ian, I'm not subject to your or anyone else's authority."

"Please allow me to set you straight on that," Plural said firmly. "During the current emergency, we are under the regulation of martial law. Everyone and everything is under my authority."

"Except for Hannah Grant, clearly."

"Oh, trust me, Mr Marshall. Hannah Grant is on a leash, just like everyone else. It's just she's allowed a lot more slack than most. You made a convincing argument yesterday for a plan that I have approved."

"A week ago, I was living in Australia. It appears that somehow, I have fallen through the rabbit hole and am now in Wonderland. I'm surrounded by egos larger than a black hole. I'm not playing these games, Admiral Plural. I'm not Hannah's property, and I'm not yours."

"Fine. What do you want in order to complete this mission?" Plural said. "Money? A position in my government? Hell, I'll even get Kensett here to go down you if you want that, but whatever it takes, I do want you on this mission."

I couldn't help but glance at Charlotte to see her reaction to this statement, but there was none. For a fleeting moment, I started to wonder what that would be like. But mostly, I was curious if she would have actually complied with that, should Plural have given her that order.

I looked back at Plural. "All I want is something you can't give me. My dignity."

"In a time of war, dignity is a luxury, Mr Marshall."

To say I was pissed off, would be an understatement. I decided that I had nothing to lose than to be as provocative as I could possibly be. "Fine. How about a night with both you *and* Miss Kensett?"

She was clearly not amused, and her eyes narrowed. "The offer of Kensett wasn't a serious one, Mr Marshall. Don't be an ass. It's unbecoming of you. I just wanted to elaborate on how important I consider this situation to be."

"I understand that, Admiral. I'm sorry, but the only thing that will resolve this situation is an apology from Hannah Grant."

"There is more chance of me putting out the sun than getting an apology from Hannah Grant, or any Grant for that matter, and you know this." She suddenly waved a dismissive hand at me. She looked at Charlotte. "I'm not going to waste any more time on this. I'm done with him." And she lifted her tablet and went back to reading.

I was about to say something, but Charlotte put her hand on my arm.

"The Admiral has concluded the conversation, Mr Marshall," she said with a pleasant smile as she stood up. I followed suit but looked down at Plural.

"It's been a pleasure, Admiral."

She didn't respond.

As Charlotte and I returned to the corridor, I glanced at her and asked, "Don't you find her talking about you like that back there quite objectionable?"

She smiled softly. "Oh, I'm only disappointed she wasn't serious and that you weren't willing to take her up on the offer."

This time, I was clearly aware that she was joking, and despite the situation, I allowed myself a grin. "Likewise, Miss Kensett, you're an incredibly attractive woman."

"Well, thank you, Mr Marshall," she chuckled.

I realised we weren't heading back the way we'd come, and I asked her, "Where are we going?"

"Admiral Plural would like you to stay as our guest whilst we resolve this difficult situation."

"And if I don't want to?"

Charlotte pondered this as if she was trying to remember something. "I don't believe that she permitted that to be an option." She looked at the anger on my face. "Oh, please don't make this difficult. I want to like you. Don't make that hard for me." She smiled.

"You just told me I'm a prisoner, and you want to be friends?" I said incredulously.

"No, not really. I just don't want this to become unnecessarily unpleasant."

We went down an elevator, and I pondered my options. It's not like Charlotte Kensett could force me to go and do anything, but it wasn't exactly that I would be able to get off the Spirit of Freedom if I didn't comply. We reached a section of the ship that looked a little out of place. There were no markings or directions to anywhere, and the doors didn't have any identifiers. This was the section of the ship devoted to Charlotte Kensett's Ministry of Internal Affairs. She led me to a room, which was fairly basic. I turned to look at her.

"How long am I expected to stay here?"

"Until you decide to be more cooperative, Mr Marshall."

"I want to see a lawyer," I said curtly.

Charlotte smiled at me and chuckled. "Oh, I didn't realise you had such a sense of humour, Mr Marshall. Let the guards know when you want to be more amenable," she said as she stepped through the door, and it closed behind her moments later. There was a click, and the light on the door's control panel lit up red, indicating it was locked.

What the fuck was going on? Did I seriously go to sleep in the M.E.T. and wake up in a world of psychotic women?

To my surprise, my stay in that cell was a little over four hours. During that time, no-one visited me, and when the door finally opened, I was surprised to see Stepanchikov standing there. One of the plain-clothes Ministry of Internal Affairs guards was at her side.

"Come on, Liam, let's get you back to the Twilight Wanderer," she said calmly.

"I'm not going anywhere with you," I said curtly.

In an unexpected move, I found Stepanchikov's hand about my collar. She pulled me up from my seat with inhuman strength and slammed me hard against the wall. "This has been a long day, Liam, and I'm tired of fucking about with you. I've had to put out fires between Hannah and Jenna about incarcerating you here, and I'm damn well tired of your shit. This isn't fucking Australia, and none of us have any fucking rights, at least for as long as the emergency exists. Hannah has told me to bring you back to the Twilight Wanderer, and that's what I'm going to fucking do, even if I have to break your kneecaps in order to get you there. Do you understand me?"

It was only then that I realised that Stepanchikov was also a GenMod. Her strength was beyond her physique, even though she was a well-built woman of almost six foot three.

I could barely answer her. Her fists were clutching my collar and pushing against my throat. She released me, and I said nothing as I followed her out. Damn, she thought she was having a bad day! We didn't speak again, even though it was several hours before I could return to the Twilight Wanderer. I was immediately led up to Hannah's quarters, but this time into her private office, where she sat with Donovan. The look Hannah gave me was one of discomfort, something I had never seen in her before, at least not since my return to her side. Without a word, Donovan got up and left with Stepanchikov, and I found myself standing facing Hannah, who remained behind her desk as silence hung between us.

"I'm sorry, Liam," she said at last. "I truly am. I enjoy being in control, and I don't plan on changing that, but I will admit to something. I'm in love with you, and I have been for a very long time. I want a relationship with you, but I want it on my terms, and that's not gonna change, love, but I did treat you with disrespect."

I was tired. So very tired.

"I think we made a mistake, Duchess. We crossed a line that we shouldn't have crossed. I think we should take a step back and forget that ever happened. The conditions of a relationship with you aren't something I'm willing to agree to."

She didn't answer immediately. She got up out of a chair and walked over to me.

"Be patient with me. That's all I ask." She stepped close to me, and once more, I felt that hot breath on my face and the smell of the ridiculously expensive perfume.

It's hard to explain the effect that a physically perfect creature could have on a man when she wanted it to. I felt my resolve start to fail me. I know it will be hard for you to understand how a man can be treated the way I had been, but then you've never been in the company of Hannah Grant.

Chapter Fifteen

Phelkar and the Admiral

My situation is only explainable by the fact that I really had no alternative. If it helps, regardless of the situation, I did indeed have strong feelings for Hannah. I can say without a doubt that despite these circumstances, I was in love with her and still am to this day. As the following days progressed, the subject wasn't raised again, and we pretty much acted like nothing had happened. Of course, the amazing sex that I continued to have with her helped me not to think too deeply about the other aspects of our relationship. Did she become faithful to me and only me over the years? No, she didn't. She was Hannah Grant. Did I remain faithful to her and only her over the years? No, I didn't.

Yes, it was seriously one fucked up relationship, but it worked, and while there were bumps along the highway, we were happy...mostly.

A couple of weeks after this incident, I was transferred long-term to the Spirit of Freedom. I was to work on prepping the team for the mission to Venus, which seemed to involve a lot more meetings than actual training. Almost every department of the government was involved. Kensett provided intelligence for the operation. Helen Tracker came on board as our technical advisor. The arrogant Tiffany Mahoney, the developer of the personal M.E.T. devices, frequently met with us. But most of my time was spent with Lieutenant Emma Dodgson, who would lead the Confederation troops under my authority.

When you first meet Emma, it is quite a surprise. The woman speaks with a pronounced stammer that makes her come across as nervous but far from it. She was a tough, no-nonsense former United States marine who was passionately dedicated to the cause of Jenna Plural, and one quickly learned not to criticise the Admiral in her presence.

Several weeks into the preparations, I was summoned to Jenna's office. I hadn't spoken to her since the incident regarding Hannah, and I admit I had some trepidation as I headed to her office. She wasn't there when I arrived, and the receptionist let me into the office to wait for her. However, instead of meeting with her that day, a rather unfortunate incident happened.

After a twenty-minute wait, a man turned up instead of Jenna. He was apparently supposed to have a meeting with her after mine, but for some reason, Jenna had been held up with other business.

"Nice to meet you, Mr Marshall." The man introduced himself with a pleasant smile and a well-educated English accent. "I'm Michael Phelkar, First Minister of Civil Affairs."

"Nice to meet you. It's good to see a fellow Englishman."

"Yes, we do seem to be a rare sight on the Freedom," I chuckled. He took a seat next to me in front of Jenna's desk. "So, how are things with Grant Industries? I'm sure working with Hannah Grant isn't easy."

"I don't have any problems with it," I said, my instinctive loyalty to her coming out.

He looked surprised. "That's not what I heard."

I narrowed my eyes. "Well, what is it exactly that you've heard."

"Oh, I heard all about that incident with you and her a few weeks back," he chuckled, which seriously pissed me off.

"Well, Mr Phelkar, if I may be so blunt, that's none of your fucking business."

His face fell, and he looked at me indignantly. "You're aware that I'm the First Minister of Civil Affairs, Mr Marshall?"

"And your point is?"

"You should be careful about how you speak to me."

"And you should be careful how you speak about Hannah Grant."

"I didn't say anything about Hannah Grant," he smirked, only to drive my ire up even more. "It's common knowledge she's one of the most difficult people to work with."

"You're aware that I'm in a relationship with Miss Grant?" I said, already wanting to punch this bastard.

"Oh, I think the entire fleet knows you're in a relationship with Hannah Grant, Mr Marshall. But then who hasn't been in a relationship with Hannah Grant?" he chuckled.

I stood up. "And just what's that supposed to mean, Mr Phelkar?"

"Well, I was in bed with her before I even knew her for an hour. "

"I'd seriously be careful what you say right now, Mr Phelkar."

Much later, I found out that his animosity towards Hannah was due to an event where she completely humiliated him to a degree, but he was now unaware of the dangerous ground he was treading on.

"Oh, I'm just trying to warn you, Mr Marshall, it doesn't take much to get Hannah Grant to open her legs."

My hands were around his collar before he even finished the sentence. I pulled him out of his seat and slammed him against the wall exceptionally hard before punching him in the gut.

Before he even fell to the ground, I felt someone grab me forcefully by the collar and pull me away.

"What the fuck is going on?" My assailant said, and I spun around to see Jenna Plural glaring up into my face.

"Educating the First Minister in a little bit of respect," I said coldly.

"Call security, Jenna." Phelkar gasped, climbing onto his hands and knees. "I want him arrested."

She let go of my collar and looked down at him with what was clearly disgust.

"Oh man up, Mr Phelkar. He didn't hit that hard. I heard what you said to him, Mr Phelkar, and while I don't condone what Mr Marshall did, you deserved that." She then looked back at me. "You need to go and calm yourself down, Mr Marshall, and we will reconvene our meeting tomorrow. I need to have a little talk with Mr Phelkar."

"Can I just hit him one more time?" I asked just to make a point.

Jenna tried to maintain that stony look with me, but I clearly saw the corners of her mouth turn up into a slight smile, but it was only fleeting. "No, Mr Marshall, you can't. I will see you tomorrow, but I think we'll do it alone this time."

I returned to my quarters, and I put in a call to Hannah, which I did every evening. I didn't tell her about the incident with Michael Phelkar, although I was sure she would probably hear about it eventually. We chatted about various bullshit such as new fashion designs Sarah had come up with and funny incidents with Bronwyn meeting with the Grant executives. It was just a really pleasant waste of time between a boyfriend and girlfriend. However, towards the end, she got somewhat melancholic.

"I really miss you, you know," she said softly. "I wanted to transfer over there while you were doing your training, but Jenna seems to think I'd be a distraction."

She rolled her eyes at this last part.

I grinned. "I miss you too, but the Admiral was correct. You would be one amazing distraction."

She grinned at this and said softly, "You really have no idea how much I love you."

Before I knew what I was saying, I said it for the first time.

"I love you too, Duchess."

For the first time in either her or my life, I found her lost for words.

"Do you really?" She said at last.

I frowned. "You doubt me?"

She shrugged and looked away for a moment. "I've never denied that I'm a bitch, Liam. Even Bronwyn points out how I treat you. I can't promise I'm ever gonna change. It's who I am. But to be honest, I don't want to change. I like who I've become." She then looked up at me. "Can you accept me for who I am?" As I went to reply, she interrupted me. "Wait, before you answer that. I want to give you a choice. I'm gonna give you this one chance to walk away from me. No repercussions. No conditions. However, this will be the only time I'm gonna make that offer. Should you not take this opportunity, I will expect your full commitment to the conditions I have stated. I don't want you with me because you're afraid to leave, but likewise, I want things my way. Can you accept that I'll be setting all the rules in our relationship?"

"That's quite an ask, Hannah," I said as her words whirled around in my head. "Can I have time to think about it?"

"No," she replied simply. "You either know now, or you don't. So, what's it to be?"

I knew full well that logic deemed that I should walk away now and never look back. However, the idea of a life without Hannah in it was painful. Her conditions were unrealistic and unfair, and I knew it, but she had a hold on me that I couldn't explain. I was truly in love with her, and the terms and conditions she set were easier than saying goodbye to her.

"I'm in all the way, Hannah," I said softly.

A smile crossed her face, which turned into a grin. "You won't regret it, Liam. I promise you that."

It didn't really sink in what I had agreed to until I went to bed that night, but the thoughts that we had just moved on to the next stage of a long-term relationship kind of made up for anything else.

I met with Jenna the following morning. I could not help but ask about Mr Phelkar's welfare as I entered. Not because I cared, but because I wanted to be difficult.

She fixed me with her trademark steely gaze. "I think his pride is more wounded than anything, but I would ask you not to do that again. Whilst I agree that he deserved it on that occasion, I won't turn a blind eye the next time it happens, are we understood?"

"Completely, Admiral," I said, unable to help but grin.

"I mean it, Mr Marshall." She then turned her attention to the purpose of the meeting. "I just wanted to know how your preparations were coming along."

"It appears to be going very well. You certainly have some very professional staff working for you. Dodgson is a little bit intense but appears to be quite capable. Provided the data that Kensett has provided us on the security setup is accurate, I can't see any problems."

"I've worked with Charlotte for a number of years, and she has yet to fail me. However, I think she's going to be more diligent on this occasion since she'll be coming with you."

"Really?" I looked surprised. "In what capacity?"

"You need someone to carry you onto the base within the portable M.E.T.s. That requires someone with an exceptionally cool head and the ability to respond to any situation. Kensett is a veritable ice queen and has a superhuman skill to get through situations such as this."

"She looks like she belongs in one of Hannah's board meetings," I responded.

Jenna chuckled. "Trust me, Mr Marshall. It is very dangerous to underestimate Charlotte Kensett."

"I'll take your word on that," I replied, still unsure.

"I need you to be ready in two weeks. Do you think you could achieve that?"

"Why the sudden rush?"

"There's an issue relating to the Martian colonies that has to come to my attention, and I'm going to need to respond to that sooner rather than later, and it requires resources currently assigned to you. The sooner you complete your mission, the better it will be."

"Then I shall endeavour to ensure that we'll be ready in two weeks."

Jenna smiled. "I would appreciate that, Mr Marshall."

"Please call me Liam."

"Very well, Liam."

"May I call you Jenna?

"No," she said, like she was declining sugar in her coffee. "So, how are things with you and Hannah?"

"They're fine," I replied, feeling uncomfortable with this inquiry into my personal life. I would eventually realise there was nothing private when it came to dating Hannah Grant.

"Is there any chance of her reconciling with her sister?"

I was completely confused by this question. "Her sister is dead. She died on Last Day back in Australia."

Jenna frowned, now looking as confused as I felt. "I can assure you, Liam, her sister is alive and well and currently living on both this ship."

"I saw her body, Admiral," I insisted. "Annabelle Grant is dead."

"No, I'm talking about Stacey Grant."

Again, I looked confused. "I think you're mistaken. I'm certain if she had a sister called Stacey, I'd be aware of it."

"I can assure you I'm not mistaken, Liam, and I'm surprised you're as unaware of it as you are."

"Well, clearly, Hannah hasn't resolved her issues, because she's never even mentioned her to me. Nor was she ever brought up when I worked for Marcia Grant."

"Well, I'm aware there was some issue between Stacey's parents, and they split up. She and her father moved to Wagga before Hannah was born. They met for the first time about a year ago and then had some falling out over something."

It was only at the mention of Wagga that a vague memory of the mention of a brother and sister in Wagga Wagga came back to me.

"Pity. Stacey is probably the closest thing I have to a best friend. I fell out with my brother. I never reconciled. I did something I very much regret."

"It's never too late," I replied.

"Oh, it probably is, Liam. This was more than seventy-five years ago, and we haven't spoken since. To be honest, I don't know if he's even still alive."

"I'm sorry to hear that. I'll talk to Hannah, but I can't promise anything. She's very stubborn."

"That's something she has in common with Stacey," Jenna said with a grin.

As I returned to my quarters, I couldn't help but be curious, and I looked Stacey Grant up on the system. It turned out she was quite a celebrity and considered one of the heroes of the Battle of Deep Space. I logged into her confidential files of Grant Industries and was surprised to find access to all her data was restricted. There's a lot of restricted data, but none of it was *ever* restricted to me, so this, understandably, made me all the more curious.

However, there wasn't much I could do about it, and instead, I turned my attention to Jenna Plural and her brother. It turned out that Jenna was one of a sort of triplets. I say sort of, because GenMods aren't born in the traditional sense, and are grown in a tank until they're viable to survive on their own. Jenna's parents must've been exceptionally wealthy, as they chose to have three genetically modified children created at the same time. Technically, Jenna was the eldest because she was the first to be taken from the tank. Her sister Jessicanna came next, and finally, her brother Jayson. *Jayson Plural?* I had worked with a Jayson Plularian back in the day. It would be far too much of a coincidence for them not to be one and the same. I pondered informing Jenna but decided to let sleeping dogs lie. I hadn't seen him in what was now over ten years.

I found myself lost in reading the history of Jenna Plural. It was hard to believe that the girl who looked barely twenty-five was, in fact, almost two hundred years old. I was also surprised she hadn't always been a Marine. Born in Ponca City Oklahoma, she attended William and Mary University in Virginia, where she studied politics and law and had intended to follow in her mother's footsteps. Her mother had been a senator in the United States government, with one failed attempt at a run for the presidency.

However, after college, Jenna appeared to disappear, and didn't turn up in records again for over twenty years. She then went to work with her father, who was an industrialist, but when he died thirty years later, the family sold the company to Grant Industries.

Once again, the record on what Jenna was doing went quiet. There was an occasional news article where she appeared in public at a political event with her mother until her mother, too, passed away. That was when it appeared that Jenna joined the military. She appeared to excel in her new career and was a rare example of someone who'd won the Congressional Medal of Honor twice. She spent a period in covert operations and, slowly but surely, rose in the ranks. It turned out she excelled in tactical planning and spent many years at the Pentagon as a general.

That was until the Grozny uprising, which changed everything for every GenMod. A group of GenMods had come to the decision that they were the master race, and in risings all over the world, they made an attempt to take over. It was known as the Grozny Uprising, because that's where it began and became its bloodiest. I was surprised to see that Jenna was instrumental in putting it down.

The Prague Convention was held soon afterwards. Seventy-five years ago, a worldwide agreement was made to halt all genetic modification of human beings. Restrictions were placed on those who were alive. They couldn't hold public office. Sit on executive boards or even own shares in companies. But most importantly for Jenna Plural, they couldn't hold a military rank higher than that of Lieutenant. Jenna was busted down to that rank and remained in that position for over seventy years.

As I thought about it, I couldn't help but feel that it was ironic, that if it wasn't for the collapse of the Pacific Alliance and the rise of Jenna Plural, Hannah wouldn't have even been allowed to own a single share in Grant Industries, let alone run it.

I then turned my attention to the reasons for my research, looking up her other sibling. Jessicanna Plularian followed in her mother's footsteps, rising to the rank of Vice President, only to lose the election when her president reached the end of his term. She married some actor and moved to Germany when she retired from politics. She became a citizen and was now listed as a European sympathiser, although there was no record of her beyond the start of the war.

Jayson Plural took a much darker path. He got involved in a gang around Washington DC, at an early age, and very quickly, misdemeanours turned into felonies. By the age of twenty-three, he had been convicted of homicide and received a life sentence, which for GenMod was sort of a long time. He served seventy-five years of his sentence, and it was at that time I saw the reason for his falling out with his sister. He served in British military intelligence before he moved off-world to Mars. The final entry of his record was that he was working as an environmental tech in one of the colonies, but that was more than thirty years ago, and there was no further mention of him.

I pondered this a moment and then submitted a request for more information to be collected on the matter. I wasn't exactly opening an investigation, but some clerk on Mars would get the memo and look into finding any records of him. In the coming days, I'd completely forget about it, and it would be some months later, when I got a response that would completely surprise me.

CHAPTER SIXTEEN

PLAN B

M ost of the Confederation contingent of my team had been selected by Jenna Plural in consultation with the unit leader, Lieutenant Emma Dodgson. The tech on the mission was a young woman called Amy Bessinger, who had been a civilian working on the moon of Enceladus until it had been liberated. She had been recruited into the military and had worked alongside Tiffany Mahoney, (Mah-hoe-knee) the developer of the portable M.E.T. device. It was her knowledge of that equipment that had got her a spot on the team. Emma's number two was a sergeant called Audra Pentauk. There was tension between them. I didn't know at the time that their relationship had become strained on a previous mission. However, Pentauk had a reputation for being one of the best, and Jenna had a reputation for not allowing personal issues to interfere with her personnel allocation.

From the Grant Industries side of things, I had Kennedy Robinson and Hailey Lipton, the cop who had arrested me, and a guy named Matt Humphries. It turned out he had been on several covert missions for Grant Industries, under the radar of the government over the years. I think he was a little peeved that I was in charge of the mission and not him, but he did his best not to show it.

Conditions for training aboard the fleet were not ideal, but we did our best to simulate the assault on the rings, with a mock-up that had been hastily built in one of the ship's docking bays that was then closed off from all other crew members. Total secrecy was the order of the day. As the time approached for us to leave, I put in a request for a couple of days off so that I could return to the Twilight Wanderer and spend some time with Hannah before I left. I admit I was a little peeved that she didn't seem too concerned about my safety and welfare. Not once did she suggest someone else take over this mission. Yet, on the other hand, I was glad that that wasn't an issue I had to deal with.

She met me personally at the shuttle when I landed back on board the luxury liner. She wasn't normally prone to public displays of affection, but she hugged me tightly when I came down the ramp. As we headed back to her quarters, we chatted idly, catching each other up on things going on in our lives. Sarah made herself politely scarce, and it was only late into our meal that I realised I hadn't seen Bronwyn.

"Ever since her injuries resulting from that M.E.T. accident, she gets these bouts of depression. You know how good-looking she once was."

"Although I admit the metal plate on her face is startling, she's still not exactly unattractive," I said. It was an offhand comment, and I really didn't know where it was going to lead, but Hannah always surprised me.

"You should tell her that." Hannah set down her fork and picked up her glass of wine.

"I'll be sure to. Should the opportunity arise."

"In fact, you should fuck her."

I choked on the piece of steak that I'd been chewing on with these words, and she waited patiently with an amused smile while I recovered. "Very funny," I replied, clearly not amused.

"Oh, I'm not joking, Liam," she replied in all serious-ness. "She could do with a good fuck. It might cheer her up a bit."

"You know, Hannah, I'm not really into this open rela-tionship stuff."

She shrugged at that. "That's really your choice."

"I thought you made it very clear that you expected me to be loyal only to you."

"Yes, well, after you left me, you made me think about it, and I realised I was being unfair. I actually agreed with you that the same rule should apply to both of us."

"Yes, well, I was thinking more along the lines we remain exclusive to each other."

"Fuck that, mate," she laughed. "I love you and no-one else. I want you to be my main man, but it's just sex, and why limit ourselves?"

I suddenly started to wonder.

"While I was gone, did you..." My voice trailed off, and I couldn't quite find the words for it. She looked at me questionably for a moment before it clicked in her head.

"No, Liam," she replied in a most sarcastic tone. "I sat here like a nun waiting for your return."

"Shit!" I muttered. "I'm not sure how I feel about that."

"It's just sex, Liam. I don't know why people make such a big deal out of it. As long as we come home to each other each night, isn't that what counts?"

"I never really looked at it in that light, and I'm not sure I can."

She shrugged that off dismissively. "Is it not better that I'm open with you about this, and not just go behind your back?"

I thought about this for a moment and then shook my head. "Am I not good enough for you?"

"It's not about good or bad. It's about variety. I like both strawberry cheesecake and black forest gateaux. Both are equally enjoyable."

"Did you seriously just compare our relationship to dessert?" I laughed.

Hannah grinned. "Liam, it doesn't matter who I sleep with. It's you that I love, and that won't change."

"It doesn't make me feel very secure in our relationship."

She stared at me a moment, then gently, she laid her hand upon mine. "How is this for security? Let's get married."

"Sorry?" I said, not quite believing what I just heard.

"I'm not about to get down on one knee, Liam," she frowned.

"This is all rather a bit sudden, and it's not something that you should ask on a whim."

"No, I've been thinking about it. I planned to ask you when you came back from this mission, but considering the situation we have here... what the fuck? Let's get married."

I stared at her wide-eyed, and I found myself saying, "Sure, let's do it."

She smiled and slipped out of her chair and, coming around behind me and leaning down, she wrapped her arms around me. She kissed me on my cheek and rested her chin on my shoulder. I felt my heart racing with excitement and fear of what I had just committed to. Marry Hannah Grant, wow...now that was scarier than being dropped into enemy territory.

"I still think you should fuck Bronwyn, though," she said casually in my ear, totally killing the moment.

The next day, I rose extremely tired from a rather wild night in the bedroom with Hannah. I took the next shuttle back over to the Spirit of Freedom. It'd been an affectionate goodbye because I wouldn't see her again until I returned from Venus.

"You better stay safe, or I'll kill you myself," she said to me with a grin.

"That's always the plan, Hannah. I can assure you of that."

I stood in the doorway as the ramp closed, looking at the most beautiful woman in the universe, knowing that on my return, she would become my wife in what would be a seriously unusual marriage.

Dodgson was in the docking bay to meet me, and we went straight into a briefing with Jenna Plural. We went through the plan one last time, concluding with the Admiral wishing us luck before I went back to the docking bay. It'd been locked down by security so that no-one would be aware of what we were doing. I oversaw the uploading of my team into the M.E.T., leaving only the senior members – myself, Dodgson, Bessinger and Kensett – downloaded. The pilot of the shuttle was a guy called Neville Batty, who had apparently previously worked with both Hannah and Jenna. Jenna had wanted Stacey Grant to be the pilot, but apparently, she was heavily pregnant and having complications.

I took a seat next to Charlotte Kensett whilst Dodgson did some final security checks, and then Bessinger did a final check on the integrity of the team in the M.E.T.

"It's going to be most interesting working in the field again," Charlotte told me as she fastened her seat belt.

"Well, I certainly hope you're as good as the Admiral says you are," I replied uneasily. "I'm not exactly a fan of the M.E.T., and I'm even less happy about trusting my life entirely to someone else."

"Oh, I'm so pleased to hear the Admiral appreciates my services, Mr Marshall. I can quite assure you that I'm very good at what I do," she smiled and placed her hand gently on my thigh. "You're in perfectly safe hands, I promise you."

"That is most reassuring, Miss Kensett," I replied, wondering whether her tactile contact with me was just simply her way.

The conversation came to an end, as Dodgson came and sat on the other side of me and began fastening her seat belt as the engines powered up. Finally, Bessinger slipped in behind us, and the craft lifted off out of the docking bay.

Once more, I took the opportunity to go through the plan before checking that we were on course with Mr Batty in the cockpit. It was time for us to be uploaded. It would take nearly two months to reach Venus.

When we arrived near the system, Batty, Bessinger, and Kensett would be downloaded, and the rest of us would automatically be transferred to the portable devices stacked up in a rack adjacent to the main system. If everything went to plan, I would 'wake up' inside one of the hubs of the rings of Venus. Mahoney's upgrades meant I no longer had to strip, and I stepped up onto the circle fully kitted out and armed. I thought about what Hannah would be doing in my absence and, worst of all, who she might be doing it with.

"See you on the other side," I said, using the now cliché term the people used when being uploaded.

There was the bright flash of light, and my world suddenly went to hell. The backdrop of the ship had disappeared from my vision, and I found myself falling to the floor. This wasn't part of the plan. Looking up, I was in a white corridor, and lying next to me was Charlotte Kensett, who was firing a snap pistol at two men in Grant Security uniforms. I instantly drew my weapon and fired two clean shots, taking them down. Charlotte was instantly on her feet, and I wasn't far behind her.

"Talk to me, Kensett," I said as I quickly scanned up and down the corridor.

"I've run into a few problems, Mr Marshall," she told me. Her breathing was heavy and laboured, and it was only then that I looked at her clearly and saw the side of her face was swollen and puffy with a bloodshot eye. She wasn't wearing her glasses, obviously. "I'm going to explain everything when we get to somewhere safely, but right now, the entire bloody station is looking for me."

It was quite bizarre seeing the prim and proper intelligence officer dressed in sweatpants, a t-shirt, and running shoes. However, there wasn't time to comment as she put those running shoes to good use and headed at a fast pace down the corridor, with me close behind. We stopped at the doorway and checked for any signs of danger before we headed through. We were in a small storeroom clearly for the use of station cleaners. As I managed to focus beyond the immediate danger, I noticed she wasn't carrying anything that could possibly have the portable M.E.T. devices in it.

"Where the fuck is my team, Charlotte?"

"I'm not entirely sure, but probably on their way to be studied by Grant Industries technicians. They seemed most interested in Mahoney's new developments."

"Yeah, I just bet they are. So, I guess its mission scrubbed?"

"That's not exactly a choice, Mr Marshall," Charlotte said considerably despondently. "It's not like Mr Batty could wait for us. The only way we were getting out of here was if we were successful."

"How is it that I'm here, but no-one else is?"

She looked somewhat embarrassed. "I took the liberty of secreting you about my person just in case such an event should arise."

"So, I did get into your underpants, after all, Miss Kensett?" I said, making light of a desperate situation.

"Well, actually, yes, Mr Marshall, you did have that privilege," she smirked.

"You know there's no possible way we can complete this mission now," I said reloading my weapon.

"Oh, don't be such a Debbie Downer, Mr Marshall. You can't possibly think I didn't consider the possibility that I'd get caught. My agents are already aware of our situation and, providing you can get me to them in one piece, we can go to ground."

Although I had memorized the floor plans of the floating hub that hung in the air of Venus connected by tubes to other hubs that encircled the planet, I'd never actually seen it, and it was much different than how I'd imagined. The wall gleamed bright white, and there were handy signs indicating directions to the different departments amid the garishly large Grant Industries logo. These made it possible to work out exactly where I was and get my bearings. However, I was in the hands of Charlotte Kensett, as she knew where she was meeting her people.

We only encountered one other person in our flight. I didn't know who they were or what they were about, but I couldn't take any chances. They were clearly scared when they saw us come rushing down the corridor, but not for long, as I dispatched them with a single bullet just before Charlotte turned down a different corridor. As we reached the end of it, a man came running towards us, and my gun quickly went up, but Charlotte pushed it aside. "That's one of mine."

He beckoned us to follow him, and he took us down a service hatch. We didn't stop for several levels until he finally took us into what looked like an engine room. As it turned out, it was the environmental system for the hub. Two other agents of Charlotte's were there, a man and a woman.

"Good to see you again, Miss Kensett," the new man said, taking her hand.

"Yes, well, I can think of better occasions and locations where we could be reacquainted, Mr Tarv, but it's much appreciated," she then looked at the girl. "You don't perchance have any spare glasses on you, do you, Miss Eden?" She smiled, reached into a small bag that sat on the counter, and handed her a glasses case, which she opened and put on the contents.

I looked at her curiously. "You anticipated losing your glasses?"

"Oh, I'm positively blind without them, Mr Marshall. Anytime I'm liaising in the field, I do my best to ensure that I have replacements on hand."

"Why don't you simply get your eyes fixed?"

She frowned at me as she pushed the glasses up her nose. "I really don't think this is the time to discuss my medical history, Mr Marshall, but if we get through this, maybe later you can give me a full physical."

She winked at me.

I didn't know the intent behind that statement, whether it was just an off-the-cuff sarcastic comment or some sort of innuendo, but she was right. This wasn't the time and place. She turned back to her little team. "We need to get the M.E.T. devices back. Do you have any idea where they are?"

"As soon as they were brought to Mr Tanner's attention, he sent them to the tech division. He's extremely excited to have them reverse-engineered," Eden stated.

"I certainly hope he's going to release the occupants before he starts tampering with those," I said with concern.

Eden simply shrugged. "I have no idea, Sir."

"Can I assume you're able to get us into this tech division?" Charlotte asked Tarv.

"We can, but I can't guarantee it's going to be a success. It will be extremely risky."

"Oh, life is full of risk, Mr Tarv," Charlotte said casually. Now I'm a professional, and I can remain calm under the most extreme of circumstances, but I had nothing on the ice queen who never once seemed to be phased by anything.

We were provided with Grant Security Services uniforms, and as we changed, I must admit I unprofessionally glanced at Kensett as she stripped down to her underwear. I was surprised at the athletic form that was usually hidden under her business-style flared pants and jacket. No doubt you've become aware whilst reading or listening to this that I did have an attraction for the attractive intelligence agent. While she didn't quite have the perfection of the likes of Hannah or Jenna, she was an incredibly handsome woman. She didn't appear to have noticed me looking, but I'm sure she probably did because, as I would come to know Charlotte, there was very little she missed. Once changed, we headed out with Mr Tarv, leaving the others behind, and walked along the corridors like we owned the place.

One of the aspects of the base that was in our favour was that anyone worth their salt would have been called up for military service. This meant most of the security of the station was run by people lacking any experience or were too old or infirm for service. No-one stopped to question us even though there was an alert out for us. Or rather just Kensett, as everyone who had seen me was now dead. No, they were looking for a woman with a bashed-in face and no glasses. Tarv, who I later found out had infiltrated into here as soon as Jenna had green-lit the mission, was clearly well known to staff. He greeted them with a smile and a hello as he passed them until, eventually, he swiped his card on the door to the supposedly highly secure tech division. It wasn't particularly large, and there were only three technicians inside whom we dispatched before they even had time to be surprised by our entrance.

It didn't take us long to search the room and find the M.E.T. devices piled up on a counter. I was relieved to see they were all still active. But my heart began to pound when I saw one of the devices in a state of deconstruction. I picked it up and looked down at the indicator. It didn't indicate any power. Each device held three people, and it was only me, Dodgson, and Bessinger who had been placed individually in devices as mission-critical personnel.

"If that was Bessinger's device, we're well and truly fucked," I muttered.

"Well, there's only one way to find out, Mr Marshall," Charlotte said as she started picking up the devices and placing them out on the floor with enough distance between them for the people to be reimaged above them. I let out a nervous breath as I started to help her, and one by one, we reactivated the devices. Confed marines began to appear in full armour and rifles at the ready. Bessinger appeared when I activated the fourth device. I was so relieved I believe I actually hugged her, which caused her to chuckle and say, "Well, it's certainly nice to be appreciated, Mr Marshall."

"This is not where we're supposed to come out? What's gone wrong?" I turned to see Dodgson standing behind me, looking very concerned, but I left it to Kensett to tell her what'd happened. Much of what the Intelligence Minister said was new to me, but as I understand it, she's written her own account of those events, so I won't go into them now.

"Okay, we are not where we're supposed to be, but we all have this place memorized," I said, taking command. "I'm going to give you a few minutes to work out the new routes to your objectives, and then we're gonna have to head out." I then turned to Mr Tarv. "Miss Kensett was supposed to return to the shuttle before it left. I'm going to leave her here with you. I expect to find her still alive when this is all over."

Tarv glared at me. "I've been protecting Miss Kensett for over fifteen years, sir. Don't tell me how to do my job."

"Oh, Mr Marshall, I didn't know you cared so much," Charlotte smirked at me.

I just looked at her with a raised eyebrow. "Would you want to explain to Jenna Plural you just lost one of her best assets?"

A smile widened. "You make an excellent point, Mr Marshall. Good luck. Don't get yourself killed. You're becoming quite an asset yourself."

Chapter Seventeen

Hostile Takeover

To make up for the loss of the three personnel in the dismantled M.E.T. device, I had to make a few adjustments to the team. Fortunately, one of the group's objectives was to destroy the portable M.E.T. devices, just in case our mission failed. We didn't want Tanner to have his hands on that little game-changer. Indeed, we hoped to complete the mission without the Peons ever finding out how we got on board.

I could now leave that task to Kensett and Tarv, and the rest of us headed out to our objectives. Dodgson had the responsibility of taking out security personnel, and most of the teams were headed for security stations. Bessinger and I had two different targets. I was to get her to the computer systems, where she would shut down all the surveillance devices and countermeasures that would stop Confederate forces from being able to land. Then, I was to make for Drake Tanner.

Bessinger was a nice kid, but she'd only made it into the military at the behest of Plural, who took a personal interest in her after some outstanding conduct on a previous mission. She was clearly a civilian tech in the military uniform. I had trained with her multiple times for this assignment, but it's a lot easier running around a plaster-board mock-up of a base in a docking bay than it is the real thing, where you can get shot.

She forgot nearly everything, and it slowed me down because I kept having to give her instructions. At one stage, she nearly got us killed, as I explained to her that she needed to work on the security locks of the door leading toward the computer centre, rather than just doing it as planned. A security patrol looking for Kensett came around the corner, and my body armour took a bullet in the back, which, although it didn't harm me, hurt like fuck. I stood between Bessinger and the guard while she worked on the door and managed to take him down. However, I must admit it unnerved me. if it weren't for my armour, I would have achieved a bullet straight through my heart, killing me.

I looked down at Bessinger, who was fumbling at the controls, her hands shaking. I crouched down beside her and placed a hand reassuringly on her back.

"It's okay, you got this. I'm not going to let anything happen to you, and we're going to get out of this alive and have a party like we've never had before."

She smiled, and although she remained focused on the controls, my words appeared to have, at least, partial success in calming her. Seconds later, the door slid open, and she stood to the side of it as I went forward. When I made sure the way was clear, I beckoned her through. I was surprised by the lack of guards in this area and had to struggle not to become carelessly confident. I would realise much later it was due to Charlotte getting caught that some idiot had reassigned the guards to find her. Any security personnel worth their salt would reinforce this area, not remove people.

When we finally arrived at the main computer area, Bessinger slid a device out of her pocket that was known as the 'Helen Tracker Special'. A device she'd designed to override security doors wirelessly when you couldn't access the control panel. As the door slid open, I stepped in with gun raised, only to find no-one was there. Oh my God, they were seriously that fucking stupid. However, that, too, I would find out, was due to an overly paranoid C.E.O., and as you will see, I don't think anyone was more paranoid than Drake Tanner. Kensett's arrival had caused him to take personal command of the security situation in the Grant Industries headquarters, and he was clearly not qualified for the job.

I felt the tension rising in me as I knew this was the moment Tanner would for sure know what was going on. Bessinger was good, but she wasn't the best, and she needed the best to talk her through it.

By this time, a couple of the Confederation frigates should have been moving into place at the limits of the base's scanning ability. However, it also enabled Bessinger to do what she did next.

"Aphrodite Drop Team, to the S.C.S. Triumphant. Come in Triumphant," she said, using our code name.

"We read you, Drop Team. Please stand by for The Panda."

The Panda was the code name for probably the most amazing engineer in history.

"Are you in position, Spanner?" the voice of Helen Tracker came back using Bessinger's code name.

"In position at the system override and security and linking you up," Bessinger replied.

"Your objective is complete, Spanner." Tracker came back after a minute or two. "I have control."

That was our cue to leave and head to our new directive. Helen Tracker would now start bringing down everything. I headed to the door, telling Bessinger to follow. But as she turned away from the screen, she suddenly looked back. She frowned.

"What's the matter?" I asked.

"I'm not sure, but this doesn't make sense." She stepped back to the screen. "She's not uploading the code I thought she was going to."

"Maybe she had to change it?" I said, unconcerned. "Is it possible that she found out something after we left? We've been away for a long time."

She didn't look convinced but merely shrugged. "I guess so."

"Come on, we have to get to the next objective." We headed back out, but I, too, became suspicious of what Helen was doing as none of the security systems seemed to have gone offline, and the camera started to follow me down the corridors.

"Mr Marshall, are you still with us?" Charlotte's voice came over my earpiece.

"Were you expecting anything different, Miss Kensett?" I replied.

"Frankly, Mr Marshall, yes, I was. The security system should be down by now, but they're not. What's going on?"

"I'm aware of that, Miss Kensett. We completed our objective, and Tracker has control, but I have no idea why it hasn't worked."

"I suggest you retreat and return here," Kensett said, her voice uncharacteristically concerned. "There is no way you're going to make it through to the corporate offices without that system being down."

"Agreed. Mongoose to all units. Withdraw to Clip-Clop's location." I ordered.

"Instruction confirmed," Dodgson responded. "What's going on?"

"Security has failed to come down. If we proceed, it's going to be a massacre."

"Understood," Dodgson replied.

"Clip-Clop?" Kensett came back once more with an amused incredulity in her voice. "Is that the best you could come up with for a code name for me? It's hardly original, you know."

"It's what everyone calls you behind your back," I grinned as a thought occurred to me. "I'm going to get Bessinger back to the computer room and find out what's happening. I'll call you when I know something. Just have everyone hunker down and wait."

"Be careful, Mr Marshall. It would be very disappointing to lose you."

"You got any ideas?" I asked Bessinger as we headed back into the computer room.

"No idea, but I can take a look." She stared at the screen again and frowned. "Okay, so she's made some routine changes to the code, which makes sense, but I think there's a line missing here."

"Are you sure?" I was confused. Tracker wasn't known for making mistakes.

"Not a hundred per cent, and I won't be, unless I spend several hours going through this. I'm no Helen Tracker, Mr Marshall."

"It was my understanding that Helen Tracker was the best of the best. How could she possibly make a mistake like this if, indeed, it is the case?" I asked.

"Everyone makes mistakes, Mr Marshall," she said defensively of her boss.

I tried calling the Triumphant, but no response came. "Well, is there anything you can do?" I asked Bessinger, trying not to sound desperate now.

"Not unless the Triumphant responds to our calls. I'm sorry, Mr Marshall, but this is way beyond my pay grade."

"Can't we just blow it up?" I asked debatably.

She shook her head. "After news got out that the U.S. Constitution was brought down by blowing up the central computer room, everyone started to reconfigure their computer rooms. Both us, the enemy, and Grant Industries. Everything's rooted through subsystems now. The only thing blowing it up would do is stop the ability to create and calibrate the defence systems, but they'll operate for weeks before that's required."

We were out of options. There was no way for us to get off this base, because even if you stole a shuttle or something, we would be shot down by the Peon fleet hanging outside. We went up against the defences, or we quit and turned ourselves over to the security services.

I tapped my earpiece. "Mongoose to all units. Objective one is a failure. However, retreat is not an option, so we gotta move forward with the understanding full countermeasures will be deployed against us. Move out and clear skies to you."

"Understood, Mr M...M....Marshall," Dodgson responded. "We will either achieve our objectives or take as many of the mother...f....fuckers down with us."

"That's the spirit, Dodgson. Good luck," I replied, but inwardly, I couldn't help but think she was just a bit nuts. We were going to take heavy casualties even if we prevailed, and if I survived, I was going to have a reckoning with Helen Tracker.

Once more, we got forced back as automated systems dropped out of the ceiling, and Dodgson reported heavy casualties. Fortunately, Bessinger and I were in the outer ring with a nice solid wall between us and space, and no-one was dumb enough to put heavy artillery where it could puncture the exterior.

Dodgson almost got shot as she came racing around the corner unexpectedly, but I managed to hold my fire just in time. Kennedy was on her tail.

Blood was soaked into Dodgson's uniform, and although she tried to brush me off when I inquired about her injuries, I simply pushed her up against the wall and opened her jacket as she glared at me.

"This is not going to look very good on my record," she said as Bessinger handed me a piece of gauze from the small med-pack she carried on the back of her belt.

"What isn't?" I asked as I shoved the gauze into the hole in her shoulder.

"I've lost most of my p...people, and we are yet to encounter the enemy," she said, wincing under my touch.

"It's not your fault, Dodgson. It's Helen Tracker's. I'm going to fucking kill her when I see her," I said as Bessinger now handed me some sealant, and I sprayed it over the wound.

"I suggest you d...don't do that, Mr Marshall. Or you'll have me to deal with."

"Are you close?" I responded as I stepped back, and we headed back toward the computer room yet again.

Dodgson grinned. "I guess you could say that. She's my w...wife."

"Really, I had no idea you were gay?" I replied.

"Did you expect me to wear a badge?" she replied as we entered the room. She stepped over to the communications console again. "Security override this is an emergency. S.C.S. Triumphant, come in."

"We already tried that." That was what I was about to say, but to my surprise, Helen Tracker's voice came back.

"Emma?" The voice was nervous and almost desperate. "Is that really you?"

"It is. B...Bessinger here is telling me there's something f...f...fucked up with your code."

There was a long pause before Tracker said quietly, "Let me take a look." There was a long pause before Tracker's voice came back uneasily. "I see the problem. Shutting down systems now."

Every ship on the base has a vibration from the power running through it. You get used to it and don't even notice it until it's no longer there. It's hard to explain, but we more felt the systems go down than we heard or saw them. "You should be good to go. Be careful, Emma. I love you."

Emma frowned and simply turned off the radio. "I love that girl to b...bits, but that was so unprofessional to say that." She turned to look at me. "Why didn't you try calling Helen?"

"I did, but she didn't reply. She didn't appear to know that you were on this mission. Did you choose not to tell her?"

Dodgson frowned. "I do not discuss my m...missions with anyone who's not authorised to know them. Everything is n...need to know, and whilst Helen was part of this mission, she didn't need to know who was actually p...p...participating in it. But honestly, I really didn't tell her because she has a tendency to worry, and I was concerned that she wouldn't do what she needed to do if she knew I was at risk."

It didn't escape my notice the sheer coincidence that Helen only answered when her wife called her. However, I didn't voice my concerns, and I only wish I did, as it may have saved some lives down the line.

As we headed back out of the computer room, the odds were now against us completing the mission, even with the security systems down. Of the twenty-man team, there were only five of us left, not counting Kensett and Tarv. Once more, we approached the corporate offices, and I was pleased to see the cameras were no longer following me, and each door that was supposed to be sealed was now unlocked. However, we still had to encounter the security personnel Drake had entrenched around his offices.

I didn't have to fear, for the bringing down of the security defences had left most of the security personnel afraid. Fighting for a pay packet isn't the same as fighting for a cause, and no-one was willing to die to save Drake Tanner. When we arrived outside the office suite, there was a security chief standing in front of the door with his hands raised. "Please lower your weapons. I'm not going to resist," he said.

"That's appreciated," I replied. "However, all I can offer you is a promise not to shoot you if you don't try anything, but we're not lowering these weapons anytime soon."

"Fair enough, but I want you to know we're willing to cooperate with you," he said earnestly.

"Colour me suspicious, Sir, but I find it difficult to believe that you would capitulate so easily," I said in a friendly tone.

"All the personnel here are former citizens of the Pacific Alliance," he argued. "Do you really think we're happy about the new direction Grant Industries is taking by helping the fucking Peons?"

"You make a good case," I admitted. "But I can see the door behind you is still sealed with its little red light on. If you're surrendering to me, why are they still locked up in there?"

"Most of my personnel are kids who, for some reason or other, weren't fit enough for military service. Frankly, Sir, they're shitting themselves. I said I'd come out here to talk to you."

I raised my hand, and Dodgson, the two surviving marines and Kennedy slowly lowered their weapons. I holstered my own and approached him, offering him my hand. "Liam Marshall, Grant Industry Special Services."

He looked confused at first. "Grant Industries? I thought you with Jenna Plural."

"They are," I said, indicating the remainder of my team. "Robinson and I are corporate. I'm here at the behest of Hannah Grant."

If I could have taken a picture of the surprise on his face, I would've framed it and hung it in Hannah's office. A wide smile crossed his face.

"Well, this is certainly a different definition of a hostile corporate takeover." He turned and banged on the door, and after a few moments, the light turned green. "Come in, Mr Marshall. Let's talk."

Chapter Eighteen

Drake Tanner

We stepped into the control station of Grant Security Services, and various eyes were peering nervously at us. They only started to relax when they became aware our weapons weren't out, and the sector chief assured them before turning back to me.

"So, what exactly is gonna happen to us if Miss Grant takes over?"

"Well, if moving forward, she has your complete and utter loyalty, nothing. However, anyone still thinking their loyalty lies with Drake Tanner will face serious repercussions."

"Oh, I think that we could absolutely assure Miss Grant that she has our loyalty," he chuckled. "None of us have been happy ever since the corporate fucker started doing deals with the enemy."

"So why did you c...continue to help him?" Dodgson asked coldly.

He scowled at her and stated irritably, "I don't know if you've noticed, Ma'am, but there's a flotilla of Peon craft outside this establishment. What did you expect us to do, and where did you expect us to go? Even if we got away from the Peons, it's not like Jenna Plural is advertising where her fleet is."

Dodgson went to protest again, but I raised a hand to silence her, and although she shot me a glare, she complied.

"So, where's Tanner now?" I asked.

"He's in the main office up above us. But I warn you, the security with him aren't Grant people and have been supplied by the Union. They're not likely to give up."

"How many?"

"Four."

"Oh, I think we can work with that." I turned to the Marine at my side. "Don't you, Lieutenant Dodgson?"

She smiled at me. "Absolutely, Mr M...Marshall."

I looked back at the sector chief. "I take it he's sealed in?"

"Locked up tighter than a gnat's chuff," he replied. "And the doors are made of mercuranium. You won't even be able to blow them off without causing substantial structural damage to the base."

"What about air ventilation?" Dodgson asked.

"Barely big enough for a cat to get through," he responded.

"We could seal it off," I suggested, looking at Dodgson.

"That would t...t...take too long. I suggest we pump nerve gas into the p...place."

I raised my eyebrows at her. "Under the '24 Galle Convention, that would be a war crime."

Dodgson rolled her eyes, looking at me like I was dumb. "The Solar C...Confederation isn't a signatory to the convention, Mr M...Marshall."

"All the same, I don't think we should go down that route," I said, trying to hide my surprise at her willingness to go down such a path. "Although, it does give me an idea." I looked back at the sector chief. "Is there any way that we can call him in there?"

"Sure," he replied. "Come over here."

He led me over to where a small communication station was. Seated in front of it was a young woman with multicoloured long hair, which I couldn't help but notice, breached the G.S.S. dress code.

"I have to warn you he hasn't been responding to our messages. We've been trying to get him to come out."

"Maybe I could be a little bit more convincing?" I said with a shrug.

"Then patch Mr Marshall through to Mr Tanner, would you, Miss Llewelyn?"

"Of course, Sir. You have a line, Mr Marshall."

I sat upon the console next to the wild-looking communications expert.

"Mr Tanner, you're no doubt aware that we have control of this base and, therefore, the entire rings of Venus. You have nowhere to go, and no-one's coming to save you. You really have no alternative, but to turn yourself over to us." I waited for a reply, but none came. "I'm not renowned for my patience, Mr Tanner. If I don't hear from you in the next sixty seconds, we're gonna to flood the ventilators into that room with a nerve agent."

Everyone found themselves looking up at the clock as the seconds ticked past, wondering if he was going to call my bluff.

"Who is it that I'm speaking to?" the familiar voice of Drake Tanner came over the speakers.

"Liam Marshall, Mr Tanner."

There was a pause. "The former Protector One who I fired? Surely, this can't be a personal vendetta? A man with your talents could certainly find another job."

"Oh, I can assure you this isn't personal," I chuckled. "At least not personal on my part, but it's extremely personal for my boss."

"I can't imagine what Jenna Plural would personally have against me. Maybe strategic, but not personal."

"Oh, you're trying to be clever and think you know what's going on," I smirked. "I'm not working for Jenna Plural, but I'm also not here to have a chat with you. Open the door, or it's pretty much it's going to be the last thing you ever don't do."

Again, a pause, and less confidently now asked, "What's to stop you from simply shooting me if I do this?"

"Nothing! You just have to trust me. You also don't really have an alternative, and if I were to shoot you, it's certainly going to be less painful than a nerve agent that will take up to three minutes to kill you as your body paralyses, and you're unable to breathe."

Again, there was a pause. "A convincing argument, Mr Marshall. Come on up. I've unsealed the door."

"Have your guards facing the walls several feet away from each other with their hands raised and touching it. If they're not in that position and we see any weapons on their person, we will come in firing. Am I understood?"

"Understood."

At that, the sector chief led Dodgson and me up a spiral stairway, down a little corridor, and to two large double doors that were standing open. As we stepped in, Drake was sitting behind an obnoxiously large desk, and as instructed, the four Peon guards were standing against the walls facing away from us.

Before I knew what was happening, Dodgson had her gun out and fired four shots toward the back of the heads of each of them. Tanner dived down behind the desk as I turned to glare at Dodgson.

"They had surrendered and weren't armed!" I shouted at her.

She merely shrugged at me. "They were P...Peons, Mr Marshall."

That finally had me convinced that the girl was bat-shit crazy psycho, but I had other things to deal with. "Please don't shoot, Mr Tanner. I have business with him," I said sarcastically. Then, after a thought, I added, "Actually, go back down with the sector chief and put a call into the Triumphant and let them know the mission was a success. Then, I want you to locate Hailey Lipton. I want to know if she's alive."

She didn't look too impressed at being dismissed, but she was under orders to obey my commands, and then I was alone with Drake Tanner, who was still hiding behind the desk.

"Come out, Mr Tanner, and take your seat. We have something to discuss."

A nervous head appeared over the top of the desk, and visibly shaken, he climbed up and allowed himself to fall back down into his high-backed executive chair.

What I was about to do next wasn't part of the plan, at least not the plans discussed with Jenna Plural. No, this was a private matter that I had agreed to do for Hannah. It was something that hadn't been easy to set up with long-distance communications down. She'd been compelled to send out Grant industry shuttles between the fleet and us at various stages. I activated the terminal on the front of his desk and tapped in the frequencies to send a message bouncing between each of those shuttles all the way back to the Twilight Wanderer. I smiled as I saw his look of surprise when Hannah's face appeared on the screen in front of him.

"Hello, Drake," she said smugly. "I couldn't let you go without knowing what was happening."

"Miss Grant, what a delight to see you," he said, but was unable to hide the shake in his voice. "I'm guessing that you're here to negotiate your position with the company once more. I can see that you're in a better bargaining position now than in our previous interactions."

"Oh no, Drake, there are no negotiations here," Hannah smiled warmly. "In fact, this isn't really business. It's more entertainment, as it's really unnecessary to do what I'm about to do, in order to further my position here. I just wanted you to see who did this to you."

"Miss Grant, you're talking like you're about to have me killed. That's murder. I don't think even you are capable of that," he chuckled.

"Oh, I can assure you that I'm. This wouldn't be the first time I've killed someone. You've lost Drake, and you've lost big time. Grant Industries is a family business, and it's back with the family."

"You will drive this business into the ground in a week, you stupid girl!" he snapped.

Hannah looked annoyed. "Oh, that can't go without being punished, right, Liam? Would you be a darling and shoot him in the leg?"

I pulled my pistol out again and fired it into his thigh. He screamed and clutched his leg.

"You fucking bitch!"

"Keep shooting him in different parts of the body until you only have one bullet left, or he stops being rude," Hannah told me. But this time, I didn't obey as he stared fearfully up at me. I fired a single shot between the temples. He fell forward, and I pushed his corpse out of his seat. I sat down to face my fiancée. "You can be such a downer sometimes, my love," she said with a mock poutiness.

"Yes, well, torturing people for you isn't gonna to happen," I said firmly.

"I've missed you," she said softly, resting her elbow on the desk and placing her chin in the palm of her hand.

"Yes, well, for me, it's only been a few hours."

"You know, maybe I'll put myself into the M.E.T. while I wait for you to come back."

"Oh, I think you're gonna be far too busy for that, Hannah. You're now the C.E.O. of Grant Industries. The second most powerful woman in the confederation, after Jenna Plural."

She smiled. "Since you've been gone. There's been talk of establishing a democratic government. She may have to fight an election to keep her position. At least over civil matters."

"You're not seriously thinking of running for public office, are you?" I rolled my eyes.

"The idea's floating around in my head, but I can't say I'm seriously considering it yet."

"Personally, I think you should concentrate on Grant Industries. You have a lot of restructuring to do."

"Perhaps you're right," she said and promptly changed the subject. "When are you gonna start heading back?"

"Well, I don't know yet what's happening with the Peon fleet out there. We do have Tanner's wing of Grant Security Services on side with us now, but I won't be happy until that fleet is gone, and Confederation traffic can start flowing in and out of this place. Maybe a few days?"

"Send me over a list of personnel that you have there. I'll go through it with Bron and see if we can come up with someone who can be an administrator on my behalf. However, make it clear that Venus is no longer the corporate headquarters."

"Are you gonna move everything to the Twilight Wanderer?" I asked.

"Well, I'm gonna be running everything from here, but for legal reasons, we need a land-based address, so officially, it will be run out of Enceladus."

I looked up to see Charlotte Kensett standing in the doorway with hands on hips and looking indignant.

"Hey, Hannah, I've gotta go. I'll give you a call before I leave. You take care of yourself."

"You too, babe, 'til next time. Mwah!" she blew me a kiss, and the line went dead.

I looked back up at Kensett, who had her head tilted to one side. "Nice of you to let me know you had taken the base and that I could leave that little tech room," she said with indignation, but there was a slight smile on her face.

"Oopsie," I chuckled. "I'm sorry, Charlotte, but I completely forgot about you."

"I'm positively offended that you could forget me, Mr Marshall." I got out of my chair as she rounded the table. She looked down at the body of Drake Tanner, and she gasped, holding her hand over her chest. "Oh my God, you killed him!"

"Oh, yes," I said, worried that she was going to make an issue of this. "Would you believe me if I told you that it was in self-defence?"

She looked up at me over the rim of her glasses and actually burst out laughing. "No, Mr Marshall, I certainly wouldn't believe that, nor would anyone else. However, I was just teasing you."

"Really?"

"Indeed. People often tell me I don't have a sense of humour, but honestly, I do."

Yeah, maybe you do, Charlotte, I thought, *but it's certainly not a funny one*. What I actually said was, "I can't possibly imagine why anyone would say that, Miss Kensett."

"Exactly. However, I suppose we should get back to work. I've got the files on all the station personnel, and if it's alright with you, I'd like to commandeer some of your staff."

"What for?"

"There were over seven thousand people scattered throughout these rings, and I need to look up the files on each and every one of them, to find out which of these peasants would be loyal to the Solar Confederation, and those who would not."

"And what happens to those who aren't?" I asked.

"Oh, you have better things to worry about than that, Mr Marshall, don't worry," she said with a sweet smile.

"I really wish you'd stop calling me Mr Marshall. My name is Liam."

"I'd be delighted to, Liam. Now, shall we get to work?"

The next few days became a blur of activity. As more of the Solar Confederation ships started to appear on the Peons radars, they did a cut and run. The frigate started to dock and drop off more Solar Confederation military personnel. In an agreement between Jenna Plural and Hannah Grant, Venus would remain civilian and under the administration of Grant Industries. Both Hannah and Charlotte were provided with the data they required, and within a day, Hannah announced a man called Sebastian Brody would be taking over as Chief Operating Officer of the Venus division of Grant Industries. It'd been intended that I would take over temporary command of Grant Security Services, but I saw no reason that the current security chief couldn't retain his position, considering his switched allegiance to Hannah.

The one thing that hadn't occurred to us was that the residents of the Venusian rings saw us more as liberators than invaders. This may not have been the case, had Tanner not thrown his lot in with the Europeans. Charlotte set up offices for the Ministry of Internal Security, and I didn't see much of her for several days as she set up her team. More of her people started to arrive, and she eventually returned the staff that she had borrowed, with a couple of exceptions, where she put in a request for their permanent reassignment to her. I couldn't help but find myself keeping track of her activities. Jenna Plural's veritable spymaster was someone I found quite intriguing, but not only that, I was curious as to what she'd actually meant about validating the loyalty of the residents.

She had all the executives who previously worked for Drake Tanner arrested, and they were kept confined to their quarters. It was left to Jenna and Hannah to decide their final disposition.

The daily meetings with everyone gradually began to decrease, as the transition started to become smoother. I started to become less and less in the loop, which was to be expected, as Sebastian Brody found his feet and went straight through Bronwyn or Hannah, rather than through me.

At the end of the second week, I started giving thought to returning to the fleet and the Twilight Wanderer, but I started getting frustrated, when I found that in my conversations with Hannah, she kept coming up with excuses to delay me. I must admit paranoia started to seep in, as to why she didn't want me to come back.

Dodgson left at the end of the second week, and I can't say I wasn't pleased. The girl frankly creeped the shit out of me. I'd hoped to go with her, but Hannah had asked me to stay to oversee security services a little bit longer, even though I'd told her on numerous occasions how smoothly things were running.

Then, my life took a little bit of a turn that I wasn't expecting.

Chapter Nineteen

Charlotte Kensett

The day after we had secured the base, I filed my official report on the mission. A copy of which would go to Hannah, and another copy would go to Jenna Plural's office. I had frankly forgotten all about it, until at the beginning of the third week, when I received a message that Charlotte wanted to meet with me. I had been assigned a personal assistant. Fazz Llewelyn, the young communications officer that I'd met when I first arrived, basically did my admin work, and liaised with other departments on my behalf. She received Charlotte's request from Charlotte's personal assistant, who I guess was probably Eden.

I don't know why, but I had Llewelyn respond with the suggestion to meet Charlotte over lunch. By this time, the various small businesses that existed to cater to the residents of the rings had begun to re-open. Charlotte sent a response to me saying that lunch sounded like a lovely idea and recommended we meet at a little Mexican restaurant called Pepe's.

I had managed to get a wardrobe of some casual civilian clothing, not wanting to draw attention to myself in uniform. I'd been held up going through some reports with Lewellen and lost track of time. As a result, I arrived about fifteen minutes late for my meeting with Charlotte.

I found she'd already been seated at the table and was waiting patiently, reading something on her tablet when I arrived. I can honestly say I don't know how it is that Charlotte always managed to have a wardrobe of business suits, and I rarely saw her in the same outfit twice. Today, she wore dark blue, and the colour of the frames of her glasses matched it. As the maître-d' escorted me to the table, she looked up and smiled, and then she looked at her watch.

"Did you forget me again, Liam?" she asked with a wry smile.

"My apologies. I got held up with some bureaucratic bullshit."

"Oh, my dear Liam, bureaucracy is the most useful tool. You can hide all sorts of interesting things within the confines of documentation that you don't want to reach the public eye."

"I'll take your word for that, Charlotte," I said, taking the menu the maître-d' was handing to me. "Personally, it just gives me a headache."

We perused the menus for a moment or two before giving our orders to an overly cheerful waitress called Kelly. When I ordered a bottle of wine, Charlotte looked up at me with a smirk. "My my, Liam, drinking on duty, you're quite the rebel, aren't you?"

"Well, I don't keep regular hours," I shrugged, returning her grin. "So I don't really know if I'm on duty or not right now, but if you want, I can cancel the bottle and order a Coke."

Charlotte pursed her lips as she rested her elbows on the table, as her eyes lit up. "You know I'm almost tempted to do that. It's been a number of years since I've been able to get my hands on an ice-cold Coke. However, the wine will be perfectly fine on this occasion."

This wasn't a particularly upmarket establishment that I had become used to in the company of Hannah, and the waitress simply poured wine into two glasses and left the bottle on the table. Once the bubbly waitress left us, I took a sip, then asked Charlotte, "So what is it you wished to see me about?"

"Oh, it's going to be straight to business, is it?" Charlotte said, feigning disappointment. At least, I assumed it was feigned. "So be it. Jenna Plural is not happy with your mission report."

"Well, that surprises me, considering, despite everything, the mission actually went quite well. What's the problem?"

This was the last thing I would've expected a meeting with Kensett to be about.

"You filed an official complaint about Captain Helen Tracker," she said, and I couldn't help but notice she momentarily averted her eyes from me.

"Yes, of course I did," I replied, not seeing a problem. "She seriously fucked up, and as a result, I lost most of my team."

Charlotte smiled. "Yes, but the problem, Liam, is the wording. You've basically accused Captain Tracker of doing it deliberately."

"No, I simply stated that I was suspicious that she'd made such an error and that I couldn't get a response from her, until she discovered that her wife was aboard the base."

"Let's not split hairs, Liam. That's tantamount to the same thing."

"I only included statements of facts that I personally experienced, Charlotte. However, that still doesn't answer the question of what it is that Jenna Plural is actually upset about."

"Helen Tracker has worked with the Admiral for over six years. She is a member of what is unofficially known as the 'inner circle'. People that Jenna trusts without reservation."

"Good for her," I shrugged. "It doesn't mean I have to trust her."

"Do you trust me, Liam?" She inquired intently.

"Do you want an honest answer to that, or a tactful one?" I smirked.

Charlotte smiled at this and said, "Well, I don't believe in the old adage that 'honesty is the best policy'. However, in this case, I would appreciate honesty."

"I trust you to be who you are, Charlotte. I trust you to do your job with, dare I say, ruthless vigour, but do I trust you to not use me for your best advantage should circumstances require it? No, I don't."

This seemed to amuse her. "Then let me rephrase the question. Do you trust me to be honest with you?"

"Unless your job requires different, yes, I do trust you to be honest with me."

"I have investigated Captain Tracker, and while she does have some reservations about Jenna Plural's way of doing things, I have been unable to prove any sign of disloyalty."

"Nice way to put it, Charlotte. You may not have proof, but you suspect her," I grinned like I had just scored a point.

Charlotte tried to dismiss that with a grin. "Oh, I'm suspicious of everyone, my dear. It's in the job description."

I shrugged. "I still don't understand what any of this has to do with me."

She frowned slightly. "Your report, Liam, like I said."

"I'm not about to change my report, if that's what you're asking. I have advised you of my concerns, and it's up to you or Jenna, or whoever, to either act on those or dismiss them. Either way, it's no longer any of my concern."

"Well, Jenna is more concerned about you discussing this issue with anyone else. She doesn't want Tracker's reputation to be damaged by rumour and innuendo."

Now, that made me angry. "Well, you can tell Jenna that I take personal offence to that. I'm a professional Charlotte, and I act like, and expect to be treated like one."

She smiled at me. "Understood, Liam."

"Was that all?" I asked irritably.

"Yes," she visibly relaxed and picked up a roll of bread to butter. "We can now enjoy a pleasant lunch together."

I sat back and chuckled. "Okay. So, tell me something about yourself."

"What is it you would like to know, my dear?" she said teasingly.

"Well, I understand that you're an American."

"I am."

"Well, you certainly don't sound American, Charlotte."

"No, as you can probably guess, I was born and raised in England, like you."

"So, what's the story?"

She shrugged. "I married an American."

My eyes widened. "You're married?"

"Don't sound so surprised, Liam," she stated with amused offence. "Not every man finds me repugnant, as you must, by your reaction. But to answer your question, no, I'm not married. I'm widowed."

"So, is Kensett your married name or your maiden name?"

"It's my husband's name. I rather unfashionably took his name."

"So, what was your maiden name?"

"Is that important, Liam?" she asked softly, pursing her lips amid an amused smile.

"No. Just curious, and you just increased that curiosity by being reluctant to tell me."

"My, my, Liam, you're wasted with Grant Security Services—you're positively a Sherlock Holmes. You should come over and work for me," she said in a pleased tone.

"And yet you still evade the question by trying to embarrass me with your sarcasm," I said, resting my elbows on the table and leaning into her. Our eyes locked, and that moment when both parties recognised a mutual attraction happened.

"And I shall continue to do so. My past is my past, and has no relevance on the now."

"You're a most intriguing woman, Charlotte Kensett," I said with a chuckle.

"I'm delighted to hear you think so," she said. She broke off a small bite of her roll and popped it into my mouth. "I must admit I find you quite intriguing, too," she lowered her hand and gently placed it down upon mine, and I didn't move it. My attraction to this woman was without doubt, and not for the first time, I thought about what it would've been like to become intimate with her. We looked at each other for a moment, and there was chemistry in that gaze, but before it went anywhere, the waitress returned with our meals.

We engaged in idle conversation as we ate, and at the conclusion, she took the bill and added it to her government expense account.

"As pleasant as this has been, it was still technically business, so I don't feel any guilt about claiming for it," she chuckled. As we got up and headed out the door, she stopped and looked at me. "That was certainly most pleasant, Liam. We must do it again sometime."

Before I knew what I was saying, I replied, "How about tonight you come over to my place? I can order in."

She looked momentarily surprised, but that quickly turned into a smile. "That would be quite a splendid idea, Liam. Eight o'clock?"

"It's a date." I had meant it as a simple turn of phrase, but it was wholly inappropriate, considering the circumstances.

"Well, if that's how you want it, Liam. I'll not object," she smirked. "See you later."

And before I realised what she was doing, she reached up and kissed me on the side of my cheek. She turned, and I watched her disappear into the crowd before I headed back to my office.

With her out of my sight, the more rational side of me came to the fore. There was clearly a thing between me and Charlotte, but seriously, should I be acting on it? I thought about Hannah and became aware that it was probably most unlikely that she had been remaining faithful to me in my absence. However, I didn't have the same attitude about an open relationship. But then there was Charlotte. Sophisticated. Beautiful. Sensual. Enticing. And just a little bit scary. Then I thought about what might be going through her head. She was perfectly well aware that I was in a relationship with Hannah, yet this didn't seem to faze her.

When I went home for the night, I found myself growing more uneasy about the prospect of Charlotte coming over. Several times, I picked up my phone to call her and cancel, yet in my heart, I didn't want to and resisted the urge. I ordered food to arrive at around 8:30 and put a bottle of wine in the fridge. I then paced around the room nervously. When 8:00 came, there was no sign of her. When my door buzzed at 8:30, I naturally assumed it was her, but it was just the food delivery. I left it on the countertop, getting cold. 9:00 came, and I concluded that she wasn't coming. I stuck the food in the fridge to use as leftovers for the next day, as I wasn't particularly hungry. I thought of calling her but found that too uncomfortable. By 9:15, I was heading to my bedroom and intended to go to sleep. Just as I started unbuttoning my shirt, the door buzzer went. Charlotte stood in the doorway looking positively amazing in a matching blouse and skirt of purest white with matching glasses and shoes.

"I'd concluded that you weren't coming," I said as I invited her in.

"My apologies, my dear Liam, for both my lateness and not informing you of it. I got called into the office at the last minute."

"No problem. Take a seat, and I'll reheat the food."

She sighed wearily as she sat down. "If it's all the same to you, do you mind if I take a pass? I'm not very hungry right now, but don't let me stop you."

"It's okay. I'm not particularly hungry, either. Would you like some wine?"

"Now, that, would be most delightful," she smiled through tired eyes.

"So, what did you get called in for?" I asked her as I went to the fridge to get the bottle.

"Unfortunately, it's nothing I can talk about. However, I really don't want to talk about work anyway."

"Well, that puts me in quite a dilemma," I said teasingly as I handed her the glass, and she looked up at me questioningly. "You don't want to discuss work, and you don't want to discuss yourself, so unless we have similar taste in movies, I really don't know what we're gonna talk about."

She rolled her eyes.

"Willard," she said as if that would mean something to me.

"Pardon?"

"My maiden name. It's Willard."

Now, that name sounded distinctly familiar to me, but for the life of me, I couldn't work out where I'd heard it from. "I appreciate you telling me," I replied, sitting down in a chair adjacent to her.

"Yes... Well... I trust you not to share it," Charlotte replied quite seriously.

"Why the secrecy? I know you're in intelligence, but it's not exactly classified information that you're the Minister for Internal Affairs."

"The name doesn't mean anything to you, I take it?"

"Well, it's certainly familiar, but I don't know where I've heard it before," I admitted.

"Ah, let's leave it at that then, although I'm sure you'll look it up later." This was most definitely true, as I was now more intrigued than ever before.

"There is an air of mystery about you that is rather enticing," I said with a chuckle.

"Enticing? That's an interesting choice of words to use," she said with an inviting smile. "If I'm that enticing, why don't you come and sit over here?"

She patted the seat next to her on the sofa. I hesitated for a moment to think about Hannah, but it was only for a moment. As I sat down next to her, she placed her hand with its long, professionally manicured red nails gently upon my thigh. She looked at me, and I looked at her, then I lowered my head down to hers and kissed her softly. When I pulled back, she looked at me with a frown.

"Oh no, Liam, that won't do at all."

She reached around the back of my head and pulled me to her, kissing me so hard it actually hurt. It was hot and feverish, and I felt her fingers tug on my hair until I felt the sharp pain of it as it was almost pulled from its roots. Not breaking from the kiss, she released my hair and began tearing open my shirt. I must admit this aggressiveness in bedroom matters was something I was entirely new to.

I made to undo her blouse, but she slapped my hand away before dropping it to join the other that was working on my belt. This whole experience was becoming a little bizarre, and I wasn't sure what to do. I had been with girls who liked it rough before, but it was usually me that was the one that was being rough. But this would go on far beyond even that.

"Call me mistress," she whispered in my ear as her hand trailed up and down my erection, which was still hidden beneath my trousers. It was an odd request, but at the time, I didn't care.

"Yes, mistress," I said, finding this situation, however bizarre, actually quite stimulating.

She moved down and began kissing my neck as one of her hands gripped the waistband of my trousers. I lifted my hips to allow them to slide down as she pulled them to my knees, and then left me to kick them off. She made no sign of removing any of her clothing, and it gave me an uncomfortable sense of vulnerability to become naked, while she remained fully clothed. She appeared to be getting aroused by my discomfort, and her breath began to increase. Eventually, she began to unbutton her blouse again, shoving my hand away when I moved to help.

Her bra was front fastening, and she quickly unclipped it, releasing a pair of beautiful, firm, rounded breasts. I reached out to touch, but again, she slapped my hand away. It was starting to get quite frustrating. As I saw the light in her eyes, I realised that was the intent. She pushed them against me. She once more returned to kissing and nibbling on my neck, and then I felt a sharp pain in my back, causing me to arch towards her, as she continued to rake those manicured nails across my flesh. In a rather odd move, she sat back and licked drops of blood from her nails with a smirk. She pulled away from me and stood up, taking me by the wrist and pulling me towards her.

"On your knees," she demanded. Disorientated and a little fearful of what she was going to do with me, I complied, for despite the oddity of the situation, the anticipation of it was rather erotic.

There I was, naked, kneeling in front of her, my eyes level with her legs as she proceeded to undress in front of me. All the while, she looked down at me with that smirk on her face. As she slipped out of her panties, she grabbed me by the hair and pulled me in between her legs, gripping me so hard that I couldn't pull away without hurting myself. She gyrated forcefully against my tongue as I pleasured her, and she reached around to the back of my head, pushing me harder against her until I actually couldn't breathe. I tried to come up for air, but she held me in place. I almost started to panic, but she simply laughed.

Eventually, she pulled my head back, and I drew in large lungfuls of breath, much to her amusement. I made to protest, but she placed her finger upon my lips, telling me to hush. She gently made me lie down upon my back on the carpet, and she straddled me, guiding my length into her. I was so confused about what this'd all turned into that I didn't resist, and as she enveloped me, I no longer wanted to.

Slowly, she began to rise and fall on top of me with soft moans of pleasure, and I gave into it, enjoying the sensation. I closed my eyes, only to suddenly open them, as a sharp pain bit into my chest. Her claw-like talons dug into me and ran down to my navel as her head hung back, and she cried out. This was seriously fucked up. But as I tried to push her off, this seemed to get her off even more, and she bucked faster as I grabbed for her wrists, but she simply leaned forward with all her weight, making it difficult to extract myself.

I felt her muscles tense as she looked down at me, still wearing those large glasses, with her hair now cascading down in front of her face, and her mouth was open in a silent cry as she climaxed. The final surprise was that when she finished, she just sat there in a state of post-coital bliss before climbing off of me. She didn't even wait for me to finish. Not that I was particularly sure that I would have in these circumstances. I simply lay there, and I stared in disbelief as she pulled her panties back on.

"Thank you, Liam, that was most diverting," she said as she picked up the rest of her clothes and began to dress. Slowly, I sat up and grabbed my own underwear from beside of the couch.

"Well, that was a little one-sided."

"Oh, I'm quite sure that you can finish yourself off when I'm gone," she smiled at me as I pulled my pants up over my underwear, glaring at her. "Next time, try to be a little bit more enthusiastic. I felt a distinct lack of commitment on your part."

"You really think there's going to be a next time?" I said curtly.

She smiled most sweetly and leaned in to kiss me gently on the cheek, whispering, "Only if I want it." She then headed out the door.

Bothered, bewildered, and incredibly frustrated, I turned away, grabbed a box of tissues off the counter, and headed to my bedroom.

CHAPTER TWENTY

A NEW BROOM

I didn't have time to ponder the previous night's events as the next morning, I found myself exceptionally busy. Indeed, I found myself woken up at around 4:30 in the morning by the security chief. Something had occurred that needed my immediate attention. By the time I was dressed and down in the central security control centre, other key personnel had arrived. Most notably Charlotte Kensett and the new administrator, Sebastian Brody. Ignoring the sly smile Charlotte gave me, I approached the security chief, who was leaning over a short-range scan of the space around the planet.

"They began turning up about an hour ago," the sector chief advised me.

I looked over his shoulder at a bunch of blips and blobs on the edge of the screen. "Just keep it simple for me, would you?" I said irritably. "I have no idea what I'm looking at."

He looked up at me. "Ships, Mr Marshall. Dozens of ships and more arriving every hour."

"Peons?" I asked, feeling an edge of nervousness begin to rise up my spine.

"Therein lies the question. They have the transponder signals deactivated. However, who else could it be? We don't have a fleet in this area."

"What defences do we have?"

"The rings were built during a time of peace, and whilst there have been some upgrades to that, it's distinctly limited. We're floating in the atmosphere of the planet, and we were already at a maximum weight capacity before the war started."

"Yes, well, that's a very nice history lesson. But what exactly *do* we have?" Charlotte asked, sounding quite bored.

"We have small-scale armaments. Rapid fire guns and low yield missiles. It could possibly help us defend against a small-scale attack, but these are frigates out there."

"Are you telling me there's absolutely no way that we can repel this?"

"Not even remotely. Even if they just tried to board us, these ships must be carrying a hundred times the troops we have here."

"Then we don't have a choice. We have to evacuate and blow this place up. We can't let the Peons take it." I stepped back from the scanner with a frustrated sigh. "Begin evacuation procedures and download the codes for self-destruct."

"Oh, I think that would be a little hasty, Liam."

I looked up at Charlotte as she spoke. "Do you have an alternative?"

"Possibly." She stepped up to stand between me and the sector chief and looked down at the scanner before looking at him. "You said they were frigates. Is that correct?"

"Frigates, destroyers, cutters. All sorts of ships are out there."

A slight smile across her face. "It's Jenna Plural. She's brought the Confederation fleet here."

"You can't be serious?" I said, finding the idea preposterous.

"I can assure you. It is Jenna."

"Wouldn't they have told us if they're bringing the fleet here?"

"Oh, not at all, my dear boy. Your mission was a risky one, and you could have been captured. Jenna has successfully managed to hide the fleet from the Peons all this time, and she's not about to advertise its movements."

"That still doesn't answer how sure you're that it's her."

"The Battle of Deep Space decimated the Peon fleet. Whilst I'm sure they are working as hard as they can to replace their losses, we have accounted for every frigate the Peon's own, and it's highly unlikely they will have a fleet of new ones in under a year."

"Forgive me for doubting you, Charlotte, but starship tech is hardly your area of expertise."

"Quite right, Liam. However, logistics is, and logistically, they don't have what's on that screen."

"Have you tried hailing them?" I asked the security chief.

"Of course, but we haven't had a response."

I looked back at Charlotte. "Surely Plural would have responded to the calls?"

"Not at all. She wants to keep the location of the fleet a secret, and even short-range communications can be picked up. She will not make contact with you until she's in range for planet-side communications."

"Here's the problem, Charlotte. If you're right, that's absolutely fantastic. But if you're wrong, allowing them to get that close will make it too late."

"Well, you're going to have to wait, Mr Marshall," snorted Sebastian Brody, the new administrator who had been appointed by either Hannah or Bronwyn. "This is a multibillion-dollar establishment circling the planet twice. It's the private property of Grant Industries, and I'm fairly certain my superiors won't be too happy if you were to simply blow it up."

"Thank you for your input, Sir. However, this is a military matter," I replied curtly.

"May I remind you, Sir, that you're not military? You, Sir, are a member of Grant Security Services. Therefore, you're answerable to me. Stand down."

He was absolutely right. I had forgotten that I was no longer in the army, but little more than a hired gun. I stood back and raised my hands in a gesture of defeat and just stood there. I was convinced that we were about to face our destruction. I stared at the scanner, and we watched the ships come closer, with ever more appearing on the edge of our scanning ability to pick them up. Then the radio came to life, and I was expecting them to demand our surrender.

"Venus base, come in Venus base. This is the Spirit of Freedom to Venus base."

Everyone released a collective sigh of relief, including myself, and before he replied, Brody shot me a contemptuous look.

"We read you, Spirit of Freedom," he replied cheerfully. "Welcome to Venus."

"Admiral Plural sends her regards and congratulates you on the successful liberation of Venus."

"Would you thank the Admiral for me?" Brody asked. "Advise her that there will be a reception waiting, should she want to grace us with her presence."

Then, another signal came through this time. It was the Twilight Wanderer.

"Good morning, Administrator Brody." The distinctly recognisable voice of Bronwyn Donovan came over the line. "Please be prepared for the arrival of myself and Miss Grant."

"I assure you we'll be ready and waiting for you," the toady gushed.

I said nothing at this point, feeling a little embarrassed. Brody spent the next hour on his communicator, preparing various receptions and other activities intent on impressing his new boss. When it was confirmed that the shuttle carrying Hannah and Bronwyn was commencing docking procedures, he made to head down to meet her, and obviously, I followed. When we reached the door, he stopped and turned toward me with an expression of disgust.

"Where do you think you're going, Mr Marshall?"

"To meet Miss Grant, of course."

"I'm quite sure she has her own contingent of security with her, and your services are not necessary. I'm fairly certain, should Miss Grant want to inspect the security, she will come here."

I was about to reference my personal relationship with Hannah, but I felt quite amused as I said, "Fair enough, Mr Brody. I'll stay here, making sure all the consoles are spick and span for her inspection."

He looked around the room and then back at me. "That probably wouldn't be a bad idea, Mr Marshall," he said with equal sarcasm and turning away, he headed out of the room.

"Oh, you are a naughty boy," Charlotte said as she headed to the door to join him. "I really should put you over my knee sometime and give you a good spanking," she whispered to me with a smug grin as she headed out the door. I just stared after her, wondering if she truly meant it.

I turned back to the sector chief. "Have everyone smarten themselves up and get ready for a V.I.P."

"You really think Hannah Grant will come here and give us an inspection?" he asked, looking surprised.

"No, personally, I don't think she gives a shit about an inspection, but she will come here fairly quickly."

"How can you be so sure?"

"Oh, just call it a hunch," I said with a grin.

In less than twenty minutes, the security centre had been cleaned up, and every member of staff had their colours buttoned and their badges polished. Oh, when the door opened, Brody entered first, holding it for Hannah and Bronwyn, who followed her. Hannah was looking quite annoyed, but that instantly dissipated into a smile when she saw me. She headed over to me with Brody at her side.

"Why didn't you explain the situation to me appropriately, Mr Marshall? It would have saved a lot of embarrassment," Brody said to me.

"He was just having a bit of fun with you, Mr Brody, so you can take that stick out of your arse," Hannah said with a warm smile, causing him to flush slightly. She glanced at me. "How's it going, babe?" she asked with a grin.

"Oh, everything's perfectly fine, Duchess. Although I must admit being a little pissed that I didn't know the fleet was coming here."

"It wasn't my call. Jenna made a security decision, in case you were captured, or communications were intercepted. It's also the reason why I kept trying to find excuses for you not to start heading back." She looked around at the people all standing at attention, looking quite uneasy in the presence of the woman who could change their lives at a single sign of displeasure. "If there's someone who can make a nice cup of tea, it would be appreciated. I'm spitting feathers here."

"I have arranged a breakfast for you in the executive dining room," Brody said with a smile.

"Well, that's certainly nice of you." She looked around the security room. "Come on, everyone, the breakfast is on Mr Brody."

Oh, the look on Brody's face as she said this was pic-ture-perfect. Everyone looked at each other in confusion, then slowly followed Hannah out into the corridor.

It was standing room only in the executive dining room, and Brody disappeared quickly to tell the chef that he'd have to prepare more food for the extra guests. I really didn't get a chance to talk to Hannah, as various execu-tives and the heads of department kept coming up to pay homage to the new boss. She remained polite and profes-sional, but clearly disinterested. It could clearly be seen by those who knew them as well as I did, that Bronwyn was the true brains behind the everyday running of Grant In-dustries. Hannah did little more than decide policy, which in its own way was no small feat. As breakfast concluded and the guests started to return to their duties, Hannah took a seat at the dining room table as staff cleared away the remnants of the meal. She had Brody sitting next to her, and Bronwyn sat opposite. It was only then that I noticed Charlotte hadn't returned with them. There also remained the various department heads who also took seats. I stood out of the way, nursing a cup of coffee.

"Okay, so I know you all need time to adjust to the new leadership, but there are certain things we have to get done straight away," Hannah started. "Who's our public relations person here?" The young man raised his hand. "The first thing we need to do is control the news cycle. The story of what happened here is going to get out pretty damn fast, and I really don't want investors shitting them-selves. We need everyone to know that the company is in competent hands."

"That's not going to be easy, if I may say so," the young man replied, but then appeared to get too nervous to continue.

"Don't be afraid to speak your mind. I don't bite."

"Well, it's like this. Drake Tanner has whittled away at your reputation over the years and overcoming that quickly will be quite difficult. To be really honest with you, the news that you're now in control of the entire company will cause major problems with stock prices."

To my surprise, Hannah took this in her stride. "That doesn't need to be a problem. Focus on Bronwyn here. She is, after all, the C.E.O. of the company. Make it out that I'm more of a...silent partner, and that she's in control of things."

"That could work. Her father's reputation as a businessman is almost on par with that of your mother's."

"Good. Get it done." She looked around the room. "There is another matter that needs to be dealt with this morning that I don't want to leave waiting. The company needs to step up its supplies to the Australian resistance. I want our people armed better than the Peons. I want them to have the best communications. And have the best tucker .... I want them to have anything they need."

"Ma'am, do you really want your first act as the owner of the company to be that we give away billions of dollars of military supplies?" asked a young American woman, who, it turned out, was the head of Grant Military Ordinance Division

There was silence as Hannah fixed her with a stare. "You can't put a dollar value on Australia. It's priceless."

"Oh, I perfectly understand, Miss Grant. However, my yearly bonus is based purely on how profitable my department is. If I have to run the division at a loss, I get penalised."

"Well, personally, I think the best bonus you could possibly have is to be able to go to Bondi Beach with your bathers on. However, I see your point. Tell you what, I'm going to link your bonus to the reports of victories we hear from the resistance. How about that?"

"That would be most equitable, Miss Grant."

"I'm so glad you're pleased." She then went on and addressed the entire room. "Okay, so this afternoon, Admiral Jenna Plural will be coming aboard. Brody will be giving her and myself a tour of the facilities. I don't need to tell you, but nearly all of our trade is within the authority of the Solar Confederation. I expect her to see Grant Industries at its best. Make sure everyone is dressed appropriately, behaves appropriately, and at least looks like they know what they're doing. Any problems, talk to Mr Brody or Miss Donovan. That's all for now."

A mumble of conversation began as everyone started to get up and leave. Hannah rose from her chair and walked over to me.

"Come on," she said to me softly. "Show me where your bedroom is. I've got some extra special duties for you."

Chapter Twenty-One

V.I.P.s

G rant Industries all but rolled out a red carpet for the arrival of Jenna Plural. There was much excitement throughout the establishment. Anyone who didn't support Jenna Plural before, certainly did now after Drake Tanner had thrown in with the Europeans. Damn hero to most, personally, I still didn't know what to make of her. She appeared to be a pretty competent and effective leader, but I still hadn't seen anything to consider her worthy of the legendary status the media would have you believe.

Hannah wanted me to go with her, but the idea of wandering around looking at corporate departments, with most executives sycophantically fawning over them, wasn't my idea of a good time. I made an excuse that I had some work to do with the sector chief. She didn't believe me; she knew it was just an excuse. But she didn't make an issue of it, nor did she seem upset about it.

As I made my way back down to the security centre, I encountered Charlotte Kensett. I had a feeling it wasn't a coincidence. She didn't appear quite as relaxed as she normally did, and our conversation went from idle chatter to something a little more serious. "I need to discuss our little liaison with you, Liam."

"What about it?" I replied coldly, still a little miffed about the way that situation had ended.

"It was probably a mistake, but it is what it is. However, it could become quite complicated, should you feel the compulsion to discuss our little indiscretion with Miss Grant."

"Surely you were aware of my relationship with Hannah before you engaged in our little 'indiscretion', as you put it?"

"Oh, I was aware that you had an intimate relationship with her, but I didn't realise how serious it was. It was only when she was talking to Brody when she arrived that I realised you're actually engaged to her. I really think it would have been appropriate for you to have told me about that."

"If you're concerned that Hannah will have an issue about it, I can readily assure you she won't. By her choice, we have an open relationship. Whilst I won't discuss whatever goes on between us, I'm not in the least bit concerned about her finding out."

"Well, you do surprise me, Liam. That doesn't happen often. So I take it that you're aware of the affairs she has?"

That was a punch to my gut. "I haven't, and I wish to remain ignorant of them intentionally. But, like I said, we have an open relationship, and I don't need the details."

"I see. You certainly don't appear to be happy about the situation," she remarked casually.

"I admit it takes some adjusting to, but it's the price I'm willing to pay if I want Hannah in my life."

"I understand. However, I still think it would be wise for no-one to know about what happened between us."

"I can live with that. So I take it you don't want to repeat that event?" I said, despite knowing full well that I had no intention of repeating it. What can I say? I was curious, and I have an ego.

"No, Liam, I don't think so. I don't do open relationships."

I couldn't help but smile at this as we reached a junction. She turned and headed off in a different direction from me.

As it would turn out, we were both lying to ourselves, for there were multiple occasions Charlotte and I would get together in private. Still, I've shared enough those sordid details with you.

The Solar Confederation had, in the last year, started broadcasting its own television channels. Nothing too sophisticated. There was a light entertainment channel that consisted mostly of quiz shows, chat shows, and the occasional comedian. It hadn't quite got to the stage of recording fictional dramas and other programming people were used to on Earth. Then, there was the news channel. It didn't take a genius to work out that the news was very much state-controlled. Everything was rosy, and reported on victories, but never defeats. It was also where Jenna Plural or one of the members of her inner circle, such as Michael Phelkar, would make public broadcasts of either an informational or morale-boosting nature. Jenna Plural had all the hallmarks of a charismatic dictator, with her picture appearing in every public institution, such as schools and administrative centres. People even hung pictures of her in their homes. And she was clearly the fantasy of many a schoolboy, if the sales of Jenna-related paraphernalia were any guide.

Today was going to be the first ever public appearance of Jenna Plural and Hannah Grant together. I couldn't help but wonder about the sight of two genetically modified women who were the most powerful individuals in this new society. Side by side, looking barely older than college graduates, they stood out like a beacon that they weren't your normal, average people. As I entered the security centre, I had them put the news on the main screen and watched as Jenna Plural descended her shuttle to be met by Hannah and other Grant executives, whilst members of the public, eager to see their leader, remained roped off.

What they said to each other couldn't be heard as they smiled, spoke, and shook hands as a news commentator discussed the trivialities of their outfits. Hannah in her formal dress, with Jenna in her rigid black uniform. Together, they walked over to a podium that had been erected in the shuttle bay for this event. Jenna stood behind it with Hannah at her side, and I noticed Bronwyn just behind her. The commentator hushed as the Admiral waited for silence to fall upon the room.

"Officers, troopers, people of the Confederation," Jenna began. "Here we are at the site of yet another amazing victory by the United Freedom Force of the Solar Confederation. For generations, the rings of Venus have been the heart of the industrial might of the solar system. Constructed more than a hundred years ago by Grant Industries, it has served our community well. As the forces of darkness grew around us, and people we once trusted fell to the lies of the enemy, they were stolen by a traitor to not only his country, but humanity itself. The great Australian institution that is Grant Industries was turned over wholesale to the evil might of the Union." Her voice began to rise. "Today, we took it back! Grant Industries is back with its rightful and patriotic owner. And what's more, I officially declare Venus as a territory of the Solar Confederation, and all its residents, citizens of the Confederation with the rights and privileges that the position holds. Today is a great victory, and I declare the next forty-eight hours a time of celebration! Enjoy yourselves. You have earned it! Come back refreshed for the next task, for this war is not over, but each day, our victory comes ever closer." She stepped down to the loud cry of cheers and applause as she spoke with Hannah, and once more, the commentator's rhetoric commenced.

"Liam, do you have a minute?" I spun around, startled to see Bronwyn coming towards me. I looked back towards the screen and clearly saw her standing there shaking hands with Jenna. She laughed at my confused look. "They're running it on a four-minute delay in case something happens and they want to cut the feed." I looked back up at the screen, and indeed, I saw her briefly talk to Hannah and nod her head before she headed out of the docking bay, no doubt for this meeting.

"Do you want to meet here or privately?" I asked.

She looked around the room and pondered this question. "Let's just go for a walk, shall we?" I agreed and followed her out. We strolled down casually towards the retail centre that was once more open for business.

"Hannah's gonna be tied up with Jenna for some time," she began. "After all the public bullshit, they're going to go into a closed meeting to discuss a rather serious issue. Venus is just the start, but the prize jewel is Mars, which recently declared itself independent from any outside authority. However, they're hoping to ally for their own safety's sake. Jenna's going to want to keep this a military matter, but we have a massive amount of investment in Mars, and Hannah wants to protect those interests. She wants you on board with whatever operation is happening, but she's not going to have a chance to ask you before this meeting, which is why I'm here to sound you out."

As she finished, we entered a small food court, and as I pondered over her words, I joined the queue to buy us some coffee.

"She should know she doesn't need to ask. Whatever our relationship is, I still work for her, and it's up to her what she wants me to do."

"She understands that, mate, but she also knows this is going to mean time away from the fleet again. She believes this is gonna involve you spending a lot of time on that planet." she said, taking the coffee I offered her as we found a fairly secluded table.

"Do you have any other information on what this is going to involve?"

"No, I don't. That is precisely what they're going to discuss, but she just wants a heads up that she can insert you into the operation, should she have the opportunity."

"Not a problem," I said.

Bronwyn stared at me for a long moment as she sat back and took a sip of her coffee. "She really cares about you, you know."

"Huh?"

"Hannah. She really cares about you. The last couple of months, she's been really pissy regretting letting you go on this mission."

"I'm sure she does to a degree, but not enough. She doesn't want to be exclusive."

"Yeah, well, I find that a little bit weird, but it's not like it's uncommon these days."

"She suggested I sleep with you."

"Yeah, she told me." She rolled her eyes.

I chuckled. "I take it from that, it's not something you're interested in?"

"I don't need a pity fuck because of this, Liam," she said tapping the plate on her face.

"Whilst it's unusual, you're still an attractive woman, Bronwyn. I feel your pain for what happened, but I don't pity you, and I never will."

A wide grin crossed her face. "Give it up, Liam. It's never gonna happen."

"Why not? It might be arrogant of me to say, but I know you're attracted to me."

"Oh sure, you have those big blue eyes and that sexy accent, and if things were different, maybe I would be interested. But I'm not fucking my best mate's bloke." I went to respond to that, but she shook her head. "Do me a favour, mate. Drop the subject and never bring it up again."

"Fair enough. Tell me, while I was away, did Hannah...?" My voice trailed off.

Bronwyn raised an eyebrow. "Do you really want to know? I'm guessing by your discomfort in asking me, that you don't."

I pondered this a moment and then nodded. "You're right."

The next few days flew by. I didn't see much of Hannah other than when she came home late in the evening, as she and Bronwyn found themselves in many board meetings. Toward the end of the week, she blindsided me when she said, "Jenna is in negotiations with the Martians about a possible alliance. She also thinks it might be a trap, so she's sending Charlotte Kensett ahead to check things out."

"Why Charlotte?"

"Apparently, she lived there for a few years on some security assignment."

"I'm guessing you're telling me this for a reason?"

"I want you to go with her. Help her out. Do whatever you need to do. Grant Industries has multi-billions of dollars of assets on that planet, so we have a huge stake in making sure everything goes well. I trust Kensett to a degree, but at the end of the day, Jenna's interest is always gonna be way above ours, and I want someone I trust to be there to make sure our interests are well above Jenna's."

"When do we leave?"

"At the end of next week."

"I was hoping we'd have more time to spend together," I said disappointedly.

"Same here. However, the clock is ticking on this one." At that point, she tilted her head questioningly at me. "And just how is it you're now on first name terms with Charlotte Kensett?" And when I flushed bright red, a huge grin crossed her face. "You dog. Seriously? You fucked Kensett?"

"It wasn't exactly the highlight of my life."

"I'm surprised your dick didn't freeze off with that ice queen."

"You Australians are always so classy."

"Yeah, well," she said, gripping the front of my shirt and pulling me towards her. "I think it's time for you to go Down Under, *mate*."

Chapter Twenty-Two

Rendezvous on the Red Planet

Teaming up with Charlotte Kensett once more wouldn't have been my first choice. While she didn't seem the slightest phased by it, I felt a little uncomfortable.

However, that was nothing to the discomfort of being separated from Hannah once more. I was also growing tired of the disorientation of large passages of time passing in an instant in that damned electronic storage machine.

With the current positions of Mars and Venus, it would take approximately six weeks to arrive. Saying goodbye to Hannah, who was temporarily going to remain within the rings of Venus, I took the shuttle back to the Spirit of Freedom with Plural. Realising that Michael Phelkar was with her, I ensured that I sat separately by going to the rear of the shuttle, only to be joined by Charlotte, who sat next to me.

"What exactly are we going to be expected to do on Mars?" I asked her, after completing the socially expected pleasantries.

"The Peons are stretched exceedingly thin. With much of their fleet having been decimated at the Battle of Deep

Space, and the need for vast numbers of troops to occupy the former Pacific Alliance states, they were compelled to withdraw most of their contingent occupying Mars. The Martian Liberation Front took advantage of this, and the planet is now independent. However, Mars has never been able to be self-sufficient. Long gone are the dreams of terraforming the world, which basically has been proved impossible. As a result, the Martians need allies. They need to be able to trade with either the Union or us. Since neither of us is going to accept Mars trading with the enemy, they have to decide which of us they want to partner with. Jenna is entering a stage of negotiations, and we are to form part of a new embassy in the capital of New Philadelphia."

"Yeah, there's got to be more to it than that?" I replied suspiciously.

"What makes you think that?"

"Whilst you can be rather pleasant, Charlotte, you're hardly a diplomat. The Admiral wouldn't be sending you unless she's expected some trouble, or wants to start some trouble."

A smile crossed her face. "How very astute of you, Liam. However, it's not my place to say any more on the matter, and it will be up to Jenna to decide what she does and does not want you to know."

I didn't have to wait long for that, because almost immediately after we docked, I was summoned to a briefing to be held by the Admiral.

There were a few people that I recognised in the meeting room, and a few that I didn't. Apart from Jenna and Charlotte, of course, there was Mr Phelkar, Emma Dodgson, and I was introduced to Commodore Claire Addison, who held the role of Jenna's second in command. I was also introduced to another marine, Abigail Thompson, and the young Japanese lady, Tamiko Sakamoto. Helen Tracker was also present, but she avoided my gaze.

"Okay, boys and girls," Jenna began almost immediately. She took her seat at the head of the table. "Thanks to Lieutenant Dodgson and Mr Marshall, we can celebrate our victory in the taking of Venus. However, there is a bigger jewel out there. Claire, if you would do the honours?"

Claire Addison rose to her feet. "The Peons have effectively been driven off the planet Mars by the indigenous people. They have a provisional government of sorts, but it's still in a big transitional stage. As you know, Mars has never been independent, nor united, with communities from all different nations that were governed by their parent countries. Although Martians clamoured for independence for generations, it's only now their situation is truly sinking in. The communities on Mars have incredible difficulties expanding. The communities can't handle the overpopulation. While they have biodomes to grow food and raise livestock, they are insufficient for the populace. As a result, they have always relied on imports from Earth. When they tried to isolate themselves from us and the European Union, all trade from and to the planet stopped. Mars now realises that it has no choice. It has to ally with either us or the European Union."

"Surely they won't ally with an enemy they just kicked off the planet?" Bronwyn asked.

"You would think not, but considering the Union has control of all of Earth's resources, it is, in fact, more logical to ally with them, than us. Whilst we are converting many ships to agricultural production, we don't exactly find ourselves in a position to meet the needs of ourselves, let alone the Martians."

"Let's be honest about it," put in Jenna. "We can pretty much offer them fuck all. However, they don't know that, and that's why we're going to need to tread carefully when dealing with the Martians. I'm hoping that now that Hannah Grant has full control of her company, she can utilise the resources of some of the agri-colonies to step up production. However, we need to ensure the Martians believe we can provide all of their needs from day one, so that they choose us as their allies."

"However," Addison continued. "We need to ensure that we have a Plan B. Gaining a foothold on Mars will be a big step for preparing for our return to Earth. If the Peons regain a foothold on that planet, it will be virtually game over. We need to prepare for the possibility Mars will side with the Peons."

"There will be two factors in the contingent we are going to send to Mars. First, a diplomatic one. Mr Phelkar will act as the Solar Confederation ambassador, with Miss Donovan as a trade negotiator. However, we have come up with a plan to ensure there is no way that the Peons are going to take control."

At this point, Charlotte rose to her feet. "Whilst Mr Phelkar and Miss Donovan are in their negotiations, Mr Marshall and I will be preparing the counter plan. As a goodwill gesture, the Admiral has arranged for relief vessels from Grant Industries to deliver much-needed supplies. However, along with those supplies will be racks filled with the new portable M.E.T. devices loaded with troops. We will ensure they are delivered to every community on the planet. Should there be a failure in the negotiations, we will have twenty-thousand troops primed and ready."

"Twenty thousand isn't exactly a lot to take an entire planet," I stated.

"In a conventional attack, you're absolutely right, Mr Marshall," Jenna responded. "However, the Martians are unaware that we now have the portable matter to energy transit devices. We'll have control not long after the Martians become aware of our presence. However, I strongly hope that the Martians will see sense and come over to us of their own volition."

It was quite an audacious plan, but I personally wasn't sure that it would work, and I was certainly not pleased Jenna had clearly dragged Hannah into the situation. If anything were to go wrong, Grant Industries would be officially recognised as an enemy of the Martians.

When we were alone again, I asked Bronwyn why she hadn't informed me of this situation. She just looked at me incredulously.

"Just because you're fucking Hannah doesn't make you my superior, mate. I don't answer to you about the executive decisions of Grant Industries."

"Shareholders already don't have confidence in Hannah. If they find out she's using resources for the war effort in a non-profit manner, this will effectively finish her."

"That's my problem to worry about, Liam. Your problem is to make sure they don't find out."

Later that day, we transferred over to a small frigate called the S.E.S. Endurance. It had clearly once been a British ship, as much of the insignia had not yet been changed. The former H.M.S. Endurance was small, sleek, and fast, with a crew of around forty-five. It was the vessel that was to take us to Mars.

Once more, I was reunited with Hailey and Kennedy. We barely had time to talk as we were led directly to the M.E.T. system. You already know the process. Needless to say, a flash and it was six weeks later, and we were coming into the orbit of the planet Mars. This time, however, I got to orientate myself. Captain Baker, the ship's commander, set us up in a briefing room where we watched a video of events of the last few weeks. Nothing much had actually changed, with the exception that Hannah had officially announced Grant Industries' independence from either the Solar Confederation or the European Union and was willing to trade with both. Jenna Plural had responded with the statement that the decision was disappointing, but didn't elaborate further. This, of course, had been expected. Hannah had made this clear in our meeting with Jenna, and it was all part of a greater plan. There had been a few shareholder complaints that costs for the company had escalated, whilst profits hadn't. This, I felt sure, was due to the company funnelling supplies and equipment to Australia via a back door. Rather expensive equipment started falling off the back of the proverbial lorry.

Our attention then turned to the situation on Mars and the division of responsibilities. Michael Phelkar was to negotiate the potential alliance with the Solar Confederation. Bronwyn was to meet with government officials to discuss the restoration of trade between Grant Industries and the planet. Me? I was listed as a member of the clerical staff working for a company executive called Lydia Williams. Of course, Lydia Williams didn't exist and looked exactly like Charlotte Kensett. She had been based on the planet for several years as a sector chief for the much-loathed United States Department of Outland Security. Therefore, the Martians had records on her, so the new identity had been created as a cover.

Down in the docking bay of the Endurance, twenty-five Grant Industries shuttles sat waiting for us, filled with much-needed supplies being donated as a goodwill gesture by the Solar Confederation. They did, in fact, store racks upon racks of Tiffany Mahoney's portable M.E.T. devices constantly on charge. Each was destined for a major population centre, and it was our job to ensure we got them through undetected.

We went ahead of these in a small executive yacht down to the capital city of New Philadelphia. We were greeted as a V.I.P.'s with a military contingent of the newly constituted Mars Defence Force and some high-ranking official who I don't really recall. Michael Phelkar took the lead with Bronwyn at his side. Charlotte and I hung back with Kennedy and Hailey, all of us dressed in civilian clothing.

After the perfunctory shaking of hands with Martian officials, we were led out to a waiting limousine. We were driven out to the acting first governor's executive mansion. A large house that stood out against the rundown community surrounding it. I don't exaggerate when I say the Martian colonies were a massive pile of shit. Large dome communities that would be generations old. The domes filtered out the harmful radiation from the sun, but it caused a light red hue wherever you went. Thin wisps of vapour that were the by-product of the artificial air generators seemed to hang motionless at various points down the street, only moving in the wake of the vehicles.

The gates of the executive residence opened, and we drove up a long path that intersected a lawn of artificial grass. I happened to notice that it had very much been styled after the White House in the capital of the United States, although much smaller.

As we got out, we once more went through the ritual of greeting executives. This time, we met the first governor, Terry Moulton, and his wife. He was a tall, bearded man who had led a rough life and was the former leader of the Martian Liberation Front who had driven the Peons off world after the Battle of Deep Space. A large scar that ran down over his right eye gave him a rather thuggish appearance, despite his smart suit and tie. I was introduced as a logistics clerk for Grant Industries here to oversee the safe transit of Jenna's donations.

Little interest was paid to my small team since Phelkar and Bronwyn were the main attractions here. As much as I dislike Michael Phelkar, I can't deny that he is good at his job. He could effectively charm a leopard into not eating him. There was a rumour that he had an affair with Jenna Plural, something he would later admit in his biography, but at the time, I didn't really believe it. I imagined her to be more interested in the more masculine type of man. As we were led into the reception, there was the ritual of posing for pictures for the Martian media, which only Bronwyn and Phelkar participated in. Charlotte made sure she was nowhere in line of sight of any photographer. The one thing you can count on is the lack of images of Jenna's number one spook. I won't bore you with the details of the reception and pomp and ceremony of the very public meal provided for us in the dining hall. We were then shown to our rooms. We didn't discuss anything related to the mission, for the possibility that we were being listened to was a real threat. The following morning, as prearranged, Charlotte, Hailey, and I headed for the city's headquarters for Grant Industries. Kennedy was to remain with Mr Phelkar.

Just like everything on Mars, the Grant Industries facility wasn't like its typical grand structures. It was small and compact. One of our first difficulties was that the Grant management on Mars had run independently of the parent company for a number of years, and as a result, were not privy to our plans. All they knew was a representative of Hannah Grant in the form of Lydia Williams was coming to take authority.

Bertram Anastasi was a Martian who had never left the planet. He had worked for Grant Industries all his life, starting at the bottom and working his way up to the managing director of the New Philadelphia office. He wasn't exactly welcoming to us.

"It's not exactly a morale boost for my hard-working team that the moment Hannah Grant takes charge, we get taken over by an off-worlder," was the first thing he said after the perfunctory greetings as he led us upstairs to his office.

"Oh, don't look at it like that, Mr Anastasi," Charlotte said most sweetly. "We are simply here to oversee the smooth running of the relief operations. It is quite a logistical task to ensure the smooth running of our deliveries."

Anastasi snorted. "And Hannah Grant in her ivory tower doesn't think us dumb Martian bumpkins can manage that?"

"Oh, I can assure you, Mr Anastasi, Hannah Grant has nothing but the highest respect for you," Charlotte replied, and inwardly, I smiled because I was fairly certain Hannah Grant didn't have an opinion on them one way or another. "Now, if you can assure me that you have extensive experience with fleet operations, I will quite happily return to the first governor for what would I be, I'm sure, quite an excellent breakfast."

That made Anastasi look uncomfortable, for obviously, he didn't have any experience dealing with a military ship and its cargo. Indeed, it was most unlikely that he had ever dealt with more than one shuttle at a time, let alone organizing multiple landings all over the planet. However, I didn't hear the rest of the conversation, for as we entered his office, something else distracted me. There was a middle-aged woman seated behind a desk. It would turn out to be his personal assistant, but it was her reaction to Charlotte that had drawn my attention. She positively looked startled as we entered and stared almost disbelievingly at her. She didn't notice me watching, and her expression went passive, and she looked away. However, there was no doubt what had just happened.

She had recognised Charlotte.

CHAPTER TWENTY-THREE

THE M.L.F.

My mind raced on how to deal with this situation. This was about to blow wide open. As Anastasi introduced us to Lucinda, for that was her name, I waited for her to comment about knowing our Minister of Internal Affairs, but although she didn't look comfortable, she shook hands politely, and when she came to me, I fixed my gaze on her to see her reaction. She looked uneasy, but quickly looked away from me.

"I heard you mentioned breakfast," she said to Charlotte. "If you haven't eaten, I'd be more than happy to go and get you something."

"Oh, that won't be necessary, my dear, but thank you for asking."

Thinking quickly, I approached. "Actually, Miss Williams, I think that would be an excellent idea. I could go with her. I'd love the opportunity to see a bit of the real New Philadelphia that's not on the tourist maps."

Charlotte turned to look at me. There was a faint quizzical look in her eye that would be indiscernible to anyone who didn't know her as well as I did. I was going off plan, and that no doubt concerned her. However, I was now about to see how much she trusted me. "I suppose it would be quite nice to sample some Martian cuisine."

"Oh, I'm sure you're far too busy to come with me. I could just run out and pick up some takeout," the girl said uneasily in a single breath, suspicious enough to even draw Anastasi's attention, but he said nothing.

"Oh, it's going to be a couple of hours before the shuttles start coming down, my dear. We have plenty of time."

We headed out into the street. She said nothing and looked pretty uncomfortable. "Is there a problem, Miss.... I'm sorry I didn't catch your name."

"Braithwaite, Lucinda Braithwaite. And no, there was no problem." However, her tone belied the truth, and she was rather agitated. We headed down the road and entered a small burger place where she ordered items off the breakfast menu. As we waited, she suddenly looked up at me and said, "I need to use the bathroom. I'll be right back." I simply nodded and watched as she walked off to the ladies' room. It was quiet, and no-one was there except for us and the staff, who were all now busy preparing our food.

Slowly, I made my way over to the ladies' room and carefully opened the door, so it didn't make any noise. I heard Braithwaite talking to someone.

"I'm telling you, James, she's here." She was inside a cubicle with the door closed, yet opened just enough to see that she hadn't locked it. There was silence as she listened to whoever it was on the other end of the line. "Don't you think I'd recognise the Bitch of Brooklyn when I saw her? I'm telling you something's going on. Charlotte Kensett is here." I sighed inwardly. I was too late. She had just told somebody. I turned around and saw a lock on the main door of the bathroom and gently clicked it over.

"Look. Meet me on the corner of Seventh and Main in about half an hour. I have to find a way of ditching this asshole that's with me, and then we can meet up."

There was a pause, and I waited patiently for her to finish. I was unarmed, since it would have aroused suspicions for me to have carried a weapon on a diplomatic mission, and that would have easily been detected when we walked through security at the docking bay. However, I waited till I heard her hang up, and then I pushed the door open. Her head spun around to me fast, fear in her eyes and the realization she had just been caught.

"How do you know Charlotte Kensett?" I said softly.

She didn't answer and immediately went to reach something behind her back. I approached and backhanded her. I brought my other hand up over her mouth so she couldn't scream as a knife fell to the floor. I looked down, and kicked it through to another stall, then looked at her again. I suddenly felt a sharp pain in my groin as a hand viciously grasped around my balls and crushed them. Despite the agony of this, I pushed her head back into the wall hard, brought my other hand up around her throat, and squeezed, causing her to let go of me.

It's a natural instinct when being choked to go for the hands, and only a trained fighter generally realises this. And I realised she was a trained fighter when she punched me in the gut. I didn't let go despite this, and she slammed her fist into my face, knocking me back out of the stall. For a relatively small woman, she could pack quite a punch. However, you can argue as much you like for equality, but the simple laws of biology gave me the upper hand. My difficulty was that I couldn't kill her as I needed to know how far the mission was now compromised.

This was a great irony, as I think back on this situation. The entire fate of the war hinged on my decision-making that day. As I fell back against the sink, she came out of the stall at a rapid pace, and her next decision was her last mistake. Maybe if she had continued attacking me, she would have had a chance, but no, she headed for the door. It took her just enough time to realise it was locked, for me to bring my arm around her neck and my hand once more over her mouth and pull her to the ground. In a moment, she was lying there, and I was on top of her, opening her arms with my knees. She tried to bite the hand that covered her mouth and was trying to buck me off with her legs. I reached down into her pocket and pulled out the phone she had just been using and was pleased to see, not only that it was unlocked, but also that it still had the contact up on the screen with a very handy photograph of a man called Riley. I committed his image to my memory, and then tossed the phone aside. I looked back down at the girl and repeated my question. "How do you know Charlotte Kensett?"

She stared at me like I was stupid, until I realised that I needed to take my hand off of her mouth.

"Because I'm from New Brooklyn." She looked at me as if that was supposed to mean something, and seeing I was clueless, she added, "Everyone remembers the Bitch of

Brooklyn. The Outland Security Sector Chief responsible for the disappearances of many people that disagreed with the American government."

"She doesn't work for the American government anymore."

She looked at me patronizingly. "Well, obviously, since there is no longer an American government. That doesn't change the fact that that woman is guilty of crimes against the Martian people. Just what the fuck is she doing here now?"

I didn't know what to make of that statement, but I didn't particularly care as I was in a quandary. I couldn't let her go, and I couldn't simply kill her and leave her in the bathroom of a takeout, only to find my face captured by the security cameras on the six o'clock news. "Who was it you were calling?"

"One of my old contacts in the Martian Liberation Front. Someone who knows how to deal with the likes of Charlotte Kensett."

"I don't know about Charlotte's past, but she's now working for the security of your planet. We're here to ensure the Peons don't return. Isn't that something you can get on side with?"

She laughed mercilessly. "She could be the Angel of Phobos, for all I care. She's a fucking demon. She's on the provisional government's wanted list for her crimes."

"If that's the case, why didn't you just call the police?"

That question seemed to throw her. "Old habits, I guess."

"I'll do a deal with you," I said, thinking quickly. "I can't give you details of our operations here, but those supplies up on the ship are genuine. If you truly care about what happens to the future of Mars, you won't say anything because if our mission here is blown, those supplies won't be coming."

She thought about this. "Is your mission more important than the life of Charlotte Kensett?"

"Yes, it is," I said without hesitation.

"Fine. You let those supplies come, but when you leave, you leave Charlotte Kensett."

After a long pause, I replied, "I can do that."

Before you think me foolish, I was under no illusion that she wasn't going to honour any agreement with me, and I'm fairly certain she was under no illusion that I was going to honour any agreement with her. However, we were both in a predicament. She wanted to get out of here alive, and I wanted to get her out of here without leaving evidence of my activities. I climbed off of her, moving to the right, and as she started to get up, I slipped my hand under the cubicle where the knife had fallen. I managed to slip it into my pocket without her seeing. We both got up like nothing had happened, and we turned to the mirrors above to sink and straighten ourselves up. Together, we left the cubicle amid stares from staff wondering what I was doing in the ladies' room, picked up the food, and headed out.

"We still have to meet Riley. If he doesn't see me there, he's gonna whip up a shitstorm that helps none of us." She needn't have worried. I wanted to meet Riley very much indeed. We made our way down to the meeting place, and I recognised the man from his picture before we even approached him. As we joined him, he looked up at me suspiciously. It didn't take long for them to show their hand as he approached me and pulled out a small snub snap pistol, typically issued to shipboard staff but very handy due to its lack of noise. He looked about, making sure that no-one noticed him, but this was New Philadelphia, the busiest city in the colonies, where no-one paid attention to anyone else.

"Talk to me, Lucy. Who is this?"

"One of Kensett's lackeys. He thinks we're here to do a deal, but you can shoot him," she said coldly, glaring at me. But clearly, this wasn't something he was going to do in the middle of a busy intersection, and, covering his gun with the folds of his jacket, he indicated for me to move down the street ahead of him. I complied, and as he stood way too close behind me and pushed the gun into my back, I knew this wasn't going to be quite an easy situation to get out of. We moved up the street, and as I suspected, he told me to move down an alley, where he was no doubt going to shoot me. I meekly complied, but when we were part way down, I brought my training into action.

His gun was so tightly placed into my back that even spinning around would move it away from me, and that's exactly what I did, bringing my fist up into his face and then grabbing his wrist. There was a snap as the weapon went off. The bullet sailed down to hit a dumpster halfway down the alley, but by this time, his wrist was broken, and his gun was in my hand. I brought it up under his jaws as he cried out, and I fired. Snap pistols have a low velocity, but even this didn't stop the bullet from coming out of the top of his head, splattering viscera over Lucy, who stood behind him. She was momentarily startled, but it didn't last long as I shot her at point-blank range in the face.

I dragged the two bodies behind the aforementioned dumpster, slipped the firearm into the back of my belt, covered it with my shirt, and picked up the takeout. As I headed back towards Grant Industries, I tried to think of an excuse for why I was returning without Anastasi's assistant. By the time I arrived, I still had none. This whole mission had just become a clusterfuck of a mess. Indeed, the first thing Anastasi asked was where his assistant was, and it was at that moment, I realised I only had one response.

"She's dead." Even Charlotte had to look at me with surprise at that one. "She tried to kill me. Said something about the Martian Liberation Front and not wanting the Solar Confederation here. Did you have any idea that you were employing a terrorist?"

Anastasi stared at me wide-eyed. "The M.L.F. has many members. Most of us played some part in the resistance against the Peons. Even I was a member, and yes, I knew Lucy was. I had no idea she was going to do that. You must believe me."

"Well, Mr Anastasi, I must say I'm not impressed with your employment practices," Charlotte said, looking most put out. "In light of this, I must advise you that only my personal hand-picked team is going to work on this operation. Nothing must be allowed to stop this much-needed aid from reaching the people of Mars."

Trust Charlotte Kensett to turn the situation to her advantage.

"Understood," he said despondently.

Charlotte sighed. "I'm afraid I have to ask you to wait outside while I discuss the situation with Mr Marshall. I'm quite sure if my boss believes us to be at risk here, she will cancel this whole operation, and we will leave, and we'll also leave you to answer to the first governor as to why we will no longer be delivering the aid we promised."

He looked like he was about to protest, but suddenly deflated and just headed out the door as it closed behind him. Charlotte turned to me. "I can see you have quite an interesting story to tell me, Mr Marshall."

I gave her a quick rundown on the events of the last half an hour, and she actually chuckled.

"The possibility of my being recognised was considered, but we thought that the odds of me running into someone from that shitty little community that I once had to suffer the indignity of serving was very remote. I must admit when she said her name, it did sound familiar. I had her incarcerated in a labour camp for unpatriotic activity against the United States, but I didn't recall it at the time because, well, I had quite a few people incarcerated in labour camps for unpatriotic activity towards the United States." At this, she stopped and pondered. "We don't really have a choice, but to now call the police. We can hardly hide the fact that you have killed two people, and being upfront about it and claiming self-defence is all we can really do."

I looked appalled at this idea. "Even a self-defence claim, they're going to arrest me while they sort it out, and it could take weeks for that to happen."

"Oh, they can't arrest you, Liam. You have diplomatic immunity. You could have buggered the girl in a public square, and the worst they could do was ask you to leave the planet."

Still unsure about this, I let her call the police, and although I wasn't arrested, I did spend the rest of the day answering questions. Charlotte informed Michael Phelkar of the incident, and he stepped in. I wasn't privy to his meetings, but I was soon informed that no further action was going to be taken, and I actually received an apology for the unfortunate incident.

It turned out that they had threatened to deport me, but Mr Phelkar had advised them that I was the only one who could oversee the safe delivery of the much-needed supplies. It would take weeks to rearrange everything. Apparently, the life of two former M.L.F. members wasn't as important as it was feeding the population.

It was late when Charlotte and I checked into our hotel rooms. We wanted to stay near where we were working, so we didn't return to the executive mansion. I must admit I pondered going to Charlotte's room to see if she wanted to work off some of the stress of the day's events, but in the end, I took a quick shower and went straight to bed.

The next day was going to be a very long one.

Chapter Twenty-Four

Infiltration

The next day, it turned out that Charlotte had been very busy working into the night. She had taken advantage of the situation to its fullest limit. Having made it clear that she no longer trusted the locals, she insisted on replacing all the staff with personnel from the Confederation. However, this actually meant we gained time rather than losing it. With all the indigenous staff removed from the building, and the shuttle delivering loyal members of her staff and the military, we no longer had to sneak around and do this under the radar. By the third day on Mars, I was busy checking with all the different cities that were expecting the shuttles to arrive.

This was a big event for the Martians, and every T.V. channel was devoted to it. People even went to the rooves of buildings in order to watch the fleet of craft coming in. It was kind of ironic that the public nature of our incredibly secret operation was on the six o'clock news. This wasn't going to be easy. It would take only one overzealous security officer to search a shuttle, and should the portable

M E.T. be found, it would be game over, because then, every shuttle would be searched.

My job was to liaise with the crews of each shuttle and keep up to date on the success or possible failure of each landing. One of the things we had on our side was the shuttles wouldn't be landing in regular docking ports, but rather in Grant Industries warehouses. However, I admit I was somewhat nervous as I waited for each ship to check in that their payload was delivered. Now, when I say payload, I wasn't talking about the relief supplies, which I frankly didn't give a shit about. I was concerned with the removal of the racks of M.E.T. devices stored with hundreds of troops. Each device only had a battery life of about three hours. As a result, they would need to be removed from the ships and placed in storage where they could be consistently charged. They would then sit there for several months waiting for the orders from Jenna Plural. The hope was that they wouldn't be needed and simply returned to the fleet after successful negotiations for an alliance were completed. However, you already know that wasn't going to happen.

One by one, the shuttle captains reported success, but as the day drew on, I grew tense when the last two or three failed to report in. However, they eventually did, much to my relief. At this point, the mission was complete. Members of Charlotte's Ministry of Internal Affairs would remain on the planet to ensure they weren't discovered. One by one, the shuttle was left, and news of the distribution of the new supplies was matched with great delight by the Martian people. We spent one more night in the hotel waiting for Phelkar and Bronwyn to complete their negotiations the following day. I got a call from Bronwyn.

"We got a deal of sorts," she told me. "They're definitely interested in an alliance, but they wanna meet with Jenna Plural personally. However, they don't want the entire bloody fleet turning up here. She has to come with one ship. I don't know how she's going to respond to that, but either way, we're done."

By that evening, we were back on board the S.C.S. Endurance. The return journey was cut in half, for Jenna had accepted the Martians' terms, and the Spirit of Freedom was headed our way. It travelled exceptionally faster than we could, and it was less than four weeks before we rendezvoused with it.

I was rather surprised to find Hannah aboard, and I didn't get an answer as to why until we were alone in her assigned quarters later in the evening on the day I arrived.

"I'm going to Mars with Jenna. Apparently, the first governor was offended that I didn't come as part of the negotiations and that I sent what he called one of my staff."

"How long have you known this?" I asked.

"Actually, it was while you were in transit. They got a message back to me after he discovered I wasn't coming."

"Why didn't you let me know? I could've waited for you back there."

She sighed and looked at me a little sheepishly. "You're not coming with me, Liam."

I couldn't help but get irritated by that. "Why the hell not?"

"They already know you. They think you're a logistics clerk who shot two Martians. You can hardly turn up as my security."

"Do you seriously think I'm going to let you go down there without me.? It's not exactly the safest place in the solar system."

"Oh, don't be difficult, Liam. It's not an option, and Stepanchikov is perfectly able to keep me safe. Whilst there is much unrest down there, it isn't exactly open warfare."

"But it's going to become open warfare if Jenna Plural doesn't get her way. We've just ensconced thousands of troops on that planet ready to take over, if she doesn't get an agreement, and that's going to happen while you're there."

She shrugged. "It is a risk, I know, but honestly, Liam, while Jenna and I have had our differences, she's so reliant on my company that she really isn't going to let anything happen to me. Trust me, I will stay as safe as I possibly can. It's not like I can't take care of myself. I survived Last Day without your help."

"Don't remind me of that," I said with a sigh. There was no point in getting into an argument about it. I wasn't going to win. At best, Hannah would listen to my advice, but at the end of the day, it was up to her, as to whether she was gonna take it. The next few weeks passed quickly, and I spent my time doing nothing. I hadn't taken a real break since leaving Earth, and there wasn't exactly much to do on the Spirit of Freedom, where private security wasn't allowed to operate. Hannah would frequently disappear into meetings either with Bronwyn, or in conference calls with Grant Industries executives and, on occasion, with Jenna Plural or members of her staff. I mostly hung around the quarters, either reading or watching movies. I started to relax and found my time with Hannah very pleasant since we stopped talking about work.

One evening, I was trying to get to sleep after a particularly intense time with my partner when she said. "We should get married."

"I thought we already decided to do that," I said sleepily.

"No, I mean actually do it."

"It's rather late, and I'm pretty tired. Can it wait till tomorrow?"

She laughed and elbowed me. "Arsehole. No, I mean, we should set a date and do it."

"Okay. I can ask Jenna Plural to officiate."

Then she laughed again. "Liam, be serious. The idea that the ship's captains can perform marriages is bullshit, and it always has been. And if you seriously think I'm gonna have some ten-minute wedding in an office somewhere, you need to get real."

"Oh fuck, you're gonna want some big fancy wedding, aren't you?"

"Too right, babe." She then giggled. "I want to get Bronwyn in the most outrageous frock as my maid of honour. She would simply die."

I chuckled at that idea. "I could see the look on her face right now. Make it bright purple to match the colour she'll turn."

"Oh, you so know, I'm gonna do it," she laughed. But she turned to face me and asked me, "Who's gonna be your best man?"

This quickly killed my mood, for as I thought about it, I realised I didn't actually have any friends. For the last few years, I've been totally devoted to taking care of Hannah, and any concept of a social life was gone. I tried to think of anyone that I was friends with, and finally, a thought occurred to me. "Well, it doesn't have to be a man, does it?"

"No, of course not. I don't even know why we still use the term, but do you have someone in mind?"

"Charlotte Kensett."

Now, she laughed quite heartily at that, until she realised I wasn't joking. "You can't be serious?"

"Honestly. Apart from Bronwyn, who is obviously going to be your maid of honour, Charlotte is pretty much the only friend I have."

"Yeah, mate. But you fucked her. Won't that be a little bit odd?" She frowned at me.

"Hey, wasn't me that came up with the idea of an open relationship," I chuckled.

She sighed softly. "Okay. I find it hard to believe that Charlotte Kensett actually *has* friends and that you're one of them, but if you want Charlotte Kensett, then ask her."

"When do you want to do this?"

"When we get back from Mars. Possibly when we rejoin the fleet, since the Wanderer has the perfect facilities for such an event."

We lay there silently for a few minutes, thinking things out. She suddenly let out a deep sigh. I turned and looked at her. "What's the matter?"

"I want my sister to be at the wedding. I want her to stand with me and be the one that gives me away."

"Seriously? I thought you hated her."

"She's a Grant. She's family, the only family I have. I can't hate her. I'm fucking angry at her, but I can't hate her."

"Then ask her."

She shook her head. "No, I can't do that."

"Why not?"

"Because she may say no."

"So?"

"I really don't want to give her the satisfaction. The only thing that exists between me and Stacey now is my pride."

"Is pride more important than your family?"

"Oh, Liam, this is the only thing in my life that's more important than my family."

She then turned on her side and snuggled up against me, as I slipped my arm around her shoulders and lay there thinking. I realised what I was going to do the next day.

Hannah had risen and left before I was awake. I wasn't sure where she went because I'd lost interest in keeping track of her various boring bloody meetings, but I had my own plans, and after a quick shower, I headed out.

Stacefield Ellen Grant is a Confederation legend. And you probably know more about her than I did at this time. The former Australian Air Force pilot set her name into the history books after her manoeuvre, taking out a frigate in the Battle of Deep Space by flying her starship into it and yet not losing a single crew member throughout the entire event.

I don't know what I was expecting, but it certainly wasn't what I encountered. It turned out Stacey was in the late stages of pregnancy. She'd been relieved from duty by Jenna, due to having considerable complications following several events where she nearly lost the child. She had been transferred to the Spirit of Freedom and was quartered on one of the lower decks, relieved of all duty.

Finding out where her quarters were wasn't exactly difficult, and I headed down there. When I pressed the buzzer to her door, there was no answer. But when I heard noises coming from inside the room, I pressed it again. Eventually, the door slid open. I expected her to look similar to her sister, but she was far from it. She was rather plain, with overlarge protruding teeth and an old-fashioned gothic hairstyle that hung over her right eye. Her visible ear was covered in an array of earrings. A thick tattoo in a bold font was emblazoned upon her neck, of which I could only read the first two letters of an H & an A. She was pale and looked quite ill.

"What the fuck, mate? What's the hurry that you can't wait for a girl to finish chundering?"

"My apologies."

"Yeah, yeah. Who the fuck are you? What d'you want?"

"I'm Liam Marshall," I said, extending my hand to her. She went to take it, but suddenly pulled it back when I added, "I'm the fiancé of your sister Hannah."

If her face was grim before, it was nothing compared to now, as it became expressionless beyond the look of contempt.

"Fuck off," she spat and shut the door. I stood there momentarily, stunned. I was about to walk away, but I became determined that I was going to do this for Hannah. After all, what can you give the girl that already has everything? I hit the buzzer again.

"Fuck. Off." Stacey repeated from behind the door, but I just simply pressed the buzzer again.

The door slid open. "Look, mate, if you don't fuck off, I'm calling fucking security."

"I just want ten minutes, Captain Grant. Just ten minutes, and then, if you want, you never have to see me again."

She stared at me for a long moment, then, with a shrug, said, "Fine. But you only fucking get five."

She stepped away from the door, allowing me to enter. Walking back into her living room, she stood there with arms folded, head tilted to one side, and stared at me.

"Do you mind if I sit down?"

"Yes," she replied. "Your time's running out here, mate. Start fucking talking."

"We're getting married."

"Whoop-di fucking doo," she said curtly with a shrug. "But that's your fucking problem, not mine, unless you want me to talk you out of it."

I laughed at that, but she didn't reciprocate, still staring at me with what appeared to be almost hatred. "No, I'm quite happy to marry Hannah. However, she doesn't want the wedding without you there."

Now, that did make Stacey snort. "Why the fuck would I be there?"

"Because she's your sister, and she's the only family you've got."

Stacey shrugged and then ran her hand over her heavily pregnant stomach. "Not for long."

"I know you don't know me and probably don't have any interest in hearing what I have to say, but...."

"You got that right, mate." She sat and glanced down at her watch. "If we are not done here, you've got two minutes left."

"Look, I don't know what the disagreement is between you and Hannah, but surely they're not irreconcilable."

Stacey snorted again. "You're fucking marrying her, yet she hasn't told you about the situation between us?"

"Yes, well, she has that stubborn Grant pride."

Stacey instantly got the dig. "Look, mate. If you can't see that Hannah's a lying fucking bitch, that's not my problem. She fucked me over big time, and frankly, you can go fuck yourself too. Are we done?"

I let out a despondent sigh. "I've worked for the Grant family for years now, and yes, I know that somehow along the line, you got screwed over, but that was your mother, not Hannah."

"You worked for my mother?" Her eyes narrowed.

"For a couple of years, yes."

Now, the look on her face was unquestionable hatred, as she pointed to the door and then venomously hissed, "Get the fuck out of my quarters. You show that fucking pretty face of yours around here again, I'll fucking break it."

I sighed. "As you wish, Captain Grant."

But as I turned to the door, she let out a sudden loud cry. I turned back and saw her clutching her belly, her face contorted in agony. Her hair now fell to one side, and I could see the artificial eye reminded me of Bronwyn.

"Are you okay?" I asked, but she didn't reply. She sank down to her knees, and I saw a large red patch of blood start to appear at her crotch. I ran over to her and tried to help her up to get her to the couch, but she was now crying out in pain. So I lifted her up into my arms and carried her over to the couch, where I gently lay her down before turning around and hitting the intercom.

"There's a medical emergency in Captain Stacefield Grant's quarters. I repeat, there is a medical emergency in Captain Stacefield Grant's quarters. I need medics now!" I turned back to the young pilot, and she was clutching at her stomach. The only time I've ever seen anyone in that much pain was on the battlefield, when one of my team members had received a gut shot. I fell to my knees beside her and gently stroked my hand through her hair reassuringly. "It's okay, Stacey, help is coming."

She suddenly reached out and gripped my hand. "Don't let me lose my baby."

"We're going to do everything we can. Help is coming." The paramedics activated an emergency override on the door and came rushing in up to her side. A gurney floated in behind them and sat in the middle of the room as the paramedics worked away on her before lifting her up onto the gurney. A tall blonde man in a white coat came rushing in and started examining her. "We need to get her down to the medical centre fast," he said with a thick Australian accent. He looked up at me. "What happened?"

I explained all I knew, which wasn't much, and he simply nodded back at me. Turning back to her, he asked. "Are you family?"

"No, well, yes. Kind of. I'm her sister's fiancé," I replied. As they headed out the door with her, I called after them. "Please let me know how she's doing. My name is Liam Marshall. You can contact me through Grant Industries."

The doctor nodded, and I was left standing in the middle of the apartment alone. A wave of guilt ran over me, thinking that it was possibly me that caused this by getting her worked up. However, later that night, I would get a message from the doctor saying she was stable, the baby was fine, and it was just part of the complications with her pregnancy. I never told Hannah anything about this.

It had been my intention to visit with Charlotte Kensett, but I was so worked up by these events that I returned to my quarters. After an hour of pacing up and down the room, I concluded there was nothing I could do, and I put in a call to the First Minister of Internal Affairs.

CHAPTER TWENTY-FIVE

BLACKOUT

"How nice to hear from you, Liam," Charlotte said when I finally got through to her. It was a normal workday, and I had to go through her assistant to get to her. "I hope it's not just for a chat. I'm rather busy today."

"I just wanted to ask you if you wanted to meet for lunch."

"That would be most delightful. Unfortunately, I'm rather pressed for time at the moment. Can I take a rain check?"

"Sure. I just wanted to ask you something, but it's not important."

"Oh, Liam, you now have got me positively intrigued. Fine, let's do lunch, but would you mind doing it in my office? I don't really have time to leave. I can order something in for us, say in about an hour?"

"It's a date," I said and instantly regretted using that term yet again.

"Oh, I wish it was Liam," she chuckled. "But let's not go down that road again. I'll see you in an hour."

She didn't wait for a response and instantly hung up. Ten minutes later, I was in the shower again and suddenly wondered why I was doing that. It wasn't like I showered several times a day, and I had decided to make myself as presentable as I could for the intelligence officer. As I got dressed, I started questioning myself about my feelings for her. Was it more than just attraction? There was something definitely sexual about the woman most people called the ice queen, but there was more than that. As I headed to her office, I tried to push the thoughts outside my head, but failed to do so.

I was made to wait in the reception for about fifteen minutes. When the door of her office eventually opened, I was surprised to see Jenna Plural step out, still engaged in conversation with her minister. She looked equally surprised to see me, but smiled and shook my hand.

"Nice work on Mars, Mr Marshall," she said with a smile.

"Thank you. I'm happy to serve the Solar Confederation," I replied politely.

"As long as there's a profit in it for Grant Industries, right?" she said before realising how offensive that comment was. I looked momentarily uncomfortable. "Do you have business with Miss Kensett?" she asked, rapidly changing the subject.

"No, simply a social call. We're having lunch together," I replied.

She couldn't have looked more surprised when I said this. "Well, I hope you enjoy it," she said and departed the room.

I turned towards Charlotte, who was standing in the doorway with her arms folded, leaning against the frame. "Oh, my dear Liam, you're going to get me quite the reputation," she smirked.

"Well, it won't necessarily be a bad one, Charlotte," I replied with a grin, as I followed her into the room.

"Lunch will be arriving soon. I simply can't wait to find out what it is you want to ask me about," she said with a smile and sat back behind her desk. I took the seat in front of her, as she fixed me with one of those steely gazes and a slight impish smile.

"Hannah and I are getting married," I said simply.

I swear a look of disappointment crossed her face, but it quickly switched to her trademark smile. "Congratulations, Liam. When is the happy event taking place?"

"Sometime after you get back from Mars."

"Well, I certainly hope I'm on the invitation list. I understand the Grant's certainly know how to throw a splendid shindig."

"Actually, I wanted to ask you to do more than just come."

Her eyes sparkled behind those large, thick-rimmed glasses as she grinned. "Oh, do tell me more."

"I want you to fill the role of my best man."

To say she looked surprised would be an understatement. The grin disappeared, and her mouth parted slightly, and she just stared back at me for a long moment. "Are you quite serious, Liam?"

"Absolutely. You're the closest thing I have to a best friend, and it'd be an honour for me to have you stand by my side at my wedding."

For the first and only time in my life, I saw her look positively flustered. Indeed, I feel sure that it was the only time in her life that she was ever flustered. "Well, honestly, I'm not sure what to say, Liam."

"Well, yes would be my preferred answer," I smiled at her.

She stared at me. "I think it would be rather awkward, to be honest. I'm afraid I have to say no."

I couldn't hide my disappointment. "Hannah said the same thing, but ultimately doesn't see a problem with it, if that's your concern."

"Hannah is aware of the incident between you and me?" For the first and only time in my entire life, I saw her look quite uncomfortable and, again, as probably the only time in her life she had ever looked this way.

"She worked it out. I assure you, I didn't volunteer the information, but nor was I going to lie to her about it."

"And she has no problem with it?"

"No," I said simply.

And then the true Charlotte Kensett that everyone saw came back, and that fake pleasant smile returned to her face. "Even so, I'm sorry, Liam, but I have to decline."

"I'm sorry to hear that. Is there anything I can do to change your mind?"

"No," she replied, but before I could say anything else, she carried on. "If you don't mind, Liam, I'm actually not feeling very hungry. Do you mind if we skip lunch?" Her intention was clear. She wanted me to leave.

"Sure," I said uneasily, getting to my feet. "I'm sorry. I didn't mean to make you feel uncomfortable."

"Oh, trust me, Liam, I'm perfectly fine. You go and have a good day now." And with that, she picked up a tablet and started to read. I hesitated, wanting to say something, but ultimately turned away and left.

"She said no to you?" Hannah frowned as I told her about the meeting with Charlotte.

"Point blank. Said it would be too awkward."

Hannah sighed. "I'll talk to her about it."

"No, there is no need to," I said, smiling at her. "But I appreciate that you care about this."

She smirked at me and said, "I didn't ask if you wanted me to talk to her about it. I just said I was going to talk to her about it. Charlotte and I have worked together for several years, and while it hasn't always been amicable, we mostly get along rather well. And anyway, you're still attracted to her, and I don't want to come between the two of you."

I frowned. "Do you have any fucking clue how weird that sounds?"

She laughed. "We may not have a conventional relationship, Liam, but we do have a good one." She reached over to me and kissed my cheek. "I love you, and you love me, and the bond between us is as strong as any so-called normal relationship."

"Yes, but we're talking about our wedding."

"I really don't get your point. I'm just going to talk to Charlotte about being your best man. I'm not going to ask her to fuck you on our wedding night." She then smirked at me. "Don't worry, my love, just leave it all to me. I'm good at negotiations."

However, I didn't hear anything about it again, and the subject didn't come up. A couple more weeks went by until it was announced we were on Mars approach. Hannah had packed like she was moving out. I couldn't even fathom why she brought so much over from the Twilight Wanderer. I say Hannah had packed, but obviously, she didn't do it herself. It did seem quite odd that it was actually Hannah leaving, and not to me this time.

No-one in the docking bay who wasn't directly involved with the operations was allowed, so it was literally outside in the corridor that I said goodbye to her. She and Bronwyn would fly down with Jenna via the shuttle, and I thought it was unfair when I saw Charlotte was also leaving. We didn't say anything to each other beyond a few pleasantries.

I returned to my cabin wishing I had access to the facilities of the Twilight Wanderer and not the restrictions of the residential wing of the Spirit of Freedom. Not that the ship was lacking in facilities, but most of them were exclusively for crew.

It was intended for Hannah to be gone for a week. As it turned out, she would only be gone for three days, but those three days were about to turn into an incredible challenge for me.

It was barely six hours later when it happened. I happened to be on the intercom ordering myself a food delivery when everything went out. The intercom went dead. The lights went out, and even the curious hum of the engines fell silent. I was plunged into total darkness, and I don't just mean the dark of night. I mean absolute impenetrable black.

I stood there waiting for emergency power to come on, but it didn't. I immediately grew concerned that there was no other reason for this, than an attack. I felt my way over to the bed, knowing that my phone on the bedside cabinet would at least give me some light, but when I fumbled around and found it and realised it was also dead and, having no connection to the ship, there was only one possible answer. An E.M.P. pulse!

I'm such a creature of habit that I managed to feel around the room to find where my shoulder holster with my firearm was hanging up with my jacket. Strapping it on, I managed to feel my way over to the front door, aware that the controls to open it would no longer work, but knowing no-one in their right mind relied on electronics to keep themselves locked in. I managed to pull open the panel and felt around until I found the small lever, which, with a hard pull, suddenly the door clicked. I then had to put my hands against it and push it aside. The complete darkness was incredibly disorientating as I stepped out into the corridor. I could hear people talking and calling out. This was the residential wing that housed mostly partners of the crew and the children, so as you can understand, there was quite a panic going on, but there was little I could do to help with that. My first thought was to get to the bridge and find out exactly what was going on, but the Spirit of Freedom isn't small, and without the use of the elevators that didn't just go up and down but left and right, it seemed an impossible task to be able to get myself across the ship.

I froze as I heard a dull thudding noise, something hitting the hull. I almost panicked, wondering if we had wandered into some sort of asteroid belt, before it occurred to me there were no asteroid belts near Mars. A troop pod had sealed itself to the hull.

Then, the sound of heating and twisting metal began. The corridor was lit up by a torch cutting through the hull, and I could now see a couple of other people in the corridor with me. To my relief, I noticed one of them was Hailey, who had been staying in quarters near us. As we joined up, the first thing I asked was, "Do you have your gun?"

She nodded and pulled the weapon out from her waistband. I indicated for her to stand on the other side of where they appeared to be cutting through the hull. Suddenly, it went dark again as the torch stopped, but then the whole hallway lit up as a circular chunk of the hull fell through into the hallway.

We waited impatiently, unsure of what to do. Hailey had gone through the Battle of Deep Space, but I had spent the entire event in oblivion and had no experience of shipboard combat. I heard voices. It sounded like a Russian to me, but it could have been any one of the Baltic countries that were siding with the European Union.

Then they came running into the ship. Fully armed in combat fatigues and snap pistols. They were obviously unaware that nearly all the military complement was down on Mars, hidden in the little M.E.T. devices. There was literally no-one to repel them. That was, of course, except for myself and Hailey, and when I brought my gun up to shoot one in the back of the head, she followed my lead. We both fired a second time, before the remaining two could even turn around.

I exchanged my handgun to one of the Peons', since they had extra clips of ammo, and I then relieved one of a belt grenades and flashbangs. Hailey immediately began copying me. Most importantly, we pulled off pairs of light-intensifying visors and put them on. I then approached the one that bore officer insignia and lying next to him, I found a tablet that had a complete layout of the Spirit of Freedom.

"Okay, Hailey, we need to make our way to the bridge. Hopefully, we can meet up with Commodore Addison and join whatever counterattacks she may have planned for this situation."

"Are the Peons gonna be landing all over the ship?" she asked, and I could hear the nervousness in her voice.

"Yes, but if I'm right, they'll be operating under the concept of a blitzkrieg. They will initially be making for key installations such as barrack rooms, armouries, weapon systems, and the like. If we stick to this residential area, it'll be a while before they come down here."

She indicated the bodies on the floor. "But this is the residential area."

"Yes, but I think they're off course, which is why they delayed coming out." I was about to indicate for her to move off but looked back down at the bodies. "We probably should take their flak jackets just to be on the safe side."

We removed the chest armour from two of the corpses, and I helped Hailey with hers before she helped me with mine. We probably looked quite funny dressed in our casual clothes, yet geared up for war. People started to come out into the corridor now that there was light, but I just shouted for them to go back to their rooms and seal the doors. Some complied. Some just stood there looking bewildered, but there wasn't much I could do about that.

We made our way down the corridor along the ship, and it was slow going. Every hundred yards or so, we had to open a sealed door manually. This blocked off sections in case of a hull breach, but now it just slowed us down.

I was surprised by how far we got before we encountered anyone. When I say anyone, I mean the enemy. We did come across crewmen who were floundering around in the dark. They couldn't see us, for we weren't using anything but the dimmest light that permitted the intensifiers to work. Everything around us was lit up in that eerie greenish colour. We didn't engage with anyone and, in fact, didn't even answer when someone spoke to us after hearing the doors where we entered opening. The last thing I wanted was to pick up a retinue of civilians I would ultimately be responsible for.

We were almost two-thirds down towards the front of the ship when I heard foreign voices on the other side of the door. I made Hailey stand back and pulled out one of the flashbangs from my belt. I knew they would hear the moment I clicked the lever to unlock the door, so the moment I did it, I only let it open a couple of inches and tossed the flashbang inside whilst turning my head away and closing my eyes. As soon as I heard the cries from inside, I slid the door open. Flashbangs can hurt the eyes at the best of times, but when people are wearing light-intensifying visors, it goes to the extreme. Four or five Peon troopers that had been heading our way now stood looking dazed, but it wasn't for long, as I then pulled out one of the grenades, hit the button on it, and threw it into the room, shutting the door again immediately. The low-yield explosion was designed to shred flesh but not damage the bulkheads. When I opened the door again, various body parts scattered the room, and I heard Hailey start to wretch next to me. I slipped an arm around her shoulder as I moved her forward.

"Keep your eyes focused ahead. Try not to look," I said, unable to avoid treading in blood and viscera as we proceeded along the corridor. Two more doors later, we were under an emergency escape ladder that headed up to just outside the bridge. Slowly and carefully, as we were approaching what would be an obvious target for the Peons, we began to climb. We continued this way for three levels and stopped just beneath the manhole. Tilting my head, I placed my ear as close as I could, listening out the sounds of activity. I could hear voices, but I couldn't make out whether it was English or something else. I had no choice. I pulled another flash bag from my belt. Slowly, I opened the manhole, trying to be as quiet as possible, ready to throw the device in my hand. It was barely open a crack when I saw the muzzle of a firearm pointing directly at me. "Freeze motherfucker!"

I froze. "I'm Liam Marshall with Grant Security Services. I'm on your side," I said quickly as the manhole cover was opened fully, and we were instructed to climb out. The corridor towards the bridge was still in darkness, but standing around me was the bridge crew. Only two of them were effective combatants, with the rest being techs, pilots, or navigators. I instantly recognised the commanding officer. She was an inch taller than me with hard masculine features.

"Commodore Addison," I acknowledged her.

She immediately indicated for her people to lower their weapons. "I'm afraid we don't offer tours of the bridge, Mr Marshall. Especially in the current circumstances," she said to me rather coolly.

I couldn't help but grin as I helped Hailey climb out of the hatch. "I thought we could help with the counterattack."

"There's not going to be much of a counterattack, Mr Marshall. Most of our troops are down on Mars. Those that remained were in M.E.T. storage."

"What can't we get them out?" I asked, and she just stared at me with a blank expression, leaving me to work it out. I closed my eyes and lowered my head as it came to me. M.E.T.s have multiple backup power facilities trying to cover every possible eventuality; however, they are all obviously based on electricity. The moment the impulse hit, anyone and everyone who was in that damned infernal machine was dead—literally erased from existence.

"So, what now? Do we abandon ship?" I asked.

"I don't have anyone I can spare to escort you to an escape pod, but you're more than willing to try to get there," Addison shrugged.

"But what about you?"

"We have to do everything we can to ensure the Peons do not take this ship," Addison said determinedly. "We may have already lost it, but we have to do everything we possibly can to try and ensure it doesn't become a spoil of war for the enemy."

Chapter Twenty-Six

Takeover

"I always thought the ships were protected against electromagnetic fields?" I asked as I followed Addison onto the bridge.

"They are Mr Marshall. The sun is one of the biggest enemies that we have out here, so we make sure we're shielded from all forms of radiation and other harmful materials."

"But doesn't that therefore mean that...?"

She didn't let me finish as she replied. "Yes, Mr Marshall, someone set it off inside the ship. Either there is a traitor aboard, or they somehow managed to infiltrate the vessel. Personally, I think it's a traitor, because it's highly unlikely anyone would get past the rigid security measures of Charlotte Kensett."

On the bridge, there wasn't a single blinking light, and the pilot was at his station looking around like a blind man. It appeared the number of light-intensifying visors that they had on hand for such occurrences was limited.

"How are you doing, Mr Batty?" Addison asked, and he turned to look vaguely in her direction, clearly unable to see her.

"To be honest, ma'am, this is kind of scary."

"Don't worry, Mr Batty, we're going to hold this position."

"Oh, it's not that, ma'am. I've been in combat multiple times with Admiral Plural. It's this whole not seeing anything that's getting to me."

"Hang tight, Mr Batty. I'll do what I can to make sure this is over quickly." She then turned to me and Hailey. "So, I take it by the fact that you're not leaving to find the escape pods, you're willing to stay on the ground with me and mine?"

I looked to Hailey to answer that first. She nodded.

"I'm at your service, ma'am," she replied.

"Likewise, Commodore," I stated.

"Okay, well, the situation isn't good. We have no communications, and I can't relay instructions to the crew. So, our first priority needs to be liberating them of their communications devices," she then looked at me again. "Am I correct in understanding that you're a former officer of the British Special Air Service?"

"That's correct."

"Well, being that I'm a Navy officer that sat behind the desk most of my life with no experience of either covet or guerrilla tactics, then I turn over my men to you."

Man! I thought, looking at the single two guards that stood at the ready by the door. I looked back at Addison. "Are you asking me to take command?"

"Well, I wouldn't go that far, Mr Marshall, but you're the strategist here."

"Well, I believe the target needs to be the Armory. We need to liberate as much ordinance as possible. The next priority is to get as many people as possible who can hold a gun. I don't care whether they're civilians, techs, or even part of the catering department. If they can shoot a gun, we need them."

"Understood, how do you...?" She stopped as the sound of gunfire came from outside in the corridor. With our weapons out, we headed to the bridge's exit, but being closer, the two guards got there before us, and suddenly fell to the ground as they were punctured with bullets. Immediately, we went to slide the door shut, and I kept myself behind it as bullets pinged off of it.

Looking through the window, I saw the Peons had somehow come up through the elevator shaft, and every member of the bridge crew that was still outside, lay dead or dying. One of the Peons stepped over a crew member who was trying to crawl her way across the floor. He simply lowered his weapon and shot her in the back of the head, then looking up at me, our eyes met. His troops were still coming out of the elevator shaft until there were at least half a dozen standing in that corridor. The Peon just stood in front of the door staring at me, and I stared back. It was made of reinforced mercuranium and would require an explosive powerful enough to destroy half the deck if he was to get it open.

Looking over his shoulder, I saw them hauling up generators, which no doubt they had brought from their own ship. One of their techs started wiring up to the elevator, no doubt wanted to power it. The person at the door didn't speak, didn't move, and just stood there staring at me like some psycho in a movie.

Addison approached me with a sigh. "Well, it looks like it's game over, Mr Marshall. If you follow any of the good religions, express a preference."

"I'm supposed to be getting married in the next couple of weeks," I said regretfully. "I really don't plan on missing that." I turned to look at her. "Whilst I hardly call myself an expert on spaceships, I do find it unlikely you don't have an escape route from this bridge."

She narrowed her eyes at me. "Are you suggesting we abandon the bridge?"

"Only when the alternative is dying on that bridge. They're going to take it anyway. At least a tactical withdrawal is warranted."

She nodded, then reaching down, she pulled one of the light-intensifying visors off of a dead guard and went over to Mr Batty. She reached out and took his hand, startling him for a moment, and she placed the visor over his head.

"Okay, let's go." She led us through to the captain's ready room and went over to a panel in the wall. She pulled down a small lever at the back of the wall and opened it. We stepped into a narrow passage where only one person at a time could move and came out into what looked like a storage room. There was rack upon rack of E.M.U. suits were hanging up in lockers by a large airlock. Opposite this, was a door that led out into the same corridor where the Peons were. I stepped up to the door and looked through the small window. They were either busy working on the generator or working out how to open the bridge door, completely unaware that we were coming up behind them now.

I unfastened a flashbang once more, and swiftly opening the door, I tossed it out, turning my head away, before rushing out with Addison behind me, firing shots into the backs of the enemy. The tech working on the generator was closer and grabbed for my gun, but I swiftly spun around and punched him so hard in the face that he went flying back down the elevator shaft with a scream. I then pulled open the control panel of the door we had just come out of and jammed an empty gun clip under the emergency lever and broke it.

"That'll only slow them down getting access to the bridge," I said with a shrug when Addison looked at me questioningly. We then headed over to the manhole I originally had come out of, finishing off anyone that wasn't quite dead with a single shot as I got there. "You better go first. You know the ship better than I do," I told Addison, and she stepped ahead of me.

"Where exactly do you expect us to go, Mr Marshall?" she asked as she slipped down the ladder.

"As I said, Armory would be a good start," I said as I followed her. Hailey had Mr Batty go next, before following him down. We went down a couple of levels before Addison jumped off the ladder onto the deck. We waited carefully for Hailey and Batty to catch up before heading back out to the corridor with our weapons primed. I checked my magazine, and seeing I only had two bullets left in it, I switched it out for a fresh clip. I can't honestly say how I was feeling during all this time. In the army, I was trained to switch off all thoughts and feelings beyond that of the requirements of the mission.

"I think you should stay here for a minute," I said. "I'm going to climb into the ventilation shaft and move ahead. Just scope everything out before we move forward."

"If you don't make it back in 5 minutes, I'm gonna assume you're dead," was all Addison said to me.

"Please be careful, Mr Marshall. I don't want to lose you." Hailey spoke for the first time in quite a while, and I smiled at her, placing a hand reassuringly on her shoulder.

"That's always the plan." I then turned back to Addison and asked, "You don't by any chance have a knife on you, do you?"

"I'm the Commodore of the fleet, Mr Marshall. I have a pen if that will help you," she said sarcastically.

"I have a pocketknife. It's not much. I don't think it's any good as a weapon," said Mr Batty.

"That would be perfect, Sir," I said, holding out my hand as he fished it out of his back pocket and handed it to me. I flicked it open and used the point to start unscrewing the nearby vent. It was quite high up, and when I pulled the grill away, Addison leaned back against the wall and cupped her hands together to make a stirrup for me to climb up into the vent. It may be obvious that this was a potential weakness in ship security, but in fact, they were covered in motion sensors and cameras, which now were totally inoperable. I made my way ahead, scoping out the corridors as I passed over the grills. All seemed to be clear, but as I was about to turn back, I heard some voices. The faint echo indicated they were also in the ventilation shaft, so I turned off in that direction. I saw a light up ahead of me and two small figures leaning over a grill, a boy and a girl—clearly teenagers. The boy was dressed in casual pants and a t-shirt. The girl was wearing a dungaree one-piece with shorts over a pink flowery shirt. The boy gripped a lighter with a naked flame as they peered down into whatever room it was beneath them.

I was about to call out to them and to get them to come with me. Not that I wanted to be saddled with a couple of kids, but I could hardly leave them here, but then I heard the girl speak.

"It should not take as long, Kaden. We can get in, get the food, and get out."

I froze, completely confused at the sound of her French accent. What the fuck were the Peons doing bringing children on board, and why the hell were they in the ventilation shaft? I couldn't fathom it, but rather than reveal myself, I backed away and returned to Addison and the others. I didn't mention the children in the ventilation shaft as I didn't want further distraction. I informed Addison the way ahead was clear, and we continued to move forward, heading down towards the Armory. But we were barely there when everything went to shit. I'm not entirely sure where they came from to this day, but as I was unlocking one of the corridor doors, a voice called out from behind us. We hadn't really been paying attention because we were fairly certain that there was no-one between us and the bridge we had left. The words were in either Dutch or German. I couldn't tell which. I just knew it wasn't French.

I spotted several Peons with weapons raised at us. There was no chance, and slowly, I raised my hands, and the others followed suit. So much for our escape. We were disarmed and led back to the bridge. Somehow, the Peons had got the door open and had full control of the area. Makeshift lights had been set up, and we removed our visors. A grim-looking officer stood in the centre of the room, overseeing things in the light blue uniform of the French army. He turned to face us as we were led inside, hands placed behind our heads. He looked straight out Addison with a smile, and I recognised him as the man who had stared at me through the window.

"Oh, Commodore, I have been looking for you!" he said in his thick French accent.

"Sorry to make you wait," she replied sarcastically.

He chuckled lightly. "I would like the security codes to your communications, if you please."

"I bet you would. But it's not likely that I'm going to give them to you."

"Oh, mademoiselle, don't be difficult. I just want to have a little conversation with your whore mistress down on Mars," he said.

"Well, considering you can use your own frequencies to communicate with her, I'm thinking you intend to pretend you're one of us," she responded.

"Oh, Commodore, how astute of you. However, I will have those codes. Even if it takes all my resources to bring it out of you, you will talk eventually, but you can save yourself a lot of pain and trouble by giving it to me now."

What happened next will forever be burned into my soul. Addison lunged at a guard and successfully managed to grab his weapon. The other guards immediately reacted, bringing up their weapons towards her, but to my utter surprise, rather than turn it on them, she placed the gun in her mouth and fired.

I admit I literally jumped out of my skin and stepped away, only to be grabbed by a guard and held in position.

"What the fuck!" I cried out as her body fell lifelessly to the ground. That was certainly some devotion to the Solar Confederation. There was no doubt with the various uses of torture and drugs, he would have wrung the information from her that he wanted. She'd just given up her life to save Jenna Plural. It took me a few moments to realise Hayley was screaming at my side, until one of the guards cuffed her around the back of the head, forcing her to stop. I looked up at the French officer, who I'm fairly certain was swearing in his own language under his breath.

He turned and looked at the rest of us before ordering something in French to one of his technicians. He approached each of us and turned and shone the light from some device in our eyes. He then looked down at the tablet before looking back at his commanding officer. When he spoke, all I could understand was when he said mine and Hayley's name and then, 'Les Industries Grant'. He then indicated Mr Batty, and I heard him say Neville Batty and some reference to the ship.

The officer looked at Hailey and me. "It looks like your lucky day. I'm under specific orders not to harm anyone from Grant Industries. Please go with my guards while I have a conversation with Mr Batty here. He has some information he wants to give me."

I glanced at the nervous pilot, but there was very little I could do about the situation, and with Hailey, we went ahead with the two guards. The elevator was now working, and we went down to the bowels of the ship. I realised we were heading towards the cargo bays. When we stopped outside of one, the door opened, and a mass of voices reached my ears. Stepping in, I realised that this was where they were holding the civilian contingent of the ship that'd been rounded up. Dozens of terrified people were sitting on the floor or wandering around, looking lost and dispossessed. Several guards stood against the walls at various points, watching everyone carefully. The guards who led us in didn't say anything. In fact, they didn't even come in, and the door closed behind us. I couldn't help but wonder how the lights were still active in here, and it wouldn't be until later that I realised that they had set up generators at various points around the ship.

"Well," Hailey said with a sigh. "What do we do now?"

I shrugged. "We thank God that they didn't kill us and pray that they don't change their mind about that," I said, as I joined the group and sat down on the floor. Hailey stared down at me, smiled, shrugged, and sat down next to me.

Chapter Twenty-Seven

The Return of Jenna Plural

I would like to say that I managed to turn the situation around and save the day like the hero of some movie, but I didn't. It wasn't like I could rally a bunch of civilians to sacrifice their lives, overtaking the guards. All I would have achieved was getting everyone killed.

We weren't allowed to move from the centre of the room, and we were under constant observation. The only time we could leave was once every few hours when we were escorted in ones and twos to go to the bathroom. Most of the time, I sat in quiet conversation with Hailey, who, I found out, grew up in San Diego, CA, before getting a job with Grant Security Services. She was twenty-five, although thanks to also spending a lot of time in the M.E.T. was actually born thirty years ago. She had been posted to the Twilight Wanderer two years into her service and had remained aboard when the solar system went to shit. Her duties had been pretty mundane, until Hannah and Bronwyn had negotiated a contract to turn the ship into support services for the Solar Confederation, at which time she was transferred to the newly established private Police Department, during which time she would eventually encounter me.

We managed to get some sleep by removing our jackets and rolling them up into pillows, and they even had the courtesy of dimming the lights, as the evening came. When I awoke the following morning, the first thing I saw was Hailey sitting there cross-legged next to me, looking down at me. I was momentarily startled, though it took me a while to remember where I was.

"Well, good morning," I said without getting up. "What's the matter?"

"Oh, nothing," she said, smiling softly at me. "I was just sitting here thinking how much I appreciate what you did for me. When Hannah Grant fired me, that was pretty much my life over. Those refugee ships are overcrowded, conditions are dire, and you barely have room to move. You literally sit there all day waiting to get a very small ration of food. Getting out of there without marketable skills is virtually impossible."

"You have skills, Hailey. You're not just your average security officer. You're licensed to be armed, and that carries a considerable amount of responsibility."

"Yeah, but there's only one company that can employ anyone in the Solar Confederation, and Miss Grant blacklisted me."

I sighed. "I have to admit Hannah can be impulsive, but you have to understand she has no concept of what it's like to be a working-class stiff, like the rest of us. All I did was put right something I believe she did wrong."

"You stood up to Hannah Grant. From my understanding, nobody does that."

I chuckled at this. "For the most part, that's true, but there's a couple of us that put our necks on the line."

"But how is it you managed this without the repercussions?" She frowned.

"I'm engaged to her, Hailey. She's my fiancée." I was surprised she didn't already know this. I thought it was common knowledge, but clearly it wasn't.

"Oh shit!" Hailey's eyes widened as she looked at me. "Are you serious?"

I laughed at this. "Why? Don't you think I'm good enough for her?"

"No, it's not that, Mr Marshall. I just don't think she's good enough for you." As soon as she said it, she flushed and backtracked. "Sorry, that was inappropriate of me to say."

I reached out and took her hand in mine as I sat up. "It's not a problem. I'm certainly not going to say anything to Hannah about what you say to me. I know full well what Hannah is like and admit she has her flaws. I'm also aware she's an incredibly hard person to work with or for."

She hesitated, biting her lower lip before saying, "Wouldn't you be more suited to someone more in your station of life?"

"What do you mean?"

She flushed a little deeper. "I mean someone you have more in common with. She's an upper-class rich girl and you're a security officer," she looked away, clearly embarrassed about something.

I grinned. "You mean someone I have more in common with, like you?"

She looked away from me. "Forget I said anything. I'm just being silly."

I reached up and took hold of her chin, gently turning her head back towards me. Slowly, I leaned up on an elbow and kissed her, and at first, she went with it before suddenly pulling away. "What the fuck?!"

Before I could respond to that, I was distracted by some Peon officer suddenly coming through the door and speaking to the guard nearest to her. That guard then hurried out the door whilst the officer went around, sending other guards out until a third of our guards remained. The officer then headed back out.

"Something's going on," I said quietly. It had been unnecessary to say anything, as she clearly saw it, too, and her eyes narrowed with concentration as she tried to work it out.

"What do you think it is?" She whispered.

"That officer looked quite harassed. My guess would be that they have a problem. My guess is someone somewhere has started the counterattack."

"What do we do?"

I shrugged. "We wait, but be ready to move when there's an opportunity."

That opportunity came sooner than I expected, for the next time that door opened, everything happened incredibly fast. Gunfire rang out before I even worked out who it was, and the surrounding guards began to fall as my eyes alighted on Jenna and a couple of troopers I didn't recognise. "Okay, boys and girls, we are taking this ship back. I want the civilians to stay in here. Any crew are to come with me."

Technically, Hailey and I were civilians, but as Jenna's eyes fell upon me, she smiled.

"Except you, Mr Marshall, you're with me." Hailey and I got up exceptionally fast and headed over to her. Jenna glanced at Hailey and then looked at me.

"This is my partner," I quickly explained, and Jenna simply nodded in response and led us out into the hall. Another trooper was there handing out assault rifles. "Do you two know how to use one of those, Mr Marshall?"

"I certainly do, Ma'am, but I thought they were dangerous to use on board a ship."

"Not on this ship." She then turned to start separating her crew members into different teams to go in different directions. Hailey moved in close beside me.

As the crew members started to move out, Jenna turned back to me. "You two with me, and Thompson, come on."

The four of us broke into a run, with Jenna at the lead, weapons primed and ready.

"When did you get back on board? You're not supposed to be here till the end of the week?"

"My daughter managed to get a message through to us from the bridge," the officer, who I would find out was Abigail Thompson, responded, sounding quite proud.

"Your daughter, is she a member of the crew?"

"No, Mr Marshall, Bridgette is a sixteen-year-old schoolgirl who is incredibly resourceful," Jenna said with a chuckle.

I remembered the girl I'd seen in the ventilation shaft. "She wouldn't happen to be French, would she?"

"Yes, she would!" Thompson suddenly grabbed me by the sleeve and spun me around to face her. "Do you know where she is?"

"I believe I saw her in the ventilation shaft yesterday, but since then, I have no idea."

There is nothing worse than the look of distress in a mother's eyes when she's worried about her child, and my heart went out to her, but there wasn't anything I could do.

"We'll find her, Thompson. I promise you that," Jenna called back, not having stopped. We ran to catch up with her.

"Is Hannah okay?" I called after her.

"She's safe, Mr Marshall. Don't worry. She's back on board the ship." A part of me wanted to go find her, but my sense of duty kept me following the Admiral.

"Where are we going?" Hailey asked.

"We're taking the bridge," Jenna called back just as I reached her side to use the emergency opening on another corridor door while I covered her. She slid it open, and at the instant sight of blue uniforms, I opened fire with Abigail Thompson stepping up beside me to do the same.

As the echoes of the gunfire died, I heard Jenna talking quietly to one side. Turning, I saw her holding her finger up to a hidden communicator in her ear.

"How did you get that working?" I asked.

"I had it before I came back aboard the ship," she said, stepping through the doorway. "Okay, I'll have all the people in position on the other side of the ship approaching the bridge, too. They've come under heavy fire, but I'm making good progress. We have to double-time it, if we're going to meet at the same time."

Once more, we broke into a run, only slowing down and taking caution if we had to change direction or go through another door. We finally reached the hatch I had originally gone up in, and being open, Jenna and Thompson went first with me, then Hailey followed behind. Before I got out, I heard Thompson scream.

"*Bridgette!*"

At the top, I saw a thick trail of blood that ran from the bridge over to where the girl I'd seen in the ventilation shaft was lying. I went cold as I was certain she was dead as her mother knelt beside her, but as I climbed out, I saw the girl's head move, and her eyes flicker open. A slight smile crossed her face as she looked up at her mother.

I didn't waste time and headed into the bridge to grab an emergency medical kit off the wall. As I turned away, I was startled to see the dead body of Neville Batty lying on the floor with his brain spread out across the room. I turned back to the door and saw Jenna standing there staring at him.

"The fucking Peon cunts are going to pay for this," she said to no-one in particular. "Trust me, they're gonna fucking pay."

I simply pushed past her and rushed to Bridgette and Thompson's side.

The girl was no longer conscious, and pulling out Batty's pen knife, I cut the straps of the little dungarees and gently pushed Thompson aside with my elbow, as I pulled them down and lifted the bloody shirt. She had lost a lot of blood, and I'm no medic, but I was convinced there was no way she could possibly survive this, but I was going to damn well try. I could hear Jenna talking on her radio again as I worked on the child.

"Have you got control of any medical facilities?" she was asking, but I couldn't hear the response. "Doctor Cooper? Good to hear you. What is your location?" Another pause: "Okay, we're on our way there. Be prepared for a sixteen-year-old girl with major bullet trauma to the stomach. She's lost a lot of blood and may need a possible infusion." There was another pause, and then she said. "Plural to Pentauk. Audra, I need you to disengage and ensure a clear path between the bridge and medical bay six on deck twelve." She then approached me and looked down, placing a reassuring hand on Thompson's shoulder as I sprayed the sealant over the wadding, stopping the flow of blood. "We're going to do everything we can, Thompson. Trust me on that."

I knelt back, unable to do anymore, but suddenly tensed as the elevator started to move. Hailey and Jenna bought up their weapons, only to lower them as soon as they saw two men in white tunics with a gurney. I didn't wait for them to come off the elevator, and I lifted Bridgette into my arms and stepped into the elevator, placing her down. Thompson came on, followed by Plural. "I want to ask you a favour, Mr Marshall." Plural said. "I'm going to break protocol here because I should stay here and keep the bridge secure. But that girl means more to me than you could possibly imagine, and I can't leave her side until I know she's okay. Will you and Hailey stay here until you're relieved by Pentauk?"

"Only if you promise to inform me how she's doing," I replied as I stepped off the elevator, and Jenna smiled slightly.

"That I can do, Mr Marshall."

I saw something that day very few people have ever seen as the elevator descended. I watched Jenna as she looked down at Bridgette and held onto her hand. A single tear ran down her cheek, and she quickly wiped it away as she disappeared from my view.

I turned back to Hailey, and together, we went back onto the bridge. Hailey removed her jacket, which she laid down over the head of Mr Batty, and then slumped into the copilot seat, which was turned to face the door.

"Please tell me it's over, Mr Marshall."

"I wish I could, but personally, I'm not going to feel happy until this ship is powered up again and helmed by Solar Confederation personnel," I said with a sigh, as I sat down in the pilot seat beside her. I placed my elbows on my knees and buried my head into my hands before I realised they were still covered in the blood of Bridgette Toussaint. We sat in silence, neither of us knowing what to do or say, only getting up and grabbing our weapons when we heard the elevator coming up once more, but looking out the door, I saw Pentauk, who I didn't know at the time, enter with various crewmen that took up positions. She approached me and gave me a mocking salute and a smile. "Consider yourself relieved, Mr Marshall."

"Do you have any idea where I would find Hannah Grant?"

"We've secured the residential wing. She should be back at her quarters." I nodded and made for the door, but she called me back. "Jenna told me to give you this." She handed me the small ball bearing-like, white plastic device, which I immediately lifted and popped into my ear.

"Thank you."

I looked over to Hailey and said, "Are you coming?"

She smiled back at me and shook her head. "No. Today's been so stressful enough without meeting Hannah Grant again."

A smile turned into a grin, and I just grinned back and turned away.

Although Audra Pentauk had told me the way was safe, I didn't let my guard down as I headed back to the residential quarters. Halfway there, my radio kicked in.

"Plural to Marshall."

"This is Marshall. Go ahead."

"I'm pleased to be able to tell you that Bridge is going to make it. The Doc's working on her now, but he's very confident that she's going to be fine."

"Well, that's good news on an otherwise shitty day, Admiral," I said, unable to hide the relief from my voice. I didn't know this Bridgette, but I felt guilty that I hadn't helped her when I'd seen her in the ventilation shaft. My war-induced prejudice hadn't permitted me even to consider there could be a Peon who wasn't an enemy. However, it is equally possible that my interference could have meant she never got the message down to Jenna Plural on

Mars, forcing her to return with troops. Although, that didn't make me feel better about my decision.

When I arrived back at the quarters, they were locked, and when I keyed in the number to open it, it remained locked. I pressed the buzzer, and a familiar voice came from it.

"Who is it?" Hannah asked.

"It's room service here to turn down your bed," I said, grinning to myself.

"You're an asshole," Hannah chuckled as the door unlocked and slid open. She positively threw herself against me, kissing me hard and holding me tight. "I thought you were dead again, you fucker!" she said as she pulled herself away from me, and before I realised it, someone else suddenly grabbed me and hugged me. Bronwyn was almost as pleased to see me as Hannah, and both started talking to me at once about their adventures. I was barely listening. The adrenaline was starting to wane, and a feeling of exhaustion was coming over me.

"As much as I'm happy to see you too, I really need to lie down. This has been one seriously fucked couple of days."

Hannah gave me one of her pouty looks, but didn't protest as I headed towards the bedroom, and they both followed me. I didn't bother to change. I just lay straight down on it.

"Those sheets are certainly ruined," Hannah muttered with a laugh.

"Oh, I think you can afford to get new ones," I said with a weary smile and fell asleep.

I only managed to get a couple of hours of sleep because I'd forgotten to remove the communications device from my ear before I lay down. A call came over the line.

"Hey, Marshall."

I was startled awake and surprised by the informality of the Admiral. "You might want to tell Hannah she's an auntie."

It took me a moment to realise what she was talking about, and I sat up.

"Stacey?"

"Yeah. I know she and Stacey have some issue going on, but I thought she had a right to know."

"Thank you. I appreciate you telling me. I'll let her know."

"No problem."

The line went dead, and I climbed out of bed and headed into the living quarters. Hannah and Bronwyn were chatting about something or other, but looked up as I entered. "I'm sorry, did we wake you?"

"No, Admiral Plural called me to let me know your sister's had her baby."

Hannah quickly got to her feet. "Is everything okay with it?"

I shrugged. "I assume so. Plural didn't say there were any problems."

"Is it a boy or a girl?"

I shrugged again. "I didn't think to ask."

"You know, mate, but you can be ten tonnes of useless sometimes," she said, before turning to her friend. "Think about what I said, Bronwyn. I have to go see my sister."

"Give me a minute to get changed, and I'll come with you," I said.

"No. If it's okay with you. I'd rather do this alone." And without another word, she headed hurriedly out of the door.

I looked towards Bronwyn, who sat staring at the floor deep in thought. "What was that about?" I asked, taking a seat in the armchair opposite her.

She looked up at me, clearly still in thought. "Huh? Oh, nothing, don't worry about it."

"If she's upset you, I'll have words with her."

She sighed, clearly pondering what to say before finally giving in.

"Hannah has offered to make me a full partner in Grant Industries. Including giving me fifty per cent of the shares she owns. She says that I put in more work than she does to make this company work, and it's only right that she makes me an equal partner."

"Well, that's excellent news. It's not like it's going to put her in the poor house. And from what I've seen, you deserve it."

She frowned questioningly at me. "Do you really think so?"

"You make the perfect team, Bron. You're the organizer, the one who gets things done and knows how to get them done. Hannah has the ideas and comes up with the policy. I think she's more concerned about what happens with the company if anything happens to her and wants to make sure it's in safe hands. I don't honestly think she's just doing this for you."

When Hannah returned, she didn't say anything about her encounter with Stacey, and it was one of those situations that you don't put pressure on it.

There was one more scare before we returned to the fleet. For a while, it was thought we could not regain control of the Freedom, and Jenna even started an evacuation. With both Bridgette and Lieberman having gone into details on that situation, I won't go into them here. Nor will I go into the details about the falling out between Jenna and Stacey because I wasn't a witness to it, and, again, that tale has been related. The death of Dodgson was a shock to me, and the real truth about that was only understood when, almost a year later, documents she had written came out, and the true level of her insanity was revealed. The exposure of Tracker as the traitor gave me a delightful 'I told you so' moment the next time I encountered Charlotte.

There was considerable tension on board the ship as it made its way to reunite with the fleet. But when the day came that we could once again transfer over to the Twilight Wanderer, Hannah immediately called a press conference. In a statement broadcast across the fleet and out into the solar system, she made the formal announcement that Bronwyn Donovan was now a full partner in the company. She concluded her statement by stating that henceforth, Grant Industries would be known as the Corporation.

There was a memorial service held for those who died both on Mars and during the assault on The Freedom. Emma Dodgson was listed as having died heroically, and I was surprised that she was committed to the deep with the others with a clean record and full military honours.

Jenna led the services and gave special mention to Commodore Claire Addison and Lieutenant Neville Batty, with whom she had worked closely for a very long time. As the bodies were ejected into space, I squeezed Hannah's hand, feeling a multitude of emotions run through me. I hated this war, and I hated the losses of good people. She looked up at me, smiled and held onto my arm. She rested her head against it. As the service drew to an end, we slipped away quietly without drawing attention to ourselves. This was a day for the dead, and not an opportunity for paparazzi to click photographs of my fiancée dressed in black.

Chapter Twenty-Eight

Weddings and Reconciliations

C harlotte Kensett slapped me hard around the face.

"Oh, my goodness, Liam, would you just stand still!"

I complied, and she continued tying the bow tie around my neck. "I'm sorry, but it's not every day that I get married."

"Yes, well, it is not every day I agreed to be the best man with someone I've been intimate with," she replied quite curtly.

"What made you change your mind?" I asked.

"Miss Grant took away my concerns," she said, actually finished, and stood back and inspected her handiwork. "Or should I start getting used to saying, Miss Marshall?"

I chuckled. "She may have opted to go for the old-fashioned walking down the aisle type wedding, but she's not that old-fashioned. We'll both be keeping our last names. To be honest, I'm surprised you took your husband's name. You don't come across as a traditionalist."

"Oh, in my case, Liam, it was a necessity of my work and situation. I had to lose the name Willard and do what I could to hide my former identity," she said like that was an everyday occurrence.

"You know, Charlotte, you should find yourself a good partner. Despite your reputation, you're a good person."

"Oh, I don't think so, Liam. I sold my soul to the devil a long time ago, and he's a jealous master," she said, sighing wistfully.

I found myself looking into those deep brown eyes shielded from me by those large, thick-framed glasses, and she looked back at me with a slightly questioning look. "You're an incredibly beautiful and intriguing woman, Charlotte. Had I met you before Hannah, then..."

She waved a dismissive hand toward me and turned away. "Oh, you couldn't handle me, Liam, and you know it." She reached over to the chair, picked up my jacket, and handed it to me. "You're going to struggle enough dealing with Hannah Grant. She is quite a dominant force, and in any disagreement, the only compromise will be to do it her way. She has that stubborn Grant pride, just like her sister."

"Oh, I'm well aware of what I'm getting into here, Charlotte, but I've loved that girl for the longest time now."

She gave me a weak smile, and looking down a little watch, she said, "Well, Liam, it's time to go."

I let out a nervous sigh and followed her out of my quarters.

It was four weeks after the events on Mars and the taking of The Freedom. The fleet was reunited just outside the detection range from Mars. Jenna wanted to be prepared if we needed to return to the planet.

No doubt you can imagine the wedding service wasn't to be a small, quiet affair and was much in keeping with the extreme wealth of the bride. The Twilight Wanderer had many function suites for many events of all types, but there was none to the scale of what Hannah had planned for. She had a docking bay cleared and completely redecorated. Even the walls had been repainted from dull grey to a creamy white and bordered with elaborate moulding that looked like it came out of the Victorian era. Over 600 chairs were laid out for guests, and there would have been more, had there been capacity. At the end of the aisle, between the chairs, an archway had been erected covered with fresh flowers. This, I must add, was quite a luxury, considering the growing of decorative flowers was hardly on the Confederation's list of much needed agriculture.

Anyone who was anyone had been invited. From ship captains, corporate executives, and senior civil servants. As I entered, I couldn't help but notice that Jenna's retinue had taken seats on my side of the congregation. This was a sweet courtesy, as I had no family or friends to invite, and all of Hannah's side was filled with personnel from the Hanwyn Corporation. However, as Charlotte and I approached the front, I smiled at Hailey, who was on my side, seated a couple of rows behind Jenna. Seated next to the Admiral was an Asian woman that I had only seen once before, but assumed she was the now recently announced replacement for Claire Addison, Tomiko Sakamoto. I saw more familiar faces, such as Audra Pentauk. As we reached the front, I turned and smiled at everyone before taking my seat and rubbing my sweaty palms on my thighs. I'm quite sure the sight of me with Charlotte Kensett raised a few eyebrows. The interstellar woman of mystery was quite the enigma amongst those who knew her, but she either didn't notice the stares or she was exceptionally good at ignoring them. Considering Charlotte observed almost everything to the most minute detail, I prefer to think it was the latter.

The ten minutes I waited seemed like hours, and when the music began, everyone fell silent and rose to their feet. Jenna got up and walked confidently over to the archway and stood behind it. I found myself staring at her, terrified to turn around and look at my bride. Jenna's eyes met mine, and a slight smile crossed her face, as she noticed what was possibly terror in my eyes. She then looked down the aisle and nodded in the direction indicating for me to turn around. I did.

My eyes almost fell out as they alighted on the most beautiful creature ever to traverse the solar system. She wore a cream-coloured gown that hung off her shoulders and trailed back many feet. The front of her dress came just down below her knees, and she wore pure white heels that rivalled those of Charlotte's, albeit the red carpet silenced any clip-clop of the heels. As her eyes met mine, a smile of pure happiness crossed her face, and they fought back a tear as I looked at the woman I would spend the rest of my life with.

As she reached the front of the arch, it was only then that I noticed Bronwyn was just behind her in a bright purple dress. On the other side of her was Stepanchikov, looking very strange in a similar dress. She had always dressed in the most masculine fashion, and it was rather bizarre seeing her in a frock with makeup. When they reached the front, both Hannah and Jenna looked at me, and I just stared at them until Charlotte pushed me forward, bringing me out of my daydream. I went up and stood next to Hannah, and Charlotte fell in beside me. As I took Hannah's hands in mine, I barely heard Jenna's words as she addressed the congregation.

"It has long been a misconception, that the captain of a ship can officiate the ceremony of marriage. However, to my delight at being asked to perform this service, I think it's a tradition the Solar Confederation should adopt. We stand at the birth of a nation, and we need to identify ourselves with our own traditions and our own way of doing things." Then she grinned. "I admit there is a selfishness in this decision. I'm absolutely delighted to play my part in the union of Mr Liam Marshall and Miss Hannah Grant. Please be seated."

I could hear the chairs scraping as people took their seats once more, but at this time, I still couldn't take my eyes off the most amazing woman I had ever known.

"Marriage is a sacred bond, but over the generations, what we have left has, sadly, become less common. It is a tradition and a union that I very much approve of, and I hope today, many of you will follow the example of these fine people before me. Today, you witness the joining of Liam and Hannah in matrimony." She then looked at Bronwyn. "Who gives Hannah Grant in their lawful duty as a guardian?"

Bronwyn took a step forward, but before she spoke, a voice in the back of the congregation said, "I do."

A murmuring went up, and everyone started to look around. At the back of the crowd, I saw a man with blonde hair standing holding a baby, but it wasn't him who'd spoken. The short, dark-haired woman at his side left him and walked up the aisle. A spattering of whispered conversation went up around the room. As she reached the front to stand by Bronwyn, she looked up at her.

"If that's okay with you, mate?" she asked.

Bronwyn smiled back at her. "Absolutely," she replied and stepped back. The woman turned back to Jenna.

"I, Stacefield Ellen Grant, of the most excellent town of Wagga Wagga, being the sister of little Miss Snooty of Melbourne, Hannah Louise Grant, give her to Liam Maddox Marshall in marriage, and may God help him."

During all this, I had been staring at her in utter surprise, but when I now looked back at Hannah, I saw a beaming smile on her face and tears running down her cheeks. I looked at Jenna, who also had a smile, but I could not help but notice that neither she nor Stacey's eyes met for the entire proceedings. "And who gives Liam Maddox Marshall in the lawful duty as guardian?"

Charlotte stepped up. "I, Charlotte Kensett, give Liam Maddox Marshall to Hannah Louise Grant in marriage."

At that point, Charlotte returned to her seat, and Stacey headed back towards the blonde-haired man and the baby. Jenna then turned to look at me.

"Do you, Liam Maddox Marshall, take Miss Hannah Louise Grant to be your lawfully wedded partner to honour and respect throughout the trials of your life until death do you part?"

I found myself almost struggling to choke out the words as I looked back at my soon-to-be wife, and then, in barely a whisper, I said. "I do."

Jenna then repeated herself for Hannah and I almost as sobbed as she responded positively.

"Having performed the legal duty required of me, I now pronounce you bonded in matrimony. May the skies be clear for you."

I just stood there staring dumbly at my wife as she stared back expectantly until Charlotte nudged me.

"Oh, my goodness, Liam, this is where you're supposed to kiss her."

My brain came back to reality, and I kissed her softly, as a round of cheers and applause went up around us.

I don't remember much about the next hour or so, and my earliest memory after the event was the reception. This was to be informal, with no head tables or anything like that and a buffet of the finest foods the circumstances had permitted. Tables were laid out, and a bar was erected. For a while, we were separated as we circulated the room, thanking our guests for coming and doing all the social norms. Finally tired of being parted from my wife, I headed it through the busy throng towards her. She turned as I approached, smiled at me, and started heading my way, but then she noticed something and paused, waiting for me to catch up. I followed her gaze and saw Stacey Grant standing there with the blonde-haired man, but this time she was holding the baby. Hannah looked at me, and I nodded, and we both headed over to them. Hannah had a huge smile on her face, but when Stacey saw her, she didn't reciprocate, and she looked quite uncomfortable.

"Thank you."

These were the first words out of Hannah's mouth when we joined them.

Stacey just shrugged and introduced her partner as Deacon Cooper. I'd heard the name before, but I couldn't place it at the time. It was the doctor that Jenna had spoken to about Bridgette back on the Freedom. Hannah and I shook hands with him in turn and shared a few pleasantries. Then Hannah turned back to Stacey. She looked down at the baby and reached out her arms. "Can I hold her?"

Stacey shrugged like she couldn't care less and handed the baby over to her. "She's your niece."

Hannah bounced the child against her chest and made the typical cooing noises before looking back up at Stacey. "I appreciate you coming and what you did."

Stacey shrugged that off like it wasn't important. "Hey, I just heard there was gonna be free grog and that you were picking up the tab, so I thought, 'what the fuck'?"

Hannah could not help but grin, and handing the baby back, she gave her the finger. "Fuck you, Stacey Grant."

Tucking the baby under her arm, Stacey reciprocated the gesture. "Fuck you, Hannah Grant." But there was a slight grin behind the glare she gave her sister. "By the way, I need a ship."

"Okay," Hannah nodded.

"To go get Bridgette and go find Harper," Stacey added as if Hannah didn't get the point.

"I understand that," Hannah replied as she grabbed a glass of champagne from the tray of a passing waiter.

"Not just any old shitty ship. I want top-of-the-range with big motherfucking guns and the latest coffee machine."

"Of course."

"And a top crew would be good."

"Absolutely. My best people."

"It better be."

"It will be. One condition, though."

"That is?"

"I get Harper, Tuesdays and Thursdays. Five till ten."

Stacey pondered this. "No trying to turn her into a stuck-up little princess with a delusion of superiority?"

"I pinky promise."

"Okay, my people will talk to your people."

"You have people?"

"No, but it sounded good. I'm hungry. Come on, Coop, let's go find some grub." And with that, they headed off, whilst Dr Deacon Cooper shot us an apologetic look for Stacey's behaviour.

EPILOGUE

HANNAH GRANT

S ix Weeks Later

  I don't remember his name. I don't suppose it really matters. I met him in one of my casinos when I had gone out for the night. Liam had been away on board the Spirit of Freedom for almost two weeks with Stepanchikov and Bronwyn.

To say that I'd been getting bored would be an understatement. I didn't gamble often, and it didn't have quite the joy it gave most people, considering it didn't really matter if I lost, and generally, I did. The roulette wheel was my personal favourite, so unlike Stacey, who I understand is quite good with a deck of cards, I had no such skills.

I rarely went out alone. Stepanchikov had made that a hard and fast rule, but I took advantage of her absence, being able to intimidate my security contingent a lot easier without her.

The man at the table with me didn't recognise who I was, which was always quite an attraction, since any interest in me would be genuine, rather than an attempt to ingratiate themselves with the boss lady of the Twilight

Wanderer and Grant Industries. The only people in the casinos, who could really afford the luxury my ship had to offer were employees of mine, which was a handy way to claw back the salaries I paid them. I highly encouraged my more affluent employees to make use of these facilities. Of course, most people present recognised me, but they knew full well not to bother me if they wanted to keep their jobs. So it was that I found myself sitting at a table, losing what, for most people, would be a large sum of money. Nothing I drank would affect me unless I took some inhibitors with this handsome young fellow, who I assumed was an American, but who I would later discover was Canadian. I'm advised that Canadians and Americans sound different, but personally, I can't notice it, and they all sound the same to me.

"Can I buy you a drink?" He asked me as his colour came up on the wheel and a small pile of chips that were previously mine were pushed over to him.

I looked down at my full glass and then back at him with a raised eyebrow. "You need a better opening line than that, mate. I already have a drink."

He didn't even bat an eyelid, which meant confidence, and confidence is quite a turn-on.

"Well, it would've been equally cliché for me to tell you how beautiful your eyes were," he smiled softly.

I returned a grin, tilting my head slightly with that look that said that his approach wasn't unwelcome, despite my teasing reproach. "Well, true, that would hardly be original either, but let's push past all that bullshit and get to the point."

He raised an eyebrow, but the smile remained as he slipped out of his seat and came to sit next to me. He no longer had an interest in the roulette table and was facing me straight on with a drink in his hand, which he took a sip from before placing it down on the table. "And exactly what point is that, Miss....?" He paused mid-sentence, waiting for me to fill in the gap.

"You can call me Han," I replied.

"Han? That is quite an unusual name for a woman."

"It's short for Hannah." If he didn't get who I was now, he was pretty dense.

"Well, it's an absolute delight to meet you, Hannah." Yep, he was dense, but it wasn't exactly his brain that I was interested in. He was buff and confident, and I was bored and horny, and he would be an enjoyable distraction for the night.

"I'm John." Like I said, I don't remember his name, so I'm just using John as a convenient place filler.

"Well, John, the point is, you either want to come back to my place tonight with me, or you want to have a meaningful conversation and then take me to meet your mother. If it's the latter, I can categorically state straight away that I'm not interested."

He looked momentarily taken aback at my forthrightness, but then the realisation of how easy I was going to make this for him turned surprise to that brief look of immaturity many men get when they realise they are going to get laid that night.

"Well, it's not like I'm looking for a long-term relationship, but who knows where this may lead."

I smiled and placed my hand gently on his. "Oh, it's not going to lead anywhere beyond a bit of fun, John. I'm quite happily married. I'm not looking for a relationship." I was always honest. It saved on drama later on.

His smile quickly vanished, and he moved back slightly. "Well, ... I..." His voice trailed off as he was stumped for something to say.

I rolled my eyes at him. "Oh, you're quite willing to pick up a girl in the bar, but suddenly, you get all prudish when you find out she's married. I don't have a problem with it, and unless you're a mate of my husband's, I don't think he'll have a problem with it. And to be honest, if he does, that's between me and him, not you." As I said this, I crossed my legs and let the split in my dress fall away, revealing my flawlessly designed legs. His eyes dropped down to my side before coming back up to meet mine.

"Well, I don't want to complicate my life more than it already is," he said, but his voice was faltering as his logic battled against temptation.

I shrugged. "My husband is on the Spirit of Freedom, and there are positively no complications, but it's up to you. I'm not playing games."

Less than twenty minutes later, we were back in my apartment on the top deck of the Wanderer. My staff had been dismissed for the night, except for one of my security officers, who was on duty. He just had to look at the expression on my face as I walked in with the young man to know that he was now dismissed.

I stood there waiting for him to leave before walking over to the bar and pulling off a couple of glasses from the shelf, before looking back at my companion. He now stood frozen in the doorway, looking around the room with a rather disquieted look on his face.

"What's the matter?" I asked irritably, although I already knew what the problem was.

"You're Hannah, as in Hannah Grant," he said disbelievingly.

"What of it?" I said, growing very annoyed. All I had wanted was a bit of fun, a nice fuck, and then get rid of him in the morning. Now, he was just going to make this uncomfortable and awkward.

"Well," he began uneasily. "You're the head of the company I work for."

"So?" I shrugged as I put the glasses back on the counter and folded my arms, staring intently at him.

"Well, it's a little bit weird, isn't it?"

"How so?" I sniped back. "Do you think I sit up here in my ivory tower, like the virgin queen overlooking my empire?"

"Well, I can't really say that I've thought about it," he said irritatingly.

"Well, that's your problem, mate. You're thinking with this." I tapped the side of my head. "I want you to be thinking with this." I pointed down towards my crotch. The guy positively flushed, and all the confidence that I'd been enjoying suddenly disappeared. This is why I positively hated fucking guys who knew who I was, but it was hard for me to avoid. "What is it you exactly do for me?"

"I'm a cargo handler," he said sheepishly.

My eyes widened. "Seriously?"

"Seriously!" he said, looking down at his feet.

"How the fuck can someone on a minimum wage job go to one of my casinos?" I said with my eyes narrowing suspiciously at him.

"I have a problem."

"You're an addict?" He didn't say anything in reply to that. He just shrugged and nodded.

I sighed softly and pondered what I was going to do next. I looked down at his hands and was surprised that I hadn't noticed before how rough and calloused they were. I had only ever been with men of my social class before. Well, apart from Liam, but he was hardly a manual labourer like this man, and the idea of those rough, rugged hands against my skin started to make my concerns disappear. I took a couple of steps towards him. The soft smile returned to my face. My anger diminished as the idea of fucking some plebeian from the docks started to restore my desires. A bit of rough and tumble for the night could possibly be just what the doctor ordered.

"Come here, John," I crooned sultrily. He looked up at me, unsure, before complying with my instruction. I reached up and placed my hand around the back of his neck, pulled him towards me, and kissed him. He was momentarily hesitant but then went with it, and his hand slipped around my waist as he pulled my body against his. I felt his arousal begin to grow and knew that any discussion on this matter was over.

However, just as we were getting going, he suddenly tensed. It was only for a moment, and I wasn't sure what was wrong, but his whole body had gone rigid, but it quickly relaxed, and he continued to kiss me, moving down to my neck as my hands ran down his back to explore his firm buttocks. Suddenly, he tensed and went rigid again. This time, with irritation, I let go of him and pushed him back slightly.

"What the fuck is going on?" I said, my anger restored. This was it. This was over. I wasn't playing games with this arsehole. However, he was clutching at his stomach with a look of intense pain. He stepped back and let out a painful groan. Suddenly, the foulest stench hit the air, and I stepped back, clutching my nose and looking at him in disgust. "Oh my God, did you just shit yourself.?"

"Something's wrong, something's really wrong," he said through clenched teeth as he gripped his stomach and fell to his knees. "Call the medics, call the medics. I think I'm dying!"

My eyes widened in horror as I watched him there on the floor in front of me, writhing in agony and stinking of shit, and I turned and ran over to the intercom.

"This is a medical emergency. Please send medics to the executive suite at once. I repeat this is a medical emergency. Please send medics to the executive suite." But no response came. I tried again and again as John started crying out in pain and rolling over onto his side, clutching at his stomach. "This is Hannah Grant, for fuck's sake, I need medics in the executive suite now!" There was still no response. I decided to switch tactics: "Hannah Grant to bridge Hannah Grant to bridge, could someone come in, please? I need medics at my suite urgently, and no-one is responding."

"Ma'am, this is Wilkes," came back the Australian accented voice of the Twilight Wanderer's third officer. "All medical personnel are tied up. We're getting reports from all over the ship of people coming down with something."

"Why wasn't I told?" I snapped back angrily, ignoring John's cries, which now grew louder.

"Ma'am, this's all just started happening in the last hour. The doctors put it down to some sort of minor outbreak. Apparently, reports have been coming in all day of upset stomachs."

"Just get medics to my room now! I don't care where you get them from or if they're doing open heart surgery. I've got some guy lying on my floor here shitting himself, and I want him out of here!"

"Medics are on their way."

I must admit that all I was thinking about at the time was how this had just ruined my evening. I didn't realise things were about to get a whole lot worse.

The medics arrived, but I just left them to it as I hurried down to the bridge to get a full account of exactly what was going on. As I headed through the corridors, I was horrified to see various people doubled up in pain in a similar manner to John. As I burst onto the bridge, they were in full crisis mode. Captain Harris, who was in charge of the ship, had been woken and was now taking control of things. However, I was immediately distracted by the communications officer, who I heard saying, "This is the Twilight Wanderer. We have a medical emergency, I repeat, we have a medical emergency."

"What the hell is she doing?" I screamed at the captain.

"Her job, Miss Grant. It's standard procedure to alert the fleet in the event of a viral outbreak on board a confined environment, such as a ship."

"That's my call, not yours. If we get locked down, we're going to lose a fortune in trade!" I said, continuing to scream at him.

"Ma'am, your authority doesn't outweigh maritime law, and it is my duty to inform fleet command of the situation here." Unlike me, he remained professionally calm.

"What exactly *is* the situation, Captain?"

"Over the last twenty-four hours, we have had incidents being reported of people with stomach cramps, and it has steadily grown worse. Nothing was reported because it didn't reach the level that required it, but now we have people dying. I recommend you go to your quarters and isolate yourself, just in case."

"Let's bring you up to date on the news, Captain. I'm a GenMod. I can't get sick, so I'm probably more useful here than you are right now."

We were suddenly interrupted as the helmsman of the Wanderer suddenly cried out and clutched his stomach.

"Tanya, take over the helm," the captain barked, and the communications officer got up as two other crewmen pulled the pilot from his seat and lay him gently on the floor as the communications officer took over the helm.

"If you want to be of any help, Miss Grant, please take over communications," the captain requested. I didn't argue, and I took the seat that had just been vacated.

"Spirit of Freedom to Twilight Wanderer, do you read me?" A familiar voice was saying.

"This is Hannah Grant, Commodore Sakamoto," I responded, and there was a brief pause before the fleet's second-in-command came back to me.

"Miss Grant, I need to speak to your bridge crew. Please transfer me back there."

"I'm on the fucking bridge, Commodore. My crew are dropping like flies here," I replied snarkily, and as if on cue, the Captain suddenly doubled over behind me, only to be caught by two of his crewmen and carried from the room where the medics had arrived.

"Tell me clearly what is going on over there," Sakamoto demanded.

"I'm not exactly sure, mate, but people have some sort of stomach pains and the shits."

"Have any deaths been reported?"

"Yeah, but I don't have any details."

Her next words weren't directed at me but came over the tannoy, as a fleet-wide emergency communication that was preceded by an alert signal.

"This is a Category One Medical Emergency. The Twilight Wanderer is in lockdown. Any shuttles in transit from that ship are to return at once. Anybody who has left that ship in the last twenty-four hours are to report immediately to the medical centre nearest to them. All medical staff are on alert. This is a Category One Medical Emergency. I repeat, all shuttles are to return to the Twilight Wanderer. Failure to do so, will result in the destruction of their vessel."

"What the fuck, Sakamoto?!" I shouted. "That's not your call."

"No, Hannah, it's my call." This time, it wasn't Sakamoto's voice, but that of Jenna Plural.

"With all due respect, Admiral, this is *my* ship," I snapped very disrespectfully.

"In *my* fleet. You're under strict quarantine, and anyone attempting to leave that ship will be fired upon. Do you understand me?"

"I understand you're going to put me out of business."

"You have just been designated a plague ship, Hannah, and I'm not about to let you wipe out this entire fleet. We're going to do everything possible to help you, but we need your co-operation. Do I have it?"

I wanted to say no, but in the rare instances of my logic outweighing my temper, I sighed. "Yes, I suppose you do. What do you want me to do?"

"I need you to put me through to your senior medical staff, and then just be patient until I get back to you. Can you do that?"

I looked at the blips and blobs of buttons and lights in front of me, and the communications officer who had previously been in my seat jumped up from the helm and came over, switching Jenna over to our senior medical personnel.

And then I did something I don't do well. I waited patiently.

An hour, maybe two, passed, and I didn't say anything. I desperately wanted Liam with me, but I couldn't even call him. It was part of the lockdown and information control. My only communications were directly with the bridge of the Spirit of Freedom. By the time Jenna came back, there were only two bridge crew members left who could work, and, of course, the ship was locked down with everything automated.

More reports came to me of victims of this unknown virus that had hit my ship, and it was looking more than likely that the entire complement of people would be affected.

Jenna eventually came back to me. "Have you shown any signs of being affected by this virus?"

"You know I can't," I said impatiently.

"Not normally, but this doesn't appear to be a normal virus, because it is acting away too fast."

Even I wasn't dumb enough not to understand the implications of her statement. "You believe this is a biological attack from the enemy?"

"Honestly, Hannah, we don't know, but we have to work on that assumption. We're also going to work on the assumption that you won't be affected. I need you to be our eyes and ears as we prepare to deal with this."

"What are you planning on doing?"

"Well, I'm advised most of your medical team is already out of the picture, so I'm putting together a team of Gen-Mods to come over there and be the eyes and ears for our scientists back here, to see if we can find a solution."

"Are there any GenMods that are qualified for this, apart from you and possibly Stepanchikov?"

"To be honest, no. However, what we really need right now are people that won't get infected. According to my records, there is another GenMod aboard the Twilight Wanderer. A man we have shaky details on, that even

Charlotte Kensett can't identify. We have records of him having changed his name at various times but being picked up on D.N.A. registers as the same person. I have no idea how he slipped past Charlotte Kensett, but he came up when we did a specific search for GenMods. I'm going to need the three of you to be our eyes and ears, until I can get aboard."

"You're coming yourself?" I asked in surprise.

"Can you recommend another GenMod with military experience to lead this situation?" she asked with a hint of amusement in her voice.

"Can I talk to Liam?" I asked, ignoring her question.

"Absolutely. He's here with me now. Come on, ladies, let's give Liam and Hannah some privacy. Call me when you're done." The last line was intended for my husband.

Several minutes passed as I sat staring at the screen in front of me before it lit up, and my husband's smiling face looked so pleased to see me.

"Well, hey there, babe," I said with a mock cheeriness that I'm sure he could see right through. GenMods could hide their emotions from most people, but when you get as close as Liam and me, it isn't possible.

"How are you holding up?" he asked, looking at me with the concern that only someone who truly loved you could.

"I'm keeping busy running the bridge. Yeah, I know you don't believe it."

He chuckled. "Oh, I always knew there was a heart in there somewhere, Hannah. I just want you to know we're doing everything we can on this side to get over there to help you. Jenna is putting together a team of GenMods. They're going to come over and fix this shit."

"They better hurry. I may have to make my own breakfast in the morning," I chuckled.

"It's a good thing Sarah went with your sister."

"I was only thinking that this morning. Sorry I couldn't call you. Communications are out."

"Oh my God, what about Stacey's baby?" he asked, almost panicking. Yeah, I forgot to mention I had persuaded Stacey to leave her daughter, in what was believed to be the safety of the Twilight Wanderer, in my custody.

"Just relax," I said, but I hesitated before admitting, "Harper Grant is a GenMod. She's immune. "

"What the fuck?" Liam blurted, completely confused.

I sighed. "Liver, something fucked up with her D.N.A., or something or other. I don't know that bullshit medical stuff. It had something to do with Stacey and alcohol abuse before she realised she was pregnant. She was infused with my D.N.A. while Harper was still in vitro. Stacey doesn't know about it. Well, not that it was me. She thinks it was Jenna's D.N.A. back before they had their falling out. Either way, it doesn't matter. Harper is safe. However, just to be absolutely sure, I've had her uploaded into the M.E.T." Okay, so that was a lie. I uploaded her to the M.E.T. every time I wanted to go out and party. I was just lucky I'd already done that earlier in the evening. "And I don't want you to worry either. I'm safe, too, and contrary to public opinion, I can take care of myself. Without servants even. Well, kind of. "

Despite me trying my best to be funny, he didn't reciprocate. "We're coming to get you, Duchess."

"Oh no, Liam, you're not coming here at all. Don't even think about it. I'll have Stepanchikov sit on your face before I let that happen," I then smirked again. "Although from what I hear from Kensett, you would probably enjoy that."

"I love you, Hannah. I love you more than anything in this universe."

I felt that warm tingle I had always felt around Liam when he was being kind to me. I'd loved that big dipshit ever since he beat up Matt outside that ice cream parlour all those years ago.

"And I love you more than anything in this universe, too, Liam. Just relax and know that no harm can come to me. We'll get through this." Then something occurred to me. "You know something, Liam, it's ironic. For most of my life, I've lived in fear about being a GenMod, and now, something I never imagined would come to pass."

"What do you mean?"

I pondered thoughtfully for a moment, staring off at the myriad of stars ahead of the ship.

"All the hate. All the fear. All the rejection. Being loathed for being what society considers perfect," I said in almost a whisper before I looked back down at the speaker. "Now, without us, humanity could be wiped out,"

"I get that, but ..." he started to say, but I interrupted him.

"Don't you see it, Liam? The day of the GenMods has arrived."

DAVID PARKER-ROSS

The End